For LOVE or HONOR

I0805665

SERIES AND INDEPENDENT NOVELS BY SARAH M. EDEN

SERIES

The Lancaster Family

The Jonquil Brothers

The Gents

The Huntresses

Hope Springs

Savage Wells

The Dread Penny Society

Storm Tide

INDEPENDENT NOVELS

Glimmer of Hope

An Unlikely Match

For Elise

Ashes on the Moor

Ashes on the Moor Collector's Edition

For LOVE *or* HONOR

A JONQUIL BROTHERS ROMANCE

FROM *USA TODAY* BEST-SELLING AUTHOR

SARAH M. EDEN

SHADOW MOUNTAIN PUBLISHING

Visit us at shadowmountain.com

Proper Romance is a registered trademark.

Printed in the United States of America
First Printing: October 2017; Second Edition: April 2021

30 29 28 27 26 10 9 8 7 6 5 4

ISBN 978-1-52440-256-3

To Liz,
by far my favorite sister

J

ACKNOWLEDGMENTS

IN RESEARCHING THIS BOOK, I read countless letters and journal entries written by soldiers involved in the Napoleonic campaigns—glimpses into their personalities, their interactions, their triumphs, and their sorrows that offered me insights into the deeply personal aspects of their experiences, which I could not have begun to comprehend otherwise. I am deeply grateful to those who took the time and made the effort to write of their experiences and to the historians who have preserved those invaluable words for more than two hundred years.

Jennifer Griffith, who read an early version of this story many years ago and offered absolutely incredible feedback and suggestions, thank you.

Thank you, Jenna Consolo, for offering her expertise on the nuances of Latin. Karen Adair, for daily support and encouragement, thank you. Thank you, Pam Howell and Bob Diforio, for their tireless advocacy. Sam Millburn, for her expert guidance in improving my words, thank you.

Thank you to my family for putting up with the frequent chaos inherent in living with an author and for taking it all in stride.

J

CHAPTER ONE

London, October 1815

"I DOUBT MARIE ANTOINETTE LOOKED half so tragic on her way to the guillotine."

Marjie had endured this lecture before. She was the first to admit she hadn't a tremendous amount of enthusiasm for their evening's social obligation, but she understood the necessity.

Marjie's sister and brother-in-law Philip, the Earl of Lampton, took active roles in the *ton* and participated in the never-ending social whirl. Marjie could not have avoided being thrust into the madness of the London Season and its horrid "marriage mart."

Embarking on the business of searching for a husband was not at all what she wished to be doing. Her affections were long since claimed by a tall, golden-haired soldier in a dashing blue uniform. Stanley Jonquil had been recalled to the Continent after Napoleon's escape from exile, and Marjie's heart had gone with him. Yet, she was required to spend the better part of each night dancing and conversing with gentlemen who paled in comparison, all the while wishing for the company of the one she loved.

Marie Antoinette's execution walk felt like an apt comparison.

"I really do not wish to go." Marjie leaned against her bedchamber door. Perhaps if she barricaded herself in, Sorrel would allow her to stay. "Must I?"

"If I can endure an evening of dancing, you certainly can." Sorrel rose awkwardly from her spot on the edge of Marjie's bed, reaching for her ebony walking stick.

Marjie recognized the tightening around Sorrel's mouth and the way her expression froze. She was in pain, more so than usual.

Marjie forced herself to stay in place. Her first instinct was always to rush to her sister's aid, but Philip had explained to her only a few weeks earlier that Sorrel did not appreciate being "smothered."

"Is the brace not helping?" Marjie asked.

"I have been a little sore today," Sorrel replied dismissively.

Marjie knew her sister did not like discussing her injury nor the frustration she had endured over the years as she'd attempted to regain her mobility. A surgery early in the summer had corrected two badly healed breaks in her right leg, but nothing could be done for her shattered hip.

For months, Philip had corresponded with a doctor whose specialty was creating braces to correct clubfoot and bent limbs in children. The doctor had fashioned something similar for Sorrel: an apparatus consisting of a wide, sturdy belt fitted snugly across her hips and a metal rod connected to the belt that ran the length of her right thigh, belting around her leg just above her knee. The doctor's theory was that the brace would hold the broken pieces of her hip in place, allowing her to walk with greater stability and less pain. The simple alteration of Sorrel's wardrobe to gowns that fit more fully at the hips made the brace easier to disguise. While Sorrel still used her walking stick, she did seem to be relying a little less on it.

Seeing her sister in so much obvious pain over the past three years had been excruciating. Marjie had taken Philip's words to heart and had not spoken her concern aloud, but she felt it every bit as much as she ever had.

"Now, come along." Sorrel reached the doorway herself. "Philip may have finished dressing for the evening and will wish to depart."

"Does it not strike you as odd that Philip takes longer to dress than you do?" Marjie said, gathering her gloves as she accepted the inevitability of the evening's schedule. "Should it not be the other way around?"

"When one is married to a gentleman whose reputation as a dandy is epic in its proportions, such things are simply assumed and accepted." Sorrel smiled, something she hadn't done a great deal of after her crippling accident. Meeting Philip had changed that.

The Jonquil brothers were, in a word, remarkable. Stanley was, of course, Marjie's favorite. Philip, the eldest, had earned both her respect and her sisterly affection simply by making Sorrel as happy as Marjie had ever seen her.

As soon as Stanley returned home, Marjie would be happy as well. He had survived Waterloo. They knew that much but little else. She had written twenty-five letters to him in the six months since he had left for war, including the one she had only just finished that afternoon and intended to post in the morning. She had saved the ribbon she'd worn in her hair the day they had said their good-byes, intending to use it to bind the letters he sent her from the battlefront. The ribbon was still in the drawer of her night table, unused.

Not a single member of Stanley's family had heard from him since his departure either. The fact that his mother had not received a letter worried the family most of all. Of the seven brothers, Stanley had always been the most attentive to his mother's needs. For him to neglect something as elemental as writing to her was very unlike him.

Marjie tried not to worry, though it was what Sorrel said she did best. She had checked the casualty lists every day after Waterloo, relieved when his name did not appear there. She prayed for him often, thought of him throughout the day, dreamed of him at night. If only she could know he was well. Though part of her worried over the possible answer, she wished she knew why he had not sent her so much as a single line, a single word.

"Do try to pull yourself into the present, Marjie," Sorrel said.

"My apologies." They had reached the second-floor landing, and she hadn't even realized it. "I was—"

"Worrying," Sorrel finished for her. "Fretting over Stanley will not bring him home any sooner. You cannot spend every moment of every day pining for a man who does not even write to you."

Heat flooded Marjie's cheeks. Everyone in the family was aware of her circumstances, but none had spoken of it quite so bluntly.

Sorrel simply did not understand. The man Sorrel loved was at her side every day. His affection for her could not be questioned. She had his attention and his love. Marjie had only her memories of Stanley's attentiveness and the distant hope that he would return to her.

"We will be back at Lampton Park in only a few more weeks," Sorrel said. Her tone had softened a bit, perhaps having realized how her words had wounded. "In the meantime, it would do you good to make friends—young ladies you might write to during the winter months and look forward to seeing again when the Season begins. And if you knew a gentleman or two, the round of balls and musicales might seem a bit less endless."

"I suppose." She had her doubts though.

"You seem to have already forged something of a friendship with Lord Devereaux." The fact that Sorrel could have a conversation while limping down the stairs was testament to her improving mobility. Stairs had once been an enormous obstacle for her. "Many people have credited his continued presence among Society to his preference for your company."

Marjie smiled and shook her head. "The *ton* has assumed too much in our friendship. We've simply found we understand one another. He misses his wife. I miss Stanley."

Sorrel sighed. "Lord Devereaux is a widower. It is understandable for him to struggle with returning to Society and for his grief to be so consuming. You and Stanley do not even have an understanding. A career in the army may very well keep him away from England for years. I do not think Stanley would wish you to be socially paralyzed by his absence."

Sometimes Sorrel could be remarkably unsympathetic.

She laid a hand on Marjie's arm, a rare moment of physical affection between two sisters raised in a family that seldom touched one another. "I do not wish to be cruel, but neither do I wish for you to look back years from now and realize you lost your opportunity for happiness while waiting on a possibility that was not meant to be."

Marjie took a quick, desperate breath, refusing to allow her emotions to surface. "I have to have some hope," she quietly insisted.

"Hope is not a prison." Sorrel gently squeezed her arm. "Hope should lessen your fears, not intensify them."

Their brother, Fennel, was supposed to be the insightful one. Sorrel was correct though. Beneath her façade of calm, Marjie was very much afraid—afraid that something had happened to Stanley, afraid he would not return, afraid he did not love her as she loved him.

A knock sounded at the front door.

Sorrel eyed the door with confusion. "Who would be calling at this time of night?"

"Was that a knock?" Philip's voice reached them from behind.

Marjie looked over her shoulder to see him descending the stairs, as impeccable in appearance as ever, though the canary-yellow waistcoat and deep-purple jacket were a bit over the top.

"Perhaps one of the neighbors has come to complain about the brightness of your attire," Sorrel suggested.

A grin spread across Philip's face. "It is rather eye-catching, isn't it?"

Sorrel shook her head even as she lightly laughed. "I thought you were supposed to be on the road to reform."

"These things take time, dear." Philip slipped Sorrel's arm through his. "You are stunning tonight, as always." He kissed Sorrel's cheek. "That shade of green is perfect on you."

She gave him a look that would have been scolding if not for the deep red staining her cheeks. Philip was the only person Marjie knew who was capable of undermining Sorrel's legendary composure.

As they reached a step low enough to afford a view of the front entryway, all three of them stopped simultaneously. A crowd of servants stood before them. Mrs. Jeffers, the housekeeper, talked incessantly but too rapidly to be understood. Her husband, the butler, rushed about the small space but not with any perceivable purpose.

"Well, my dear, it appears the staff has finally lost their minds," Philip said.

"It was bound to happen." Sorrel almost sounded like she meant it.

"Jeffers." Philip's voice, authoritative without being raised, cut through the chaos below them, and all eyes turned toward the three of them. "I am expecting a very entertaining explanation of all this."

"My lord." Jeffers turned wide eyes on them, his hands fidgeting and a look of flustered amazement on his face. Marjie had never before seen the butler anything short of completely composed. "It is only that it is so unexpected. None of us had any idea. Had we been warned, perhaps . . . Even then . . ."

"Mrs. Jeffers? Would you like to attempt a less rambling explanation?" Philip led Sorrel the rest of the way down the stairs. Marjie followed behind.

The housekeeper, suddenly silent, shook her head, wiping at her face with an enormous handkerchief.

"Well, I, for one, am dying of curiosity." Philip glanced around at the assembled staff.

Marjie was no less intrigued. While Philip had an easy way with his staff, they were never lax in their duties.

"Obviously something has overset the lot of you," Philip said. "Would you care to tell me what?"

The crowd parted in answer, revealing a soldier, thin and pale, sitting on the footman's bench to the side of the front door, his threadbare blue uniform hanging from his frail form. He looked up at Philip, dark circles beneath his deep-blue eyes.

Marjie's throat tightened. Her heart beat hard against her ribs. Even haggard, she would have known him anywhere. Stanley. But not at all as she remembered him. He was too thin, too still. Had he been ill? Injured? When had he returned home? Why had they not been told? She could not voice a single question.

"How—? When did—?" Philip was not usually inarticulate. "When did you get back in England?"

Stanley's posture slumped further, and his eyes dropped to his gloved hands, which rested on a rough-hewn walking stick. "I suppose I should have sent word."

CHAPTER TWO

It was not the homecoming Stanley had anticipated. He hadn't planned on one at all, truth be told. The chances of any soldier surviving the largest battle in the history of modern warfare weren't very good. He'd somehow managed it though, and there had been many times in the four months since Waterloo that he had wished he hadn't.

"When did you leave France?" The shock on Philip's face was understandable.

Stanley obviously had not been expected, and even a simpleton would notice his altered appearance. He avoided looking at Marjie. He could not bear to see the look of horror that was surely on her face—and she didn't even know the worst of it.

"I left the Continent yesterday morning." He leaned more heavily on his walking stick, tired despite being seated. Every part of him ached. He was, in a word, exhausted. Not just in the moment but all the time. He struggled to simply remain on his feet. It was little wonder he had been sent back to England. "I have been granted a temporary leave of absence."

"How long before you are recalled?" Philip asked.

Not long enough. "I am here only until Lord Hill orders me to return."

"*Lord Hill* sent you back to England?"

Stanley reached into the pocket of his uniform and pulled out a sealed letter. "I was told to give you this."

Philip took it, examining the address and seal before returning his gaze to Stanley. Even dressed as the most frivolous of dandies, Philip could give one a look that pierced as though he were examining one's insides and uncovering secrets one had no intention of revealing.

"Jeffers, see to it that Captain Jonquil's things are placed in his room, and have Cook prepare a tray and send it to my book room."

"Yes, my lord." Jeffers seemed to have recovered his professional composure.

Stanley was quick to recover his as well. He sat up straighter, squared his shoulders. *Always a soldier.* His first commanding officer had barked out those three words whenever the men grew too relaxed. Staying alert kept them alive. Focusing on being a soldier prevented the horror of it all from ever truly sinking in.

Philip continued addressing the butler. "Send one of the footmen to Her Grace with our regrets. We will not be attending her ball this evening after all." Philip turned to his wife. "I hope you are not overly disappointed, dear."

Sorrel actually snorted. Philip laughed, and Sorrel's scolding look transformed to amusement in an instant.

Stanley held his face expressionless. The army taught a man to shut out the world in the name of duty and dedication. He tightened his grip on his crooked walking stick until the inflexible skin of his horrifically burned right hand ached in protest beneath his powder-blackened glove.

"Why don't you and Marjie repair to the drawing room, dear," Philip said. Stanley kept his eyes directed forward and his back ramrod straight. "We'll join you after we've had a moment in the book room." He turned to Stanley. "Come along, Stanley." He made the request as if it would be very simple to carry out—as if Stanley weren't apt to fall quite ignominiously on his war-ravaged face in the attempt to obey.

He shifted his weight, leaning on his stick more heavily. Getting to his feet always constituted something of a risk. He planted his left foot firmly on the ground. His walking stick provided some additional balance. Slowly he rose. For a fraction of a moment, his right boot slid beneath him, threatening to send him sprawling to the floor. He shifted his weight, gripping his stick more desperately, and held his breath for a moment, waiting to see if he'd compensated sufficiently. Everything appeared steady. He carefully straightened, assuming his soldier's posture once more.

They were all watching him again. The staff had taken Philip's earlier instructions for the dismissal that it was, but Philip and Sorrel yet stood at the base of the stairs. Their looks of surprised alarm hardly registered. Marjie's expression, however, hit Stanley with the force of a brutal wind. She pressed her gloved fingers to her heart, her mouth forming a perfect O. Her eyes grew wide and unblinking.

She was, it seemed, beginning to realize what had become of him.

He pulled his gaze away. "To the book room?" Stanley asked Philip, trying to sound unaffected and unconcerned.

Philip grinned, holding a fist in the air as if leading an advance. "Charge!"

Stanley flinched. That word echoed in his mind in myriad different voices, many of which had been forever silenced by war. The Jonquil brothers had shouted that so many times as children as they'd played on the banks of the River Trent, but the dreamlike quality of those games had long been shattered by the nightmare of real warfare. Stanley closed his eyes against the images of young boys lying still and lifeless. His shoulders slumped under the weight of everything he tried to forget. *Always a soldier*, he reminded himself and instantly corrected his posture.

Stanley walked stiffly in Philip's wake. The clunk of his right boot against the floor filled the silence around him. He refused to look at Marjie as he passed. He could not endure the sight of what certainly must be her growing revulsion, not when he was exhausted to the point of being ready to drop. He would face that particular mountain later. He told himself that a lot. Whatever happened, he would face it later. Then he simply put off later indefinitely.

Philip closed the door to the book room once they'd entered. He pulled off his shockingly purple jacket and flung it on the back of a leather armchair, then motioned for Stanley to sit in the chair opposite.

Sitting was far simpler than rising. Positioning himself over the seat, he allowed himself to drop back, essentially falling into the chair. Philip sat more gracefully. Indeed, he did most things with a degree of elegance that bordered on absurd. It was one of the most enjoyable things about Stanley's eldest brother. He could lighten the atmosphere in any setting.

"You are injured," Philip said, that penetrating gaze turned on him once more.

"I was," Stanley replied, sitting with his back so straight it didn't even touch the chair.

"*Was* is past tense," Philip said. "You are presently not moving well."

Stanley's right leg seemed to twitch, as if reminding him of his near immobility. "I am moving better than I once was."

Philip leaned his head against the outstretched fingers of his right hand, his right elbow resting on the arm of his chair. He studied Stanley's face. The scrutiny was uncomfortable, but Stanley knew the worst of his physical alterations weren't visible.

"How long ago were you injured?" Philip asked.

"Waterloo." Stanley swallowed against the word. The name alone brought back unwanted smells, sounds, and sights, all of which would have haunted even the most callous of men.

"That was four months ago." Philip's gaze focused further. "Obviously you are still not well. Have you seen a doctor? Has everything possible been done?"

"Trust me," Stanley said. He barely managed to keep the bitterness out of his voice. "*Everything* has been done."

The silence that followed was both heavy and awkward. Stanley hadn't intended to be cryptic, but he did not at all wish to discuss his injuries nor the treatments they had necessitated. He wanted nothing more than the quiet of his room and to be left alone.

Philip sighed, a sound of exasperation rather than weariness. He opened the letter Wellington's second-in-command had ordered be given unopened to the Earl of Lampton. Stanley had no idea what Lord Hill had written. He had accepted his orders without question, like any good soldier would.

Philip's expression grew more perplexed as he read. He raised his eyes after a moment and looked directly at Stanley. "Perhaps you could shed a little light on this very odd letter." Philip held the folded sheet of parchment up before lowering it again and reading aloud. "'Lord Lampton. With heaviness of mind, I send to you Captain Stanley Jonquil.'"

Heaviness of mind did not sound promising.

"'I commend your good mother and the late earl for raising a young gentleman of such stalwart character. I fear, however, this war has asked too much of him.'"

Asked too much of him. Stanley shifted his gaze to the dark windows on either side of the fireplace. He clamped his jaw shut so he wouldn't actually speak the words that flew instantly into his mouth. *The war has not merely taken "too much." It has nearly taken everything.*

"'Captain Jonquil will require time to heal, and I feel confident that his chance of recovery would be best amongst his family. In a few weeks' time, I will send a representative to check on his progress. Yours, etc., Hill.' That was rather ambiguous, don't you think? Even for the army?"

Stanley didn't return Philip's gaze. Speaking of the war was always easier when the discussion felt impersonal. From the sound of Lord Hill's letter, Stanley was only to be granted a brief reprieve. He had been hoping for more. Still, he kept his tone neutral. "Lord Hill told me I was returning to England to recuperate for a time, just as his letter said."

"Four months *after* your injury?" Philip asked. "Why were you not sent home sooner?"

Stanley had managed to make himself useful, even after everything that had happened. He had ridden from Belgium to France to rejoin his men only to watch them be picked off one at a time by embittered French soldiers hell-bent on revenge. No peace treaty on earth seemed capable of stopping the bloodshed of that war.

"What is going on, Stanley?" Philip asked. "You haven't written to anyone since you left in March. Now you return unannounced, obviously unwell and injured severely enough that it has reached the attention of Lord Hill, though your own family knew nothing of it. Not a single letter. I have never known you to neglect Mater."

Their mother was better off not knowing the particulars of his last six months. Father had told him again and again as a boy that easing Mater's burdens was the duty of each one of the brothers. *Do not add to her troubles*, Father had told him. Stanley had done just that and would continue to do so.

"And what of Marjie?" Philip asked. "She has written to you regularly despite never receiving a reply."

Marjie. Her letters had been both treasured and torturous. Her words had forged a connection between the idyllic weeks he'd spent with her and the life he'd been living ever since. The contrast had been horrifying, an inescapable reminder that her world of peaceful innocence was no place for someone who had seen and done what he had.

He looked back at Philip at last. "How is Marjie?" The question emerged almost breathless, almost soundless.

"She was standing right next to me. Or didn't you notice?"

Stanley had most certainly noticed. Her hair was still the color of a newly minted guinea, her complexion as soft and pink as the gown she'd been wearing. She probably even smelled the same, with just a hint of roses. She hadn't smiled, however, as he remembered her doing so often during their time together. Faced with his transformation, though, what reason would she have had to do so?

Stanley shifted in his seat, realizing his soldier's bearing had slipped. He corrected his stance and reminded himself of his duties.

Philip released a slow breath. "I'll have the dinner tray sent to your room. You appear in rather desperate need of rest."

Stanley nodded. Rest would be welcome, but he would have to settle for the usual ineffective sleep.

Philip rose in one fluid motion. Stanley pushed through the belabored steps required to get himself upright. Philip studied him, watching every painstaking moment. Stanley stood as tall as his battered body would allow.

Expression devoid of emotion, standing almost as if he were before his commanding officer, he offered a crisp, "Good night, Philip."

He had a lot of practice on stairs, and it paid dividends in that moment. Relying heavily on the banister kept him upright—that, and his determination to reach his room and escape into the cocoon of solitude. His ascent was slow, but he managed it.

Pluck, a young soldier who had assumed the role of batman—Stanley's personal servant in the army—shortly after Waterloo, would have the ointment ready when he arrived.

Stanley reached the door of his bedchamber to find Pluck, as expected, ready and waiting.

"Laws, Cap'n. I always knew ye was a toff, but you never said ye was an aristocratic-type cove."

Stanley sat on the edge of his bed but kept his posture as rigid as ever. Lud, he was tired.

"I heard so many 'my lord this' and 'my lord that,' I blasted well thought I was in church."

"Quit being blasphemous, and grab the jar of ointment," Stanley said. "Thought he was in church," he said under his breath, smiling a little in spite of himself.

"Is your hand givin' ye grief again?" Pluck asked, crossing to the shaving table.

"When is it ever not giving me grief?" Stanley grumbled. He winced as he tugged at the fingers of his glove.

"I told ye to leave the glove off," Pluck said. "Gotta let your hand have some fresh air, I say. Cain't expect it to heal up iffen it's stuffed into that coffin ye put it in."

His hand jerked the rest of the way out of the glove, pain searing across the back of it. He clenched his jaw, pulling a hissing breath in through the minute spaces between his teeth. "A glove is not a coffin."

"Might as well be." Pluck spoke with all the assurance of a general, though he was only a seventeen-year-old private. "That hand of yours ain't seen the light of day in months."

"No one needs to see this." Stanley glanced only briefly at the mangled mess that had once been his right hand. The basic shape was still there, all five fingers, but the skin was pulled and melted, the color a grotesque and ever-changing mixture of deep reds and purples. Every time he looked at it, the smell of burning flesh returned to his mind.

"It looks better, Cap'n," Pluck said.

"Apparently this isn't enough like a church to stop you from lying."

Pluck laughed. "Ain't lying. The putrification's cleared up."

His hand had been quite obviously infected only forty-eight hours earlier. Could it really have cleared up so quickly? He looked more closely. The swelling along the back of it and the bright redness between two parallel ridges of warped skin had lessened. The oozing had stopped entirely. "Hmm. Look at that."

"Told ye the liquor'd do the trick." Pluck grinned triumphantly. Pouring a half bottle of brandy on his hand had been one of the more painful of Stanley's recent experiences—and that was saying something. "Me dad drank more gin than any person I ever knowed. And he weren't sick a day in his life. Till he died, leastways."

"That is very comforting," Stanley said. "Fetch the ointment and get on with it."

"Off with the uniform first," Pluck said. He always grew nauseatingly chipper when Stanley least wanted to be cheered up. "Ye must be happy to be home again, what with that Miss Kendrick you was always talkin' about living here and all."

That had been an unexpected stroke of bad luck. It had been easier when she was more of a distant memory, when he could keep in his mind the image of her thinking of him the way he had been before.

Pluck helped him free his arms from the sleeve of his jacket. Stanley tensed against the agony of rough fabric pulling against the open sores on his hand. Pluck applied the ointment. It stung at first but quickly soothed a day's worth of irritation and chafing. He often wondered if the skin would ever heal entirely. It wasn't as sensitive as it had been four months earlier.

Pluck took Stanley's walking stick and leaned it against the wall near his bed, then stood there for a minute, not looking at Stanley. "You ready?" he asked.

It was Stanley's least favorite part of the day. He could almost pretend everything was normal until that moment each night when lying to himself didn't do any good. He hadn't written to Mater or Marjie or any of the others. Most men in his situation died of infection; there was no point putting his family through the worry of knowing all that had happened when he would likely end up dead anyway. He knew his duty: do not add to their troubles.

A few more months and he would be returning to the killing and inhumanity. It would be best to let them think he was going back whole.

"I'm ready." Stanley sat so straight and stiff his back ached with the effort.

Pluck tugged at Stanley's boots, dropping them one at a time on the floor. "None of them knows, do they?"

"They don't need to know."

He pulled up the leg of his trousers. The carpenter in Belgium had done a very good job—the basic dimensions were right, and when the replacement was hidden beneath the fabric of his clothing and the rigid leather of his right boot, no one would guess at the deception.

Stanley worked through the ties and buckles that held everything in place. It was so frighteningly easy to take off now. Four months ago, the process had been excruciating.

Pluck stood, holding his hands out like he always did, not quite looking Stanley in the eye. It was an unspoken rule between them, a way of not acknowledging everything that had occurred.

Stanley pushed back a sudden rush of angry tears. He hadn't cried about this in months, not since the moment the surgeon had first approached with his saw. He took a deep breath, pulling himself together. "Always a soldier" echoed in his mind.

He yanked the lifeless slab of wood off the stump of his leg and shoved it into Pluck's hands.

"Ye ought to tell them, Cap'n," Pluck said, looking uncharacteristically solemn. "They ought to know. They ought to know what a blasted miracle it is that you lived through it all."

Stanley dropped back onto the pillows. He snapped the blanket over his battered and broken body. "Not a miracle," he muttered. "It's a deuced shame."

CHAPTER THREE

"Sally Jersey specifically asked if you would be attending Almack's this evening."

Marjie recognized Philip's voice coming from the book room. The only person in the household whose attendance at Almack's was in question was Stanley. Marjie paused outside the door, listening for his answer.

"Then I hope you specifically told her I would not be."

Marjie's heart dropped to her feet.

She had hardly seen Stanley in the five days since his unexpected return home. She couldn't very well go into his bedchamber, and he very seldom came out of it. He had not made a point of seeking her out, and other than the occasional "good day" uttered in passing, he had not spoken to her.

"The rumors of inedible food are, I assure you, a bit exaggerated," Philip said.

Marjie slipped quietly inside the book room. Stanley sat near the fireplace, thin to the point of alarm. Before leaving for the Continent, he had been healthy except for a slight weakness in his right arm. Now dark circles marred his undereyes. He'd aged years in those brief months. He limped more than Sorrel did.

"There is absolutely nothing worth drinking, but the company is congenial." Philip leaned against the back of the chair opposite Stanley, his relaxed posture and flamboyant attire painting a unique picture. He would most certainly be the only gentleman at Almack's that evening wearing yellow silk knee breeches. His efforts at subduing his wardrobe were apparently falling short.

"An evening of dancing is entirely out of the question," Stanley said. He sat rigidly upright. His words came out tense.

"Sorrel is attending," Philip said.

"Her mobility has improved since I last saw her."

"She will never be able to dance," Philip said. "Yet she attends every Wednesday."

"I don't—"

"Do come, Stanley." The words simply fell out of Marjie's mouth, a plea that had hovered anxiously near the surface ever since she'd entered the room.

Both gentlemen turned at the sound of her voice. Philip smiled at her. Stanley looked more surprised than happy.

"Yes." Philip motioned her over. "Please help me convince him."

Marjie rushed across the room. How she had dreamed of having Stanley at her side at Almack's and the theatre and the dozens of other gatherings she had attended. If only she could persuade him.

She sat on the footstool just to the side of Stanley's chair. He shifted a little away from her and tucked one hand between his leg and the arm of his chair. His posture grew stiffer. His eyes focused on the fireplace.

He had never been like that before. Always when she had spoken with him, he'd looked at her, truly listened. She had seldom been given such consideration at home.

But, then, he had been ill. He hadn't said as much, but his appearance told her the truth of the matter. Some leniency must be granted to one so obviously afflicted.

"Please come," Marjie said. Her eyes never left his face, though he still did not look at her. "Philip, as you know, never holds still for five minutes, and Sorrel spends the evenings talking with the other married ladies. I am not asked to dance very often." Her face heated at the admission. "And I grow terribly lonely sitting by myself. I have so few friends and—" She faltered. Stanley's eyes had very abruptly focused on her, a look of confusion on his face. Even thin and weary, it was *his* beloved face. How she longed to reach out and simply touch his cheek to assure herself that he was real. They had embraced only once, on the day he'd left for the Continent, but she had longed to touch him ever since.

"You do not get asked to dance?" Stanley actually seemed shocked, upset even.

The heat in Marjie's cheeks stole down her neck. "I am not very popular. Brunettes are all the rage just now."

Stanley shook his head. "Did the gentlemen of London go blind while I was gone?"

Marjie laughed nervously, his scrutinizing gaze sitting heavily upon her. Did he notice how pallid she appeared in the pastels required of a young lady making her come out? She hoped not.

"Many very pretty young ladies are out just now." Marjie tried to make the comment sound light. "They receive a great deal of attention."

"And you don't?" His voice was soft, compassionate, the way it had been so often before his departure.

This was the Stanley she had missed so dearly. Perhaps he had not changed so entirely.

"No, I do not." The less-than-flattering opinions of others, though they stung a bit, did not weigh too heavily upon her; she had already found what she was looking for.

"So they are blind *and* stupid." Stanley's lips twitched upward for the briefest moment.

Marjie smiled back at him. "Please come," she said. "Come sit by me. I won't be lonely with you there."

Stanley shook his head. "I doubt you'd wish to be seen with me."

"Of course I would," Marjie said. She clasped her hands together on her lap, the temptation to reach for him growing with every passing moment.

Stanley's forehead creased, his eyes still on Marjie. Was he at least considering coming?

"I daresay you would clean up nicely," Philip said. Marjie had forgotten he was even there. "A haircut and a good close shave ought to do the trick."

"Please, Stanley." Marjie's eyes didn't leave Stanley's weary face. He would improve with time, she was certain of it. But when he was well again, he would leave. She wanted every moment with him she could possibly have.

"You could wear your dress uniform," Philip said. "It is in far better shape than the rags you showed up in."

Marjie could see indecision in Stanley's eyes. Perhaps they had convinced him. Her heart flipped in her chest. She would not have to endure another evening of thinking of him in his absence.

"Of course," Philip continued, "you would have to wear it with knee breeches. The patronesses are very strict about that requirement."

"Knee breeches?" Stanley didn't seem happy about that.

"Yes. You know, the lovely little knickers that buckle just below the knee so we men can display our well-shaped calves in silk hose and dancing shoes."

"I know what they are," Stanley muttered.

"Come on, then," Philip said. "Drag yourself upstairs and get cleaned up. We can wait."

Marjie smiled at Stanley. They could most certainly wait.

"I don't think so, Philip." Stanley's gaze moved back to the fireplace, his expression cleared of every identifiable emotion. "Give Lady Jersey my apologies."

"She won't be happy," Philip said.

"She will recover."

"Then you're not coming?" Marjie could hear her own disbelief. Stanley had seemed nearly convinced, and then he'd abruptly decided against Almack's.

Stanley shook his head but didn't look back at her.

"Because . . ." She tried to piece it together. "Because of the knee breeches?"

He didn't answer.

"I realize they aren't fashionable, but—" No. There had to be another reason. "Certainly you could endure knee breeches for one evening."

He shook his head again. Every inch of him radiated tension. Was he upset or merely extremely opposed to the fashion requirements of the invitation?

"I would have to sit by myself." Marjie blinked against the sting in her eyes. "You would abandon me because of knee breeches?"

"I'm sorry," Stanley whispered.

Marjie sat watching him, confused. What had happened? What had changed? Stanley had spent nearly the entire Christmas house party where they'd met sitting with her and talking to her. Now her company was not even worth the inconvenience of uncomfortable attire.

Philip sighed quietly. "Come, Marjie. As soon as Sorrel is ready, we'll leave."

Marjie nodded mutely and rose to her feet. Stanley still watched the embers in the fireplace. "Will you come with us to the theater on Friday?" she asked him.

Stanley's posture did not give an inch.

"There are no wardrobe requirements." The words broke a little as she spoke them. How had she sunk so low in his esteem as to rank below his clothing consideration?

"I will think on it." He didn't even look at her.

"Marjie," Philip whispered. He had come to stand beside her. "Come along."

Marjie allowed Philip to lead her away, though her gaze remained on Stanley. His brows were pulled together, his forehead deeply creased. His expression was not dismissive nor uncaring. Rather, he appeared burdened.

She didn't realize she'd stopped walking until she felt Philip tug lightly on her arm.

"Something is weighing on him," Marjie said as Philip walked with her out of the book room.

"I've noticed that myself," Philip said. "Sorrel is nearly out of patience with him."

"Patience never was Sorrel's strongest trait." They had reached the front entryway.

"Oh, I wouldn't say that. She has endured a great deal these past months and has been remarkably patient through it all."

"Patience with other people, then," Marjie said. "She was always the strong one in the family. Fennel was the insightful sibling."

"And you?" Philip asked. "You are named for marjoram. I believe Sorrel said marjoram was a soothing herb."

"Yes. We've each made a point of living up to our names."

"How patient are *you*, Marjie?" Philip suddenly turned quite serious. "I am worried about my brother." He glanced back toward the corridor they had just walked down before returning his gaze to her. "He was prone to heavy moods after Orthez but never this severe."

Nervousness tugged at Marjie's stomach. "What can I do?"

"Help me sort out what is wrong with him."

"If he won't even talk to me or spend time with me, how am I supposed to—"

"Don't give up on him," Philip said. "He was happier in those few weeks he spent with you than he had been in the months he'd spent at home before that. He needs you."

Marjie shook her head. "He didn't even want to come tonight."

"I know, and I am sorry for that."

"I'm afraid I may have misread his feelings for me. If he really— He hasn't even spoken to me." Marjie pushed out a breath. She hadn't let herself think about it, let alone speak the words out loud.

Philip watched her closely. "If he didn't love you"—Marjie winced—"would you help him anyway?"

"I would," she answered without hesitation. "I would do anything for him."

"Then be his friend," Philip said. "I have my suspicions that you stand a better chance of piercing his armor than any of the rest of us."

"I am not at all sure of that." She did not even detect signs of friendship in him, let alone anything beyond.

"But you will help?"

"Of course."

A moment later, she stood alone in the entryway. Philip had left to seek out Sorrel.

Marjie closed her eyes. In her mind, she could see Stanley as he'd been during those beautiful weeks of the Christmas season and again in the days before he'd been recalled to his regiment. He had suffered a shoulder injury at the Battle of Orthez and had frequently been in pain, but he had been happy. His smile had come easily; his laughter had warmed her to her very core.

Was *that* Stanley—the Stanley she had fallen so deeply in love with—still there somewhere? She had seen a glimpse of him for just a moment in the book room.

When Sorrel had been so ill at Christmastime, Stanley had listened to all Marjie's worries and concerns. He had been an unfailing source of support to her.

Marjie took a deep breath and solidified her resolve. Stanley had stood as her friend during her difficulties. No matter his feelings, no matter the eventual outcome, she would do the same for him.

J

CHAPTER FOUR

"I MUST HAVE LOST MY mind." Stanley eyed his reflection in the mirror in the entryway. The uniform he wore hadn't seen a single day of battle and was, therefore, in remarkably good condition.

"Lost it? Pffft. I'd say ye finally found that rattlin' old bacon canister of yours."

Bacon canister? Pluck had an odd way of saying things. He held Stanley's shako out to him. It was not the most flattering of hats but was a requisite part of the uniform. Thankfully, so were gloves. "Cain't think why ye'd be wantin' to sit around all night with nothing but your own breathing to keep you company when you've a right dimber mort wishin' for a bit of your time."

Perhaps bringing Pluck home with him had been a bad idea. "You cannot call any of the ladies of this house a 'dimber mort.'"

"It ain't an insult," Pluck insisted.

"I know." Years in the army had lent Stanley a remarkable familiarity with cant expressions. "But that does not make it appropriate."

"Don't make it untrue either. You've a fine lady wanting you to go to the theater with her. Only a man with a vacant upper story would turn up his nose at that opportunity."

Some opportunity. He'd probably be only half awake by the first intermission. Attending would require being out in public. He would be stared at by strangers and asked probing questions by acquaintances. He really ought to do all of them a favor and stay home.

"We are going to make a devastating pair tonight." Philip came down the stairs, graceful as always. He had toned down his look a little: a dark-blue jacket and matching pantaloons. If not for the orange waistcoat, he might have looked subdued. "It's a shame the dragoons' uniform doesn't have a bit more dash."

"The hat adds a bit of interest." Stanley placed his shako on his head, careful to center it exactly. One learned the importance of precision in the army. Perfection often kept a soldier alive.

"True." Philip stopped next to Stanley, their reflections side by side in the long mirror. He seemed to study them both. "You're missing something."

A leg, Stanley silently thought.

"You're not wearing your sabre. Is that not part of the uniform?"

"Cap'n Jonquil doesn't wear his sword anymore, Yer Grace." Pluck bowed so formally and low his nose nearly touched his knees.

"You don't address an earl as Your Grace," Stanley said.

"Yer Most High and Mighty Lordship," Pluck corrected, still bent nearly in half.

Stanley shook his head and pulled Pluck upright by the back of his collar.

Philip grinned. "Where did you find this gem?"

"Loading the guns." It was the barest version of the truth and the only one he could manage without thrusting himself back into unwanted memories. "He was horrible at it."

"I'm a much better batman," Pluck said.

"That's debatable," Stanley muttered.

Pluck just laughed.

"He seems to be doing well as your valet," Philip said. He eyed Stanley in the mirror again. "He's turned you out nicely, even if he did forget your sword."

"I told ye, Yer High and Mighty—"

"'Lord Lampton' or 'my lord' would be sufficient, Pluck," Stanley said.

Philip stopped him. "No, I like the 'high and mighty' part. I think everyone should begin addressing me that way." Philip grinned at Stanley the way he always had when as boys he and the second oldest, Layton, had undertaken their usual mischief.

"Cap'n Jonquil don't wear his sword anymore," Pluck said. "Not since—"

"Pluck." Stanley snapped out the single syllable. Any one of his men would have recognized his tone for the warning it was.

Pluck didn't even pause. "Waterloo. Lord Hill told him he was supposed to wear it, seeing as it was part of his uniform."

"And he still didn't?" Philip asked.

Pluck shook his head. "Told ol' Lord Hill to go to the devil."

Stanley turned to face Pluck but wasn't given a chance to say a single word.

"Was this before or after Lord Hill ordered Captain Jonquil back to England?" Philip asked, suddenly as sober as a judge.

"Before," Pluck answered. His eyes darted to Stanley, his look clearly one of defiance.

"And he wasn't court-martialed?" Philip's attention didn't waver from the overly talkative batman.

Pluck shook his head. "Lord Hill likes our cap'n. Everyone likes our cap'n."

"That. Is. Enough." Each syllable cracked against the walls of the entryway. "You have work to do."

"Aye, Cap'n." Pluck grinned. "Have fun at the theatre." He snapped a rather cheeky salute and sauntered away.

"Your valet has a great deal of nerve," Philip said.

"Yes, well, Pluck isn't his Christian name."

"A name he earned, then." Philip chuckled.

"Thoroughly." Pluck had more courage than many grown men.

"Why did you decide to make him your personal servant if he annoys you so much?"

"It was *his* idea."

Philip laughed harder. "I like that boy."

"And what boy would that be?" Sorrel asked as she made her way down the stairs toward them. She had nearly as much trouble on stairs as Stanley did.

"Stanley's valet," Philip said. "The boy has a mouth like a river: it never stops flowing."

"Has he been telling secrets?" Sorrel's nearly constant solemnity stood in stark contrast to Philip's unending joviality.

"Of course he has." Philip took the hand Sorrel wasn't using to hold her walking stick and pulled her arm through his own. "That's why I like him so much."

"Encouraging insolence among the servants." Sorrel shook her head. "What will you think of next?" Her gaze settled on Stanley. "You look very nice this evening. Are you joining us?" She compressed her lips and narrowed her eyes on him as she waited for his answer.

"I thought I might." Stanley felt like a schoolboy nervously speaking to the schoolmaster.

"And the sight of Philip's wardrobe disaster didn't change your mind?"

"Disaster?" Philip scoffed. "It's a masterpiece, a tribute to—"

"The dangers of orange silk?" Sorrel tipped her head and raised an eyebrow. She looked Philip over with theatrical disapproval.

Philip's look of feigned shock very nearly slipped into a grin. Sorrel was good for him. She had managed what none of the rest of the family had. She had broken through Philip's dandified mask.

"Stanley?" His heart jumped at the unexpected sound of Marjie's eager voice. "Are you coming with us?"

Stanley watched her practically skip down the stairs. A breathtaking smile lit her face. Her eyes shone as brightly as he'd remembered them every single night he'd been away. He'd hated himself for tainting his memories of her with the sounds and smells of the battlefield, but without her to focus on, Stanley knew he would have gone mad.

Marjie came directly to where he stood, gazing up at him. There was something almost blasphemous about looking at her with the same eyes that had watched men blown to pieces.

"I had so hoped you would," she said. "This is to be our last trip to the theatre before we return to Nottinghamshire." She watched him, uncertainty in her expression.

He managed a small smile. His heart thudded against his ribs at the smile he received in return.

"I think you will like the show," Marjie said, her enthusiasm returning. Stanley had nearly forgotten how joyful she always was. That aspect of her character had drawn him to her from the beginning—his life as a soldier was nearly devoid of happiness. "Lord Devereaux will be there. He was at Almack's Wednesday night, and when I told him you might join us at the theatre, he said he would come along too."

"Lord Devereaux?" Stanley looked to Philip. Who was this Lord Devereaux, and what had he to do with Marjie?

"You may have met him," Philip said. "He is quite close with the Duke of Hartley. Active in Lords but has an atrocious sense of fashion."

"Which means he actually dresses like a reasonable person," Sorrel said, her tone dry as dust.

"I am astounded by your lack of enthusiasm, my dear." Philip pressed a hand dramatically to his heart. "One cannot underestimate the importance of one's wardrobe." Mischief twinkled in his eyes once more.

Sorrel simply shook her head, tilting the sides of her mouth at an amused angle.

"Lord Devereaux is older than you are," Philip said to Stanley. "He's been out of Society since his wife died. A fine gentleman, though, and apparently anxious to be in your company."

"You'll like him, Stanley," Marjie said. "I am certain of it."

An elderly widower seemed relatively unthreatening. Perhaps Lord Devereaux had reached the age of severe near-sightedness and would not notice anything amiss in Stanley's appearance. A certain degree of deafness would help as well. Lord Devereaux would be far less likely to ask questions if he were unable to hear the answers.

Thirty minutes later, however, Stanley felt like the veriest fool. Lord Devereaux arrived in the Lampton box shortly after they did. The elderly widower Stanley had been expecting proved to be quite young, surprisingly good-looking, and obviously in the pink of health. He greeted them all cordially and seemed genuinely pleased to meet Stanley, insisting "Miss Kendrick" had spoken highly of him.

Lord Devereaux was offered the seat beside Marjie as the curtain rose. Stanley found himself relegated to the seat beside Philip. He'd agreed to come to the theatre only because the idea of being with Marjie for the length of an evening had outweighed his desire to remain at home.

"How old is Lord Devereaux?" Stanley whispered partway through the first act.

"Thirty-two. Thirty-three," Philip whispered in return. "His wife was very ill for quite some time. She died quite young."

Stanley watched Marjie lean closer to Lord Devereaux for just a moment to say something to him. He could tell from Lord Devereaux's profile that he smiled back at her.

"He seems very . . . friendly."

"Those two are like a couple of hens," Philip said. "One would think they had been friends from the cradle the way they've taken to each other."

"Except, when she was in her cradle, he would have been"—Stanley calculated quickly—"fifteen years old, or so."

"That's not so unusual," Philip replied.

Stanley did not once turn his attention to the stage. Instead, he watched the exchange between Marjie and Lord Devereaux.

"The late Lord Techney was nearly two decades older than his wife," Philip whispered.

"*Wife*?" Stanley's eyes snapped to Philip. "Things lean that way?"

Philip shrugged. "I don't know if it is as serious as all that, but they have been very good for each other."

"Good in what way?" Stanley's gaze returned to Marjie.

"Marjie is not one for superficial friendships," Philip said. "The *ton*, on the other hand, specializes in empty associations. So Marjie has been a little lonely. Lord Devereaux has struggled since losing his wife. His required period of full mourning ended more than two years ago, and yet he has not been seen anywhere other than Parliament. That is, until this past month or so. Marjie appears to have helped him begin to work through his grief."

"Like his guardian angel." Stanley tried to breathe through the tension in his lungs. Throughout the past six months, he had thought of Marjie as *his* guardian angel.

"Most of Society is quite interested in the outcome of their association," Philip said. "Speculation is rife. Most, I think, feel they will eventually make a match of it."

Stanley didn't hear a single word spoken on the stage below. Philip had gone back to whispering with Sorrel. Stanley's eyes stayed on Marjie and Lord Devereaux, who never ran short on topics of conversation. They appeared wholly charmed by each other.

Stanley had told himself again and again during the months before Waterloo and the excruciating recuperation afterward that Marjie deserved better than him. She ought to marry a man who did not have blood on his hands, a man who wasn't a cripple, who wasn't so mutilated he could no longer write a simple sentence.

His angel had found someone better.

The pain of cracking skin told Stanley just how tightly he had wrapped his fingers around the arm of his chair. His heart thudded high in his chest, tattooing out a rhythm of grief. He couldn't watch them any longer. He groped in the dark, searching for his walking stick.

"Stanley?" Philip's whisper was loud enough to be heard over the pounding in Stanley's ears.

"I'm tired. I'm returning to Lampton House."

"On foot?" Philip asked.

"Don't be an idiot." Stanley rose as quickly as he could to his feet, using his chair for balance, then corrected his posture to that of a career soldier. "I will send the carriage back for you."

"You're certain you want to go by yourself?"

"I doubt the few miles across London will be any more dangerous than six years on the front lines," Stanley said. "I'll have Pluck read me a bedtime story if I have nightmares afterward."

"You are very suddenly in a bad mood," Philip said.

"I—I'm only tired," Stanley said and moved toward the door. "See you tomorrow."

"Don't you wish to say good-bye to Marjie?" Philip had followed him to the back of the box.

Stanley resisted the urge to look back toward the front of the box where Marjie sat. She, no doubt, would still be talking with *him*. He did not wish to see that any longer.

"If she asks"—the word *if* sat sour in his mouth—"tell her I was—"

"Tired?"

"Exactly. Deuced tired of this whole blasted mess."

"I didn't think the actors were that horrible," Philip said.

"Not the play," Stanley grumbled.

"Then what 'blasted mess'?"

Stanley shook his head, feeling as weary as he'd claimed to be. He was tired of it all. "Life, Philip. Life."

CHAPTER FIVE

Marjie had no idea why she was crying. Judging from the look on Lord Devereaux's face, neither did he.

"Have I said something to upset you?" he asked, forehead creased, his expression growing ever more confused.

"Not at all. I am not even certain why I am crying." She wiped at the tears that refused to stop. Thankfully, no one else in the drawing room seemed to have noticed. Explaining the downpour would have been both difficult and embarrassing. "I suppose I am a little weary. We were out late last night."

"Yes, I know. You were worn to a thread when you left the theatre. That is the chief reason I asked how your day had been. I hadn't meant to upset you with the question."

The tears picked up pace. Marjie almost laughed out loud at the look of near horror on Lord Devereaux's face. Why did gentlemen panic at the sight of tears? "I have had a difficult day," she confessed, attempting to smile.

"Tell me." That had become something of a regular expression between the two of them.

They had first met at a ball. Marjie had seen him sitting beside a pillar, alone, his spirits clearly depressed. Her heart had gone out to him; she had been feeling precisely the same way. Although Society would have condemned the forwardness of it, Marjie had made her way covertly around the room to where he'd sat and taken the seat beside him. His discomfort had been evident, but only a moment's conversation had overcome the awkwardness of their unconventional introduction.

She had learned that he was returning to Society for the first time in more than three years since his wife had died. He had not been at all certain of the wisdom of attending the ball. Not having his wife beside him at the very events she had once attended with him had proven far harder than he had anticipated. Marjie had told him of Stanley and how she missed him most during evenings just like that one.

The next evening he found her at a musicale. The Duke of Hartley, an acquaintance of Philip's and one of Lord Devereaux's closest friends, performed the required formal introductions. She and Lord Devereaux spent many an evening in one another's company, understanding, often silently, the loneliness the other endured. Whenever either noticed the other appeared particularly burdened, the phrase "Tell me" became a lifeline of compassion and empathy.

"I am worried about him," Marjie said, coming back to the present.

"Captain Jonquil?"

She nodded even as she forced the tears to stop. She simply could not break down again in a drawing room filled with half a dozen people in attendance for Sorrel's at-home.

"He left so suddenly last night," she said.

"Yes, I noticed his rather abrupt departure." Lord Devereaux had the oddest look on his face, as though Stanley's leaving had been almost expected and he found it a little amusing. "The daggers I could feel being thrown at the back of my head quite suddenly disappeared."

"Daggers?" What an odd thing to say.

Lord Devereaux didn't explain. "And does the good captain seem well today?" He sighed. "Here come the tears again."

Marjie shook her head at herself. "I am afraid I am a very emotional person. My sister finds me exhausting and regularly tells me so."

"You may tell your sister I find you delightful."

"She would never believe you." Marjie laughed lightly. She took a shaky breath and a moment to regain her composure. Lord Devereaux was a very patient and kind man, precisely the sort of gentleman she had always wished her father had been. "I believe I am under control now."

"For the moment, at least."

She smiled at him. "You're teasing me."

"Only a little," he said. "I think you need to be teased. Obviously, you have been far too often distressed lately."

Marjie sighed but, remarkably, didn't feel a single tear threatening to spill. "I simply don't know what to make of the change in him."

"Has he been unkind to you?" Lord Devereaux's tone grew concerned.

"He has not been kind nor unkind. He has been absolutely nothing." Marjie twisted her handkerchief around her fingers. "He does not speak to me or seek me out. He seldom even looks at me. I don't know if he is unwell or if his experiences changed him or if—if he does not—" *If he does not care for me anymore.* She couldn't force the words out.

Lord Devereaux took hold of her hand, his grasp light and comforting. "I learned through difficult experience that it does not do to ask 'What if?' What will be, will be. Only when you allow yourself to stop worrying over those things you cannot control will you truly have any hope in your life."

"Hope should lessen one's worries," Marjie said. Sorrel had told her that.

Lord Devereaux squeezed her hand and released it. She glanced up at him. His expression had grown sad once more—he was thinking of his wife again and missing her.

"I am sorry to be burdening you with my concerns," Marjie said. "I know you have enough of your own."

"Time spent with a friend is never a burden." And yet his words and expression were not light.

"You must be eager to accept the Duchess of Hartley's invitation to her Christmas house party." Marjie knew he was anything but eager, but she further knew attending would do him a world of good.

"The fact that I am even considering attending is remarkably uncharacteristic," Lord Devereaux said. "I doubt Her Grace has yet recovered from the shock of not receiving an immediate denial from me."

"I hope you do go," Marjie said. "It would be a very merry way to spend the Christmas season."

"Merry is not my usual style."

"I think it once was."

The drawing room had thinned of all visitors except Lord Devereaux. Sorrel sat on the sofa reading a book. Philip had left at some point.

"When do you leave Town?" Marjie asked.

"At the end of the week," Lord Devereaux said. "I have delayed my departure longer than usual."

"Will you be attending Lord and Lady Techney's ball tomorrow evening?" Marjie asked. She hoped he would be.

"Yes, it will be my social swan song for the remainder of the year," Lord Devereaux said. "I hope you will save a dance for me."

"Save a dance?" Marjie smiled. "Do you really think I will so suddenly be in demand?"

"Pardon me for saying so, but I sincerely hope not." Lord Devereaux looked a little embarrassed by the admission. "I would miss your company if you spent the entire evening being squired about by all the young bucks of the *ton.*"

"Captain Jonquil will not be dancing," Marjie said. "Perhaps he will sit with us and you will finally have a chance to truly know him." Lord Devereaux had expressed a desire to meet Stanley but had not been granted the opportunity beyond the very brief introductions the evening before.

"I suspect, Miss Kendrick, that Captain Jonquil would not care to sit with the two of us."

"Why not?" She was absolutely certain Stanley and Lord Devereaux would like each other.

Lord Devereaux smiled briefly. "My dear girl." He shook his head. "Sometimes you are far too sweet natured for your own good."

"Sorrel always says I am too vexing for my own good."

"I think I need to have a talk with your sister. She does not appreciate you enough."

"That is a very kind thing to say."

Something seemed to catch his attention, and Lord Devereaux's gaze shifted away from her. "Captain Jonquil," he said, rising to his feet.

Marjie turned. Stanley stood not ten feet from them, leaning on his walking stick, his eyes locking with hers. He never allowed his gaze to linger, a tendency he had acquired since their separation in March. She couldn't look away, the unexpected contact entirely capturing her.

Abruptly, his gaze darted to Lord Devereaux. Stanley bent at the waist, though he seemed unable to make the required bow. "Lord Devereaux."

Stanley's eyes returned to Marjie, and she had to concentrate on simply breathing. The shadows of illness still marred his face, but his eyes were as captivating and beautiful as ever. "Miss Kendrick." Again he managed a semblance of a bow.

"Good afternoon," Marjie said.

"You've been crying," Stanley said.

"Only a little," Marjie said.

"Why was she crying?" Stanley's gaze skewered Lord Devereaux. His question sounded far more like a demand.

Lord Devereaux didn't flinch, didn't look remotely intimidated. "Why don't you tell me?"

"Me?" Stanley looked and sounded confused. Marjie was confused herself. "I haven't been anywhere near her all day."

"Thank you for making my point," Lord Devereaux said.

"Ah, Lord Devereaux. I hoped you were still here." Philip's voice cut through the thick tension. "Could I have a moment?"

"Certainly." Lord Devereaux turned back to Marjie. "Miss Kendrick, it has been a pleasure, as always." He bowed over her hand. "I look forward to seeing you tomorrow evening."

"As do I," Marjie said.

Lord Devereaux made his farewells to Sorrel. He gave Stanley a look that could be described only as a challenge as he passed. What had come over him? Lord Devereaux was generally very quiet and even-tempered.

"Where are you going tomorrow evening?" Stanley asked.

"Tomorrow evening?" Her eyes returned to him once more.

"Lord Devereaux said he would see you tomorrow." Stanley's brow pinched as he watched her.

"Lord and Lady Techney's ball." She resisted the urge to smooth his forehead with her finger. A man who, by his own admission, hadn't been near her all day would likely not welcome such liberties. "He will be attending, and so will we."

Stanley did not look away, neither did he speak.

"Lord Devereaux does not ever dance, and I seldom do." Marjie tended to ramble under the influence of uncertainty. "At most balls, we spend a lot of time simply sitting and talking. I told him I thought you might enjoy joining us, but he seemed to think differently. I can't understand it. He seemed to wish to make your acquaintance when I told him you had returned home, but just now, he was a little unwelcoming when I suggested you could sit with us tomorrow evening. It was almost as if he didn't want you there."

Marjie wasn't certain that was quite the right interpretation of Lord Devereaux's reaction, but it was the best she could manage. He certainly hadn't agreed that Stanley would enjoy the arrangement.

"I'd wager he *doesn't* want me there." Stanley spoke so quietly Marjie wondered if she was meant to overhear. His eyes had swung to the door Lord Devereaux had left through, his expression thoughtful. "What did he do to make you cry, Marjie?"

"He didn't make me cry. He simply asked me a question I wasn't expecting."

Stanley grew quite still. "He asked you a question? One that made you cry?"

Every ounce of color drained from his face. Marjie reached out in anticipation of a collapse. His glove pulled tight around the top of his walking stick, and his posture grew rigid.

"Stanley?" She touched his arm.

He still did not look at her. "Did you answer him?"

Had she answered the question? "Not entirely," she said. "But I imagine he'll ask me again."

"What will your answer be?" His eyes bored into hers.

What would she answer the next time Lord Devereaux asked about her day? "I hope I will have a very positive answer."

His hand caught hers, and his searching blue eyes grew intent upon her face. "But you aren't certain that's how you'll answer?"

"No." How was she supposed to know how some future day would go?

"Excuse me." He pulled away without explanation or preamble. His bow, though less graceful than Lord Devereaux's, was everything that was correct and proper.

Not another word between them was spoken. Stanley turned and walked unevenly out of the room.

J

CHAPTER SIX

"Oh, you're just so dashing in yer uniform, Cap'n Jonquil." Pluck flipped an imaginary lock of hair behind his shoulder and batted his eyelashes. Stanley was absolutely certain Pluck's voice hadn't been so piercingly high in a decade or more. "I'd be honored iffen ye'd sit beside me at this bang-up ball we're attendin'."

Stanley kept himself from smiling right up until Pluck started prancing around the room, humming several octaves above what was natural. Stanley actually laughed out loud when Pluck attempted a flitting leap.

"Oh, Cap'n, yer lyrical laughter is just music to me dainty, girlie ears!"

"It's a very good thing you didn't enact something like this on the Continent," Stanley said. "The rest of the artillery would have strapped you to the cannons."

"They'd have laughed till they wet themselves," Pluck said. "Those boys was always laughin' at somethin' or other."

"I know. We could hear the gunners laughing all night long." Stanley turned toward his mirror, checking his appearance again. His face had filled out a little since his return, though he still wouldn't be considered healthy looking by any stretch of the imagination. "I always wondered what was so blasted funny about gunpowder and exploding balls of lead."

"We weren't laughin' about guns, Cap'n." Pluck didn't actually roll his eyes, but he sounded very much as if he had.

"What, then, were you laughing about?" Stanley asked. War was not at all funny.

"Stories from growin' up. Jokes we'd heard along the way." Pluck moved closer and gave Stanley a look over. "Most of us was from London—street kids—ye know. We seen some funny things, heard some jokes that'd make a man laugh till he cried, but not the sort ye'd tell to yer mum."

"I would imagine not."

Pluck straightened Stanley's collar, then looked him up and down. "Ye look a regular rum duke, Cap'n," he said.

Stanley doubted he cut such a handsome figure as all that.

In the next instant, Pluck's expression showed similar doubt. "That walking stick's something of a sorry sight. Thing ain't even straight. Makes ye look pathetic, it does."

"Yes, but less pathetic than I would look sprawled in a heap on the floor." Stanley limped away. He didn't need to be reminded of the picture he made. Lord Devereaux would be reminder enough. The man was almost ten years older than Stanley but looked younger than he did. Lord Devereaux was fit and would be considered handsome. And apparently, he and Marjie were far more than friends, despite Philip's explanation at the theatre earlier that week.

"I ain't suggestin' ye go without a walking stick," Pluck said. Stanley could tell he had followed him across the room, but he didn't look back. "Just that ye not use that one."

"You have a walking stick simply lying around, I suppose." Stanley carefully smoothed his right glove. The skin beneath was tender, as always.

"Might happen to."

Stanley did not at all like the sly edge to Pluck's voice. He turned, careful not to dump himself on the floor in the attempt. His inert right leg did not always turn with him.

"How did you come to be in possession of a walking stick?" Stanley asked warily. "I doubt you carved it yourself."

"I stoled it." Pluck shrugged.

Stanley's stomach dropped. "Pluck." Growing up in the seedy parts of London, the young man was bound to have picked up a few undesirable habits. Stanley had not thought he was a criminal. "You cannot—"

Then he noticed Pluck was grinning. Stanley knew that look. "Where did you really get it?"

"From His High an' Mighty Lordship," Pluck said. He reached behind the chest of drawers and pulled out an ebony walking stick.

"The earl gave you his wife's walking stick?" That didn't seem likely. Sorrel couldn't walk far without it.

"Nah." Pluck spun the stick around in his hand. "It's his High an' Mighty Lordship's own twig, it is. Says he don't carry it no more, seein' as how his lady cuts a finer figure with hers—she makes him look like a bumblin' noddy by comparison."

"It looks just like hers." Stanley would have sworn it was Sorrel's.

"Aye," Pluck said. "An' it'll look right nice with yer uniform." Pluck tossed the stick, and Stanley caught it with his left hand.

It was lighter, much less clumsy than his own. One would purchase just this type of fine walking stick with the intention of using it for years on end. His stick was meant as a temporary fix to his rather permanent problem. One of his men had carved it for Stanley to use while they waited to see how long he lived before infection set in.

"I don't know." Stanley eyed the smooth, polished wood. It wasn't the type of implement he'd take back to the Continent with him. Practicality always trumped appearance in the army.

"C'mon," Pluck said. "Your lady's nearly engaged to some nambsy swell, an' you're gonna arrive at the ball with a log of wood what makes you look like a common beggar? What kinda soldier are ye? Cain't head off to war with slingshots when the enemy's armed with muskets. Even those who volunteered for a folorn hope were given ammunition, though they knew they was signin' up for almost certain death—chargin' the enemy first, like they was."

"I was part of the forlorn hope at Orthez, Pluck. You don't have to give me details."

"An' ye didn't survive it by goin' in with a target on your chest and a big sign sayin' 'Shoot me,' did ye?" Pluck pulled Stanley's outer coat from the clothes press. "Ye went in fightin', even though everyone knew the slim chances of success."

"Are you saying this endeavor faces similar odds?" Stanley gripped Philip's walking stick ever tighter. He didn't want to hear Pluck's answer, though he knew perfectly well what it was. A hardened, broken man like he was had little to offer a beautiful, joyful young lady like Marjie.

Pluck shrugged. "Lord Devereaux's staked his claim, and he's claimed the stronghold. You're rushin' the defenses, puttin' yourself in the line of fire. Maybe ye'll come out the winner; maybe ye won't."

"Most men don't survive a forlorn hope." It seemed an appropriate metaphor—men rushing to death and glory in the name of battle strategy. There was a reason volunteers were used for the first attack against a fortified enemy stronghold. No one should be forced into a suicide mission. "It's generally a lost cause."

"When did ye begin giving up on lost causes?" An earnestness overtook Pluck's words. "Even when a roaring fire trapped a whole battery of artillerymen, ye didn't ride off like all the others. Ye didn't say 'Bad luck,' and get on with it." Pluck's voice grew thick. Stanley knew the boy was reliving those moments at Waterloo when he could very easily have been burned alive. A sheen of tears too minuscule to be noticed by anyone who didn't understand the devastating impact of battle memories hung on Pluck's lashes. "Ye pulled a worthless street orphan outta the flames 'cause ye didn't give up on 'im."

Stanley squared his shoulders against the weight of his own recollections. Soldiers never permitted their emotions to surface. "Pluck—"

"A man who'd do that ain't the sort to let some highbrow cove run off with his woman."

"Miss Kendrick was never actually mine." Even the tentative claim he'd once had was no longer valid. He'd been whole before physically, if not entirely mentally. Though the war had taken a toll before Waterloo, he'd had some hope of putting the years of bloodshed behind him. That hope had drowned in the muddy fields near Brussels.

Exasperation filled Pluck's eyes. "Ye didn't let the Frenchies have Orthez. Don't let ol' Lordy-Pants have your lady."

"*Ol' Lordy-Pants*? That is an expression you'd best not say in front of anyone else."

"Time to be a man, Cap'n. Rush the wall. Fight for what's yours."

"You are missing a rather vital aspect of the analogy, Pluck." Stanley, however, had caught on immediately. "In the end, we gave Orthez back. It never belonged to us."

"Aye, but it didn't belong to ol' Nappy, now, did it?"

"Are you comparing Lord Devereaux to Napoleon?"

"I'm only sayin' if you ain't planning to try and win Miss Kendrick for yerself, at least make certain she's getting a good deal, you know?"

"Save her from the cruel clutches of a heartless dictator?"

"An' if you steal a bit o' her heart along the way"—Pluck managed to look almost coy—"well, them's the spoils of war. And it's somethin' to carry back with ye when Daddy Hill comes a-callin'."

A little bit of her heart. It was more than he deserved, but heaven help him, he needed it. He needed the reassurance that there was some part of him that was good and unsullied enough for an earthbound angel to love.

"So what's it gonna be, Cap'n?" Pluck asked. "The target-on-my-chest, shoot-me-sign walking stick or the fancy, look-out-Lord-Nimbsy-Bum-I'm-watchin'-ye one?"

"*Nimbsy-bum*?"

Pluck didn't answer beyond a crisp nod.

Stanley tossed his rough-hewn walking stick to Pluck. Philip's stick fit oddly in his scarred hand, but he would adjust. He was determined to.

"Forlorn hope?" Pluck asked with a grin.

Stanley nodded. "Time to rush the wall."

Pluck shoved a fist in the air.

"Don't you dare start prancing around like a little girl again."

"But, Cap'n Jonquil, ye're just so han'some and heroic," Pluck answered in that ridiculously high voice he'd used before. He batted his eyelashes again, so Stanley shoved him with his free hand.

Pluck laughed, and Stanley couldn't help doing the same.

A knock echoed off the door. "Stanley?" What was Marjie doing at his door?

"Rush the wall, Cap'n."

Stanley hobbled in that direction. "You've got it wrong, Pluck. She is the city, not the wall."

"Either way."

Stanley opened the door, his heart thudding far too loudly. He'd done his best to look presentable but knew he paled in comparison with Lord Devereaux.

"Good evening, Mar—" Her brows were drawn, her eyes pleading. "What is it?"

"I went down to the entryway to wait, and Sorrel was there, sitting in a chair. She looks ill. She's pale, and her eyes are glossed over." Marjie wrung her hands. "She hates when I fuss over her, but I'm worried. I am certain she is on the verge of one of her fevers. She would let Philip help her—I know she would—but I don't know where he is."

"He's probably in his rooms." Stanley looked over his shoulder at Pluck. "Deliver a message to his lordship. Tell him his wife appears to be ill and he is needed in the entryway."

"Yes, Cap'n Jonquil." Pluck snapped a salute that was, for once, not even remotely cheeky. He left quickly, an advantage to having a young, energetic valet and a reasonably well-trained soldier.

Stanley turned back toward Marjie. The worry hadn't left her eyes. "You and I will go down to the entryway and see that Sorrel is well."

He stepped from his room, intending to make his way downstairs. Marjie didn't follow as he'd expected her to.

"But Philip says I'm not supposed to make a fuss over her," she said. The lines of worry hadn't left her forehead.

"No fuss," Stanley said. "We'll simply keep an eye on her."

Marjie nodded, though she still seemed hesitant.

"If they voice any objections, we'll tell them it was my idea," Stanley said.

Marjie smiled a little. "They'll never believe you."

"I'll take my chances." Stanley motioned for her to come with him. "Let's go make sure Sorrel is well. It may take Pluck a minute or two to track down Philip."

For a moment, he lifted his arm, intending to offer his hand. She looked very much as if she needed a reassuring touch. He realized almost on the instant that he required both hands to navigate the stairs. His hand fell back to his side.

Rush the wall. How ridiculously pompous it sounded. He could hardly walk down a flight of stairs.

"I hope Philip can convince her to stay home tonight," Marjie said as they walked slowly down the stairs. "Sorrel can be very stubborn about these things, and she ends up only more ill than before. I don't want her to suffer."

When a man loved a woman, he simply didn't allow anyone or anything to hurt her, not if he could possibly prevent it. Philip loved Sorrel. He could be trusted to do all he could to secure her welfare.

Marjie's compassion had always astounded him. Her beauty had taken his breath away from the first moment they'd met. Her sweetness had been a balm to a soul ravaged by the violence of war.

He would never let anyone hurt her or make her unhappy, even if it meant making sure she found a gentleman who was better for her than he could ever be.

J

CHAPTER SEVEN

Sorrel looked precisely as Marjie had described her. She sat on a chair near a tall window in the entryway, pale and still.

"Stanley is coming with us this evening," Marjie said to her sister. Stanley could hear the edge of worry that colored her tone, though she did an admirable job of sounding casual.

"Pulled himself out of his exile, did he?" Despite the show of wit, Sorrel's words were noticeably belabored.

Her lack of coloring and the weariness of her posture spoke volumes about the state of her health. There was no evidence of fever in her eyes. He'd learned to look for that in the army. Once illness clouded a soldier's eyes, it was time for the doctors to intervene.

"You have a new walking stick," Sorrel said. "A definite improvement."

"I was told the last one was pathetic."

She shook her head. "The last one was a concession."

What did she mean by that? And why did his choice of walking stick matter so much to her? She had been out of patience with him since his return. She hadn't been that way before he'd left for the Continent.

She closed her eyes and rubbed at her left temple with one hand. The other hand, Stanley noticed, was balled in a fist on her lap.

"Lady Techney, I have heard, has decorated her ballroom to look like an ancient Grecian temple." Marjie's words sounded forced. Her hands grasped one another, and her eyes never left her sister. "White pillared columns and hanging vines." She continued her description as Stanley turned toward the stairs, hearing light footsteps descending.

Philip's eyes met Stanley's, a question evident in his expression. "How ill is she?" he whispered as he came to Stanley's side.

"Not too bad off," Stanley said, whispering as well. "But she is certainly unwell." He spotted Pluck standing quietly in the shadows beside the stairwell.

"How long do you think she has before it reaches its height?" Philip asked.

Stanley suffered from the same ailment as Sorrel: recurrent fevers following a very severe injury. The shoulder wound he'd received at Orthez would begin to swell, and his entire right shoulder would grow warm to the touch. Within a few hours, his body would grow lethargic and achy. The fever would begin within a day, reaching its climax after two or three days had passed. "Two days," Stanley answered. "Perhaps fewer."

"Lud, I wish there were a way to get out whatever it is that keeps causing these infections," Philip said. His eyes were on his wife, frustration pulling his mouth in a sharp line.

"But there isn't," Stanley said. He understood that well. The universal opinion of his own situation was that a piece of shrapnel was still embedded in his shoulder but too deeply to have been seen when the wound was originally cleaned. Should it someday work its way close to the surface, it could be removed and the fevers might stop.

"Well, time to beard the lion," Philip said. "This is always something of a delicate undertaking."

"She does not like being fussed over." Stanley had seen Sorrel pull up stiff at anything she considered coddling.

"It is more that she does not like feeling broken. Reminders of her delicacy are unwelcome, to say the least."

Stanley could appreciate that. He watched Philip cross to where Sorrel sat. No one seeing his not-a-care expression would ever guess he was worried.

"Anything else ye be needin', Cap'n?" Pluck had slid up to him.

"Not at the moment," Stanley answered. "But be on the ready. I have a feeling we're about to break camp."

"Aye, Cap'n." A well-executed salute signaled his departure.

"Have you finished reconstructing Rome?" Sorrel was saying to Philip.

"My dear, do I look finished?" Philip scoffed. He was without his jacket, though the rest of him was done up to completion.

Sorrel's mouth tightened, the knuckles of her fist turning white. "Someone sent for you."

Stanley felt Marjie's eyes on him, and he flicked his own gaze in her direction. How was it that she could look at him in such a way that every protective instinct he possessed was suddenly at the ready? He motioned her over to him. If Sorrel meant to get spitting mad, Marjie ought to be out of firing range.

"Oh, Stanley," Marjie said.

Stanley kept his hand on his walking stick, forcing himself to ignore the temptation to pull her into his arms. She was practically engaged to another man.

"I don't want her to be angry with me."

"Sending for Philip was my idea," Stanley reminded her. "I will tell your sister as much if she makes an issue of it."

"Why would someone send for me?" Philip asked Sorrel. He raised an eyebrow as if to say he knew full well the reason but intended to make her admit that she'd kept something from him.

Sorrel looked away from him, her mouth shut in a straight line.

Philip sighed. He knelt on the floor in front of Sorrel, something no true dandy would ever do. He touched his hand to her forehead. Dropping it back to his side, he asked, "How long has this been coming on, love?"

Sorrel didn't look back at him. "I have been a little sore this last week or so." She waved a hand as if dismissing the complaint.

Philip took her hand and held it in front of him. "A week?" He sounded frustrated, a little upset even. "How is it that you have been ill for an entire week and didn't tell me?"

"I haven't actually been ill. Only sore."

Stanley felt Marjie's hand grasp his arm. His heart rate nearly tripled.

"It always starts with her being sore," Marjie whispered.

"Philip will look after her," Stanley whispered back. He laid his hand on hers, where it rested on his arm, savoring what was sure to be a fleeting moment.

"Let's go home, Sorrel." Philip lightly touched his wife's face. "Lampton Park must be horribly quiet with all of us gone."

"You had not intended to leave Town this early," Sorrel said.

"True, I did not."

She shook her head, slipping free of Philip's touch. "I promised myself I wouldn't be a burden, that I wouldn't let my struggles, my worries be—"

Philip pressed his fingers to her mouth, stopping her words. "There are no *your* worries and *my* worries any longer. There are only *ours*. In this moment, our only true worry is whether or not we can pack up this ridiculously large entourage of ours before you are entirely delirious." Stanley could hear a smile enter his brother's tone. "Although that could be entertaining."

Sorrel smiled indulgently but not very broadly.

Philip stood once more, holding his hand out to her. Once she was on her feet, they walked toward the stairs. Her limp was noticeably more pronounced.

Marjie's hand tightened around Stanley's arm. He was certain she was struggling not to "fuss," as Philip had apparently labeled her attention to her sister's well-being. Marjie would worry until they were back at Lampton Park, where Sorrel could rest and recover.

"Philip." Stanley stopped him as he passed.

With his head turned toward Stanley and away from Sorrel, Philip's face transformed from merely attentive to fully concerned, something he apparently did not wish Sorrel to see.

"If you'd like to leave in the morning, I will see to it," Stanley said.

"Could you truly manage it?" Philip looked hopeful.

"I have helped to orchestrate massive troop movements," Stanley said. "This will be far simpler."

"I would appreciate it."

Stanley nodded. "Have yourselves ready with the most basic necessities. I will see to the rest."

"Thank you." Philip grasped Stanley's upper arm for just a moment before continuing to walk with Sorrel toward the stairs.

Neither Stanley nor Marjie spoke as Philip and Sorrel made their way up. Marjie laid her head against his arm. Stanley closed his eyes and simply felt her there. During the months of their separation, Stanley had easily pictured her. He had vividly remembered the scent of her and the sound of her voice. But he had been utterly unable to fully replicate in his memory the impact of her touch.

He'd tried to imagine it countless times during tedious hours of marching, on the night before Waterloo, through the excruciating pain of amputation and the horrendous weeks that had followed. Nothing had filled the void. Nothing had taken away his pain. It lingered still, gnawing away at him. But in that moment, he felt relief, however small and fleeting.

"Is there anything I can do to help?" Marjie shifted and abruptly broke the contact between them.

He wanted to beg her to not step away, to tell her how desperately he needed her close to him. *Do not add to her burdens*, Father's voice commanded in his mind. Stanley pushed the emotions away, reminding himself he had a task, an assignment. "Have your abigail pack enough for the journey. The rest will follow later."

"I hope we are easier to deal with than an entire regiment of soldiers," Marjie said, smiling at him.

"I think nearly anything would be easier than the army in wartime." He'd meant his response to sound light, but his mind instantly filled with voices shouting over exploding cannon fire and the chaotic rush of men attempting to maintain rank and fulfill orders in the face of shattering fear. Stanley pushed it all back, reminding himself that a soldier kept marching no matter what.

"I am glad we are returning to the Park," Marjie said.

Stanley nodded, though he didn't agree. He had dreaded returning to a place that had always felt peaceful, knowing he brought with him too many regrets and wounds for even that haven to offer an escape.

"I should probably send Lord Devereaux a note explaining why we were not at the ball." Marjie's expression had grown thoughtful. "He will wonder why we did not attend."

A surge of jealousy shot through Stanley. "Do you write to him often?"

"Actually, no. I cannot say that I have ever personally sent him a letter. Philip or Sorrel send him invitations and notes when necessary. They say it wouldn't be proper for me to write to him because we are unwed and unrelated."

Stanley nodded. He did have one thing Lord Devereaux did not: twenty-four letters in Marjie's own hand. Stanley kept them with him always. "Perhaps Philip could send around a note in the morning before we leave."

Marjie smiled once more. "I'll ask him. In the meantime, I suppose I ought to start Jane on the packing."

"A very good idea." Except doing so would necessitate her leaving his side, something Stanley could not conjure any enthusiasm for.

Marjie touched his arm again. He stiffened his posture and pulled his mind out of the moment, just as he'd learned to do in the aftermath of a battle. Doing so had kept him from breaking down.

She deserves better, he reminded himself. *Do not add to her burdens.* Still, another part of him shouted, *Rush the wall!*

"Sleep well, Stanley." Marjie's blue eyes looked directly into his.

He nodded. "You as well."

He stood in place, watching her as she made her way up the stairs. She reminded him of a butterfly flitting around full of energy and life. Forcing her to be his solace and comfort would drain that life from her. War did that; it destroyed everything it touched.

"Ye shoulda kissed her, Cap'n."

Stanley jerked his head toward the sound of Pluck's voice.

"A woman don't look at a man like that unless she's wantin' some affection." Pluck walked to where Stanley stood, the lone occupant of the very empty entryway. "This ain't exactly my idea of stormin' the citadel."

"'Rushing the wall,' Pluck. Try to keep the metaphors straight."

Pluck crossed his arms in front of him. Every hint of soldier had disappeared. Stanley couldn't begin to count the number of times he'd nearly snapped, "Always a soldier" at Pluck. He never had though. Being a soldier hadn't yet destroyed Pluck's *joie de vivre.* Stanley couldn't bring himself to be the one to turn the boy into a hardened cynic.

"Aye. So what is it you're doin' if ye ain't rushin' the wall? Maybe I weren't in the army long enough to learn the official word for 'just sittin' on our bums waitin' to be blown to bits.'"

"We are breaking camp," Stanley said. He walked toward the book room, motioning for Pluck to follow him. Even with a limp, Stanley moved with the determination born of more than half a decade of marching across Europe. "I need you to take down a list for me."

Stanley couldn't write with his right hand anymore. He'd discovered, however, that telling Pluck something was as good as etching it in stone. Pluck couldn't write much other than his own name, but he never forgot anything. He'd been utterly wasted in the artillery. The boy ought to have been in reconnaissance. In the end, Pluck had, as Stanley's batman, been put to good use conveying information between the various commanding officers who had been charged with putting the Continent back together after nearly two decades of war.

Pluck tapped his finger against his head just above his temple. "Ready when ye are, Cap'n."

J

CHAPTER EIGHT

"Remind me to always bring Stanley along when I travel," Sorrel said as their carriage rolled up the drive to Lampton House. "He managed to orchestrate the closing of Lampton House in mere hours, something that usually requires a week or more."

"He didn't reach the rank of captain by being inefficient, my dear," Philip replied.

That was most certainly true. Marjie had never in all her life seen anything as efficient as Stanley's oversight of their departure. With only twelve hours' notice, he had arranged for breakfast to be delivered to all of their rooms on trays and for the carriages—one for Philip, Sorrel, Marjie, and Stanley, and the other for their personal servants—packed and ready to depart an hour after their morning meal. A hot brick had already been placed inside, leaving the carriage interior comfortably warm. A basket of food had been provided for their journey. The London staff had been left with very specific instructions for packing those belongings left behind and sending them on to Nottinghamshire. He had drafted a list of individuals to whom Philip's social secretary would send regrets and notices of the family's removal to the country in lieu of the usual calls of farewell. Everything had been seen to.

Stanley was certainly efficient, though *magnificent* felt like a better word.

Philip walked with Sorrel up the front steps of the manor house at Lampton Park, and the butler and staff greeted them. Stanley remained behind to issue directions to the footmen and stable hands. Marjie hovered in the doorway, watching him, worried.

Stanley rolled his right shoulder as if to work out a tight spot in it. Whatever injury he had sustained to his right leg had rendered his gait a little stilted and caused obvious stiffness in his ankle, but the effects of long hours in the carriage had not intensified his limp nor really changed it in any way. She hoped that was a good sign.

"Miss Kendrick."

She turned at the sound of the housekeeper's voice. Mrs. Beck, who oversaw the running of the Jonquils' country seat, smiled sweetly and indicated the maid waiting to divest Marjie of her coat and bonnet.

"His Lordship asked that you come along to the drawing room, Miss Kendrick."

Marjie nodded and looked one more time out the front windows at Stanley before walking down the corridor toward the drawing room. She had lived at Lampton Park for a month before going with Sorrel and Philip to London. Her mother had decided shortly after Sorrel's marriage that she did not at all like living at their home in Kent and, having declared herself free of the burden of caring for her crippled daughter—not that Mother had ever expended an ounce of energy on any of her children—wished to enjoy her freedom. She had taken up residence in Tunbridge Wells, where a childhood friend lived. Marjie had been sent to live with her sister. Fennel, their younger brother, was away at school.

Philip stood at the mantel in the drawing room. His mother, the Dowager Countess of Lampton, sat on a nearby sofa. She was remarkably unpretentious for a woman in possession of more titles and social standing than most anyone Marjie had ever known. Sorrel was not in the room, owing to her ailing state of health, no doubt.

The dowager looked up as Marjie entered. "Marjie, how wonderful to have you back."

"I am very happy to be back, Mater."

The dowager countess had insisted Marjie call her Mater, just as all her sons did. Marjie had come to think of the kindhearted woman as a surrogate mother. While in London, she had truly missed Mater's quick wit and humor, her affectionate nature, even the perpetual black she wore in mourning for a husband who had been dead for a decade. Marjie's family had not mourned their father at all in their hearts and had put aside their mourning clothes the very day convention had allowed them to.

She sat beside Mater, contentment settling over her like a warm blanket.

"Now, Philip." Mater exuded a fierce focus, her gaze not shifting from him in the least. "Where is my boy? I was specifically told by you, you will recall, *not* to come to London when he so unexpectedly arrived. You have brought him with you, have you not?"

Philip snapped his fingers. "I knew we forgot something. Maybe Sorrel remembered to stuff him in the boot with the luggage."

"None of your jesting, I warn you."

Philip smiled kindly. "Of course we have brought him home, Mater. He is outside playing general. He'll be in by and by."

Mater laughed lightly. "I remember the lot of you playing soldiers down by the Trent for hours on end when you were young, even including some of the neighborhood children on occasion. Little Arabella Hampton was always willing to join in the fun. Though *you* were the one playing general then." Tenderness filled the dear woman's eyes. "Your Father and I watched more reenactments of the War with the Colonies than I can even recall."

"Yes, but *we* actually won," Philip said. "It's amazing what one can do when historical accuracy is not a consideration."

Mater's smile remained only a moment before slipping noticeably. "How is he, Philip?" she asked. "Truthfully."

Philip hesitated. His brow furrowed. "He is not well, Mater," he finally answered. "He has sustained some sort of injury to his right leg, though I do not know the details."

Marjie saw Mater pale, so she took the woman's hand in her own.

"And if I am not mistaken, something has also happened to his right hand."

His hand? Why did Philip think something was wrong with Stanley's hand?

"He is right-handed, but he now eats exclusively with his left and puts on his hat with his left. The few times he has shaken a gentleman's hand, I've seen him wince, as if the gesture is painful. He tries to hide it, but I've noticed."

Marjie hadn't been as observant as Philip had been. What else had she missed?

"And otherwise?" Mater asked.

Philip pushed out a long, strained breath. "I think he is very unhappy."

Marjie's heart plummeted. Philip had quite succinctly expressed what she had been trying to identify ever since Stanley's return. He seldom smiled. He did not spend time in the company of other people. When in public, his rigid posture never eased into anything resembling comfort.

Marjie felt Mater squeeze her hand. How embarrassingly ironic. The dear lady's son was struggling and she had to comfort Marjie.

"He is home now," Mater said. She had straightened her spine and pushed back her shoulders. Marjie saw a little of a general in Mater as well. "We will see to it that he is well again."

Philip smiled and leaned against the mantelpiece, not far from where they sat. "I have already recruited Marjie to help in the effort. With the two of you joining forces, I don't see how we can possibly fail to pull our Stanley out of this state of blue devilment he's in."

Mater nodded her emphatic agreement.

An echoing click made its way in from the corridor.

Marjie was well acquainted with the sound of a walking stick and recognized it instantly. "I believe he is coming," she said to Mater.

A moment later, Stanley stood in the doorway. Marjie couldn't help thinking he looked apprehensive, nervous even.

"Oh, my dear boy." Mater's watery words accompanied her very sudden dash across the room. Her arms were around her son hardly before Marjie realized she had moved.

For just a moment, he looked like he might lose his balance, but he remained upright. Slowly, uncertainly, his left arm made its way around his mother, his right still grasping his walking stick. All the Jonquil brothers were tall—it was one of their more identifiable traits, one they quite obviously had inherited from their father. Mater's head did not even reach Stanley's shoulder.

"Oh, Stanley." Mater's words were muffled, her head pressed into Stanley's chest. "Forgive me for turning into such a watering pot. I have simply missed you so horribly."

"Don't you know a soldier likes to have a pretty lady cry over him?" Stanley's arm could not have been applying more than the lightest pressure against his mother, as if he was avoiding actually embracing her.

"*Pretty lady*? You boys and your glib tongues." Mater pulled back, her head moving as she looked him over, though she did not entirely release him. "You have come back to us whole," she said. "I prayed and prayed for that. The heavens must have listened."

Stanley nodded, his eyes moving away from her.

"Oh, my sweet Stanley." Mater touched Stanley's cheek. "Promise you will stay with us for a while."

"Until I am required to go back."

"Then let us hope that is not for a long while yet." Mater might very well have been speaking on Marjie's behalf.

Suddenly, there was a look of such intense sadness on Stanley's face that Marjie's lungs compressed painfully at the sight of it. What was he thinking of? What had upset him so entirely?

"Stanley?" Mater pressed.

As quickly as it had clouded, his expression emptied, and he stepped back. "I am a little fatigued from the journey," he said, his words halting. "I would like to retire for the evening. If you will excuse me."

He didn't wait for a response but moved quickly from the room. Marjie looked from Mater's surprised face to Philip's concerned one.

"He is not well." Mater still stood where Stanley had left her, looking in the direction of his departure. "I have never known him to be so distant and unaffectionate."

"I wanted to see how he would interact with you," Philip said. "I knew it would be more telling than almost anything else."

"He was always so attentive, caring to the point of being a bother at times." Mater turned back to face her eldest son. There was pain and worry etched in every line of her face. "The embrace he offered just now hardly counted as one. He said not more than a few words, none of them personal."

"Something happened to him, Mater." Philip looked weary, weighed down. "Mariposa said the war was destroying Stanley's soul. At the time, I thought she was exaggerating—she does have a tendency toward the dramatic."

Mariposa's flair for the dramatic was one of Marjie's favorite things about that particular Jonquil sister-in-law. Mariposa had known Stanley while she had lived in Spain and later in France. She had seen him as a solider and had lived through battles herself.

"I am beginning to think the newest Mrs. Jonquil was spot on the mark," Philip said. "I very much fear we are losing him."

Marjie would not allow Stanley to slip away from them all. His soul was worth fighting for. She would help him, whatever it took.

As if placed there by some invisible messenger, an idea formulated in her mind. Marjie excused herself and made her way from the room. She caught up with Stanley in the corridor leading to all the family rooms. She had been given the bedchamber she was told had once been Jason and Corbin's and was, therefore, very near Stanley's. Though she would have denied it had anyone asked, she had sat in Stanley's bedchamber during his absence, feeling closer to him by simply being in a room where he had spent so much of his life.

"Stanley," she called out to him.

He stopped only a few steps from his doorway and turned. She came to a stop directly in front of him. She stood close enough in that moment to smell his shaving soap, a scent she had become familiar with during her time spent sneaking into his empty bedchamber.

"There is something I have been meaning to give you." She rushed her words, attempting to get them out with what little air she could manage to press out of her suddenly tight lungs. "Would you wait here, please, while I retrieve it? I know precisely where it is and shan't be but a moment."

"I—" He looked uncomfortable. "I rather need to sit, actually." Was he blushing? "One would think after two days of sitting, I wouldn't have to do so again, but—"

"Of course."

His injury, whatever it might be, had begun to bother him again, and she was keeping him standing in the corridor. What a widgeon she was!

"I will bring it to your room. You can sit in there." She happened to know that a very comfortable armchair sat near the fireplace.

Not wishing to cause him any further inconvenience, Marjie hurried into her own bedchamber and directly to the portable writing table she'd brought back with her from Town. She opened the lid and shuffled around the stack of stationery, pulling out the sealed envelope beneath: her most recent letter to Stanley, the one she'd written in the hours before his unexpected arrival.

How she had longed for a letter. Had she ever received one from him, she was certain that would have brightened her spirits on even the darkest day.

She rushed back down the corridor. Stanley's door stood fully open. She knocked lightly before stepping through. Though being in his room with him, alone, was pushing the bounds of propriety almost beyond bearing, his door had been left wide open, and she meant only to be there for a brief moment. He hardly had the strength to stand; she couldn't be faulted for not insisting he suffer in the name of strict acceptability.

He was inside, just as she'd imagined him so many times. His presence changed the room entirely. Where she had once felt peaceful and filled with longing, she now felt anxious and as tense as the strings of a harp.

She pushed out a quick breath. She would not lose her courage.

He rose as she approached. She opened her mouth to insist that he need not but stopped herself, convinced that saying as much would only wound his pride. "I wanted to give you this." She handed the letter to him, feeling terribly uncertain. Was she doing the right thing? Would it even help?

He looked perplexed. "A letter?" he asked.

"I had intended to send it to you, but you returned before I could. I sent one every week you were gone. I am not certain how long they took to reach you or if they reached you at all—one can never be sure. It is probably silly to even give it to you. I doubt you actually want it." Why did she always ramble when she was nervous?

"Why would you think I would not wish for a letter from you?" Stanley's eyes were on the folded parchment he held, an intense look on his face.

"I—" She swallowed against the thickness in her throat, dropping her gaze to her hands. "I never could be certain you didn't find my letters more of an annoyance than anything else."

"An annoyance?"

She felt the softness of his glove on her chin and the gentle pressure as he tilted her face upward. Their eyes met, and her heart lurched inside.

"I was the envy of my entire regiment, I will have you know. Not a single one of them had such a faithful correspondent."

"But you never wrote back," Marjie whispered. That had hurt more than she had ever let on. Why would he not write if he truly cared for her?

"Life for a soldier is either excruciatingly dull or too horrific for a lady to read about," Stanley said.

"I would have been happy to receive a single line to say you were well."

"And if I wasn't well?" he asked. His hand had moved to cup her face, his gloved fingers lightly touching her jaw.

"I would have liked to have known that too." She closed her eyes, wanting nothing to interfere with the memory she was creating of the feel of his fingers on her face. Even through his gloves, the touch was magical.

"You would have only worried," he said.

She could feel the warmth of his breath against her face. He must have moved closer. She kept her eyes closed. Her heart raced. "Worrying could not have been worse than not knowing."

"Some things are better left unknown." His hand dropped away, and the warmth he'd offered fled.

She opened her eyes. He had, indeed, moved farther from her, and not just physically. His expression had closed off; his eyes were focused out the windows and away from her.

Some things are better left unknown. That admission held tremendous significance: an acknowledgment that he purposefully didn't speak of the things he'd experienced. Marjie felt to her very core that if he would just speak of and share his burden, he would improve. He would heal.

"Good night, Stanley," she said, wishing he would reach out to her again.

His gaze returned to her. "Good night."

Marjie turned and walked toward the open door. Her "quick" visit had lasted longer than she'd expected and had proven, for a moment, quite personal. The scheme, it seemed, had been a rather foolish one.

"Marjie." Stanley's voice stopped her in her tracks, though she didn't look back. "Thank you for the letter."

The tiniest whisper of a smile tugged at her mouth. Perhaps her idea had not been futile after all. "You're welcome."

J

CHAPTER NINE

HE'D ALMOST KISSED HER. THAT thought ran endless circuits in Stanley's mind all that night and into the next morning. As he always did, he told himself he would think about it later, but his mind refused to be fobbed off.

She had stood so very close. He'd been enveloped in that unique scent of hers. Hearing that she had wanted a letter from him and had been disappointed not to receive one touched him deeply.

Her words notwithstanding, he could not have written. Before Waterloo, there had been nothing he could have shared. Afterward, there had been nothing left of him worth sharing.

The head of Philip's stick was narrower than the one Stanley had been using, and therefore, the skin on his hand pulled more and the stretching was painful. The disfigured skin had broken across the joints of his hand. In the back of his mind, he knew infection, even amputation, remained a possibility.

He had not been back at Lampton Park twenty-four hours yet, and he already felt deucedly uncomfortable.

"You've come back to us whole," Mater had said with such obvious relief and satisfaction when he had first arrived. His being whole was important to her—she saw it as an answer to her prayers. Stanley would not disillusion her.

She had not received any letters from him and had apparently decided he could make up for his oversight by sitting down for a cozy chat in which he would share all the details of his six-month sojourn. He'd extricated himself with a vague reply and a noncommittal suggested postponement.

Philip had issued an invitation for him to join Philip and Layton, whose estate bordered the Park, for their morning gallop. His refusal must have seemed out of character for a man who had made a career in a mounted unit of the army. But he knew the awkward picture he made attempting to mount a horse. There would be no avoiding questions—nor the expected answers—if he were to provide his brothers that spectacle.

For such an enormous house in which only two of the original seven brothers were currently residing, Lampton Park felt suffocatingly crowded. If the weather hadn't turned nasty and wet, he would have walked down to the Trent in search of peace and quiet. As it was, he couldn't seem to escape. Even the servants made a point of smiling at him, the butler and housekeeper asking after his health and expressing joy at his return.

After glancing through the door of the conservatory to make absolutely certain the large indoor garden was unoccupied, he hobbled to the wrought-iron bench beneath the far windows.

Blessed quiet. No questions or stares or need to attempt to look happy. Rain ran in vertical rivers down the walls of glass, the wind blowing the trees outside. He took a deep breath and silently watched nature relieve her tension. He'd wept enough the day he'd lost his leg to rival any English rainstorm. It hadn't helped.

Pluck had told him later that during the amputation, when the pain had left him delirious, he'd cried out for Mater, had begged his father to make them stop, and had pleaded with everyone from the sawbones to Pluck himself to find Marjie—he had insisted he needed her with him. Someone, Pluck said, had pulled Marjie's letters from Stanley's satchel and had read them to him until he'd lost consciousness from the unendurable pain of it.

"At least ye shut yer mummer," Pluck had said. "'Bout near had me weepin' like a baby, ye did, crying fer yer mum like that. An' hearin' ye call for yer father was worse, seein' as how all of us knew he was dead an' had been since ye was a boy. I knowed ye was outta yer head then."

He had told Stanley all of that less than a month after the amputation. They hadn't spoken of it since. He'd been fitted for a counterfeit leg, had watched for infection, and had gone on as if nothing had happened. When the misery of it all became too much, he would take Marjie's letters out and read them again, though they were memorized. Then he would return to soldiering, walking upright and unflinching into the purgatory that had become his life.

The rain continued to pour outside. He pulled from his pocket a folded sheet of parchment. The handwriting and seal were identical to the twenty-four others he had in his room. This letter was not worn at the folds or spotted with stains, the origins of which he refused to contemplate. It was crisp and unsullied and unopened.

He had very nearly broken the seal the night before but hadn't been able to. He knew it was the last letter he would receive from her. So long as he remained at home, she wouldn't write, and he entertained significant doubts that she would write to him once he left again. Lord Devereaux would not approve of her doing so. He hadn't even wanted Stanley to attend the same ball as Marjie.

Once Stanley opened the final letter, that lifeline would be cut off. But he was drowning. Pluck would attack him with barrels of alcohol as soon as he saw the newly broken skin on his hand, and that would hurt like the devil. His family wasn't likely to leave him be either. Eventually Marjie's engagement would become official, and he would lose her despite never having had any real claim to her affection. He needed another letter the way so many of his fellow soldiers had come to depend on laudanum or alcohol to survive all they'd been through.

Stanley held the letter in his hand for a moment, simply looking at it. Not opening the blasted thing wasn't going to change the fact that he wouldn't receive any others.

He flipped it over. The Jonquil family seal pressed in deep red wax was affixed to the back. The seal Marjie had used had changed when she'd moved in with Philip and Sorrel. Somehow, he'd been under the impression it was merely a temporary arrangement, that she would be living with her mother again after the summer ended. He'd been so eager to read her letters he hadn't bothered to contemplate the significance of her continued use of the Jonquil seal and not the Kendrick one. If he'd paid attention to that detail, her presence at Lampton House might not have caught him so off guard.

"So, Marjie," Stanley whispered, slipping his finger under the seal. "This is to be your farewell."

The hardened wax gave way without the slightest fight. Still, he hesitated. His eyes swung back to the rivulets of rain wiggling their way down the glass surrounding him. It was an appropriately dreary day.

The stiff parchment rustled as he unfolded it.

Dear Stanley,

She probably should not have addressed him by his Christian name—they were not actually brother and sister, and there was no understanding between them—but he had no intention of correcting the lapse. Let Lord Devereaux make an issue of it if he chose. He had never heard Marjie refer to her soon-to-be-fiancé so intimately.

> *I have missed you. That is not a very sophisticated way to open a letter, but there you have it. The weather is turning cold, and I find it horribly sad. I hope the sun is shining where you are.*
>
> *Have you ever wished for something so fervently that when you opened your eyes you half expected to find your wish had been granted? That is how I feel about spring. I spend each winter wishing for the return of longer days and bright-green budding leaves. Mostly, though, I long for the flowers to return. The world is a far less dismal place when it is blooming.*

A whisper of a smile touched his face. She wrote to him of flowers and spring. Was it any wonder her letters had become a soothing medicine to him?

*Jason and Mariposa are now both away from Town, spending time with her family at Thornton Manor. While I do enjoy visiting with your brother and new sister-in-law, I regret most of all the loss of their butler's company. Black was quite possibly my favorite butler of all time. Again, I am probably proving myself terribly unsophisticated, but I confess I enjoyed the short intervals I spent with him. He tries so very hard to be the perfect butler and succeeds only in being very earnestly unsuccessful. Jason and Mariposa would not replace him for the world, however. I do believe they have grown attached to him. How very un*ton *of them! What shall we do, Stanley, with this very unfashionable family of yours?*

He knew Marjie well enough to recognize the implied humor in her anecdote. The brother just older than he had recently married, and according to Marjie's previous letters, Jason and his new bride had acquired a remarkably ragtag assortment of servants of whom they were inordinately fond. Had Marjie not been the very embodiment of honesty and had he not known Mariposa very well from the time he'd spent on the Continent, Stanley might not have believed it. Jason had ever been the overly proper, strictly civilized brother. Mariposa, it seemed, was good for Jason.

I fear there is little else to report. I have discussed with you the weather and gossiped quite horridly. All that remains is to comment upon the latest fashions, and we will have engaged in a very British conversation, indeed.

Except that only I have spoken. I shall do as always and imagine your replies, though I draw the line at actually speaking to myself. Poor Jane will think I have run mad should I begin doing that.

Please be safe, Stanley. Bask a moment in the sunshine of the Continent and think of me lonely amidst the fog and continuous drizzle of England. I have decided to no longer pester you for a reply—I am certain you have your reasons for not writing to me. I will simply continue to think of you and pray for you and miss you most acutely.

Yours, etc.,
Marjie

Expressing her desire to hear from him had ever been the closing thought in Marjie's cherished missives. But it seemed she no longer intended to ask.

She had given up on him.

Unexpected footsteps broke the silence of the room. He refolded his letter and slid it carefully back inside his pocket. He would place it with the other letters when he was next in his room.

The swishing sound of skirts told Stanley the arrival was female. He did not hear the tapping of a walking stick, so the newcomer was not Sorrel. Mater wore the heavier fabrics common amongst ladies of her generation, and the sound was not quite the same as he remembered from his days of long walks with her after Father died. Either a maid had come in to tend to something or Marjie had just entered Stanley's temporary sanctuary.

Thoughts of her upturned face inches from his own instantly filled his mind. She had stood there, a breath from him, with her eyes closed as if his touch had been as powerful for her as it had been for him. If only he'd been able to touch her face without the necessity of his gloves. He couldn't very well have taken off one and not the other. Seeing his discolored, misshapen hand would have led to unanswerable questions and looks of revulsion or, worse yet, pity.

From around a row of bushes, Marjie came into view. He saw her before she saw him. For that brief moment, he studied her, memorized the sight of her. She was the very picture of fragile English beauty, with her golden hair piled on her head, her pale skin soft against the powder-blue of her simple gown. She had an unspoiled sweetness one seldom found in the population at large.

For perhaps the thousandth time, he cursed Napoleon to perdition for leaving exile. Stanley had been far from blameless before returning to the war, but he'd had fewer lives on his conscience, fewer faces that swam accusingly through his thoughts, fewer regrets.

Marjie must have sensed his presence; her eyes stole about the room for a fraction of a moment before settling on him. He braced himself. How would she react to him after their near kiss the night before? Would she be offended? Wary? She was nearly engaged, after all.

A brilliant smile lit her face. "Good afternoon, Stanley," she said with every indication of pleasure at seeing him.

I hope the sun is shining where you are, she had written.

In that moment, it most certainly was.

J

CHAPTER TEN

If Stanley were smart, he would excuse himself and find a place far from the magnetic pull of Marjie's cheerfulness. He needed to learn to live without it. Yet, Pluck's words echoed in his mind. "Steal a little of her heart."

Heaven help him, he wanted just a piece.

"How are you today?" Marjie asked.

"I'm fine." It was the response everyone expected and, therefore, the one he always gave. "How are you?"

"Splendid." Another smile lit her face. "This is my favorite room in the entire house."

"Is it?" Stanley very nearly returned her smile.

"In here, it is always spring."

He absently pressed his hand against the outside of his pocket where her letter sat. Marjie had written that she longed for spring.

"A conservatory always feels very alive." She glanced around the room, a contented smile on her face.

He gazed around as well. The place teemed with vitality.

"May I sit by you?" she asked. Hope sparkled in her eyes.

Her request was unexpected. "Of course." The words sputtered a bit on the way out. He slid down the bench, moving to his right so she would be seated on the left. Though his right hand was encased in a glove, as always, and his artificial leg was beneath both his pantaloons and the thick leather of his boots, he felt less uneasy with her seated on his whole and unmangled side. No sooner had she sat beside him than Stanley realized having her that close undermined any sense of ease he might have felt, regardless of the side she occupied.

"Doesn't it smell wonderful in here?" she asked.

All Stanley could smell was her, though he couldn't begin to explain how he could distinguish between the rosewater scent she wore and the profusion of flowers blooming in abandon all around them.

"I came here every day before we left for Town." Marjie seemed quite content to talk without a reply, which suited Stanley perfectly. He enjoyed listening to her and knew that if he had something to say, she would happily listen. "I always wanted a conservatory growing up so I could enjoy flowers year-round. My father, however, believed conservatories and succession houses and the like were blasphemous."

"Blasphemous?"

She turned her head in his direction. Her smile had grown a little strained, though it had not disappeared entirely. "He had very decided opinions on God's view of things—he considered himself something of an authority, in fact. I asked my father once if we might have a conservatory, even a small one. He said that God had made the seasons and that He had intended for the world to be bleak and despairing in winter, and it was not for us to override that decree by recreating the warmer seasons."

"Did he object to warming the house in the wintertime?" Stanley asked.

"No." Marjie's expression grew just a touch ironic. "His condemnation of conservatories stemmed from the fact that their purpose was to grow things out of season. Also, he would have been remarkably uncomfortable in an unheated house, and I do not think he considered seeing to his own comfort a blasphemous endeavor."

"What of the comfort of his family?"

Marjie looked away again, out over the sea of greenery. "We learned to stay out of his way."

"He hurt you?" Every muscle in Stanley's body suddenly tensed at the thought.

"He never struck any of us. But his words were invariably unkind, and his evaluation of us all was harsh and condemning." Marjie took a deep breath, almost an inward sigh. "I envied Fennel's opportunity for escape to Eton, then, later, Sorrel's one Season in London. She had always been good at deflecting him. Those few months I spent without her were almost unendurable."

"Did your mother never intervene?"

Marjie looked at him once more, a sadness in her eyes that cut at him. "You have met my mother. Did she seem to you the sort of woman who would make an effort on another's behalf?"

Answering her question honestly would not be terribly gentlemanly of him.

"I tried to copy Sorrel's air of indifference," Marjie said, apparently not needing a response. "She would offer a slight shrug when his words stung, as if it didn't matter at all. I was never quite as good at that as she was. Father would simply laugh at me because I acted like I was unaffected even as tears rolled down my face."

If the man had still been alive, Stanley would have hunted him down.

"I used to pray that he would stop tormenting all of us. After Sorrel's accident, he became positively barbaric. She was the only one he could never reduce to tears, and I honestly think he hated her for it. He gloated over her near-death and the painful crippling that followed. He declared it the will of God, a sign that the heavens disapproved of her."

Stanley hadn't realized he'd taken her hand until he felt it tense inside his grip.

"I prayed harder than ever after that. I feared she would die, that I would fail her in that. Father didn't allow her to be seen by a physician, so I was all she had."

"You were so young."

"I prayed fervently, desperately pleading with God to just make our father stop terrorizing everyone so Sorrel could heal, so we could all live in peace." Her brow furrowed, her eyes gazing ahead as though she was completely lost in her thoughts.

Stanley squeezed her fingers.

"One morning," Marjie continued, "his valet came down to breakfast to inform us that our father had died during the night. The local physician believed he'd suffered a stroke. I told Sorrel; she had been confined to bed with a fever. That was the only time in my life I ever saw her cry."

Stanley laid his right hand atop hers, ignoring the pain that seared through him at the movement. Her hand sat encased in both of his, shielded the way he wished she'd been during those difficult days.

"'If I lived and he did not,' Sorrel said, 'then maybe God hated him more.' That was all she said. Sorrel improved quickly after that. Fennel was almost instantly more cheerful. Even Mother was happier."

"Were *you*?" Stanley asked.

"I tried very hard to be."

"But if your father made you so miserable, why were you more upset by his passing than the rest of your family was?" He could not bear the thought of her having been unhappy. He gently rubbed her hand, hoping to give some comfort.

"I worried that I had prayed him into his grave. I still am not entirely certain I did not. I have struggled to reconcile myself to that fact."

"Marjie, you couldn't possibly—"

"I knew the only true escape for any of us would be his death or our own." Her interruption was more heated than Stanley would have expected, although he did not think she was upset with him. She fidgeted, her brow furrowing under the influence of these memories. "Fennel, being the heir, is tied to the estate. Father would never have given his blessing to a potential suitor for Sorrel or me who wasn't precisely like himself. I realized beforehand that begging the heavens for release was tantamount to praying for someone's death. But I was infinitely glad in the end that he had died and not I."

"Oh, Marjie." The words were little more than a sigh.

He could not condemn nor dismiss her remembered concerns. He understood only too well the feelings she had described. He regretted every single life he'd taken as a soldier, and there were many. Yet he knew on an intellectual level that if he hadn't taken the lives he had, he himself would have been killed.

There were two stark differences between their situations, however—the first being that Marjie was grateful to have been the survivor and Stanley struggled at times to feel that way. The second was that Marjie hadn't actually taken her father's life. Too many moments flashed regularly through Stanley's memory for him to lay claim to that same innocence.

Marjie laid her head on his shoulder, her gaze out on the flora once more. "I do love coming here. It is so peaceful."

Stanley kept her right hand in his left, though he pulled his right back once more. The throbbing of open wounds had become too painful to endure any longer.

The atmosphere was indeed peaceful as they sat there in the quiet of the conservatory, with her leaning against him. For once, the distant echo of the battlefield didn't linger in the back of Stanley's thoughts.

"Do you remember the day we met?" Marjie asked.

Remember? He thought of that day with increasing regularity. "I do."

"You said your brothers had all refused to play backgammon with you and would I be interested in playing?"

Gads, he'd been nervous asking her that. He'd hardly been able to keep his eyes off her from the moment she'd arrived at Kinnley for Lord and Lady Cavratt's Christmas house party. He had never been adept at the lighthearted flirting most young gentlemen used to gain a young lady's attention. Like an idiot, he had grasped at the first opportunity to secure her company he could find. His shock and relief had probably been painfully obvious when she'd agreed, though she had appeared reluctant.

"You seemed a little wary," Stanley said, still remembering.

"My father used to rage whenever he lost at anything," Marjie said. "But if I lost, he would belittle me for my stupidity."

Stanley laid his head on the top of hers. It was very nearly an embrace, though they were seated side by side and facing forward, their hands still entwined on the small sliver of bench that separated them.

"I worried that you would be as difficult a game partner as he had always been."

"Then why did you agree to play with me?"

"There was so much kindness in your eyes. There still is."

As compliments went, it was a good one. Perhaps Stanley had found the piece of Marjie's affection that he could lay claim to—she saw kindness in him when he struggled to see it in himself. With Marjie near, he felt kind. He felt almost like a good person again. It was no wonder he had needed her so desperately during his time on the Continent.

He turned his head enough to look down at her golden hair. He knew she'd been partial to him before he'd left in the spring. Part of her seemed to care for him still; he'd felt it in the brief moment he'd touched her face the night before and again when she'd sat beside him just now. Obviously she was not averse to him.

There was a chance he might win her heart. Her engagement was not official, after all. Lord Devereaux was probably the better choice for her; he didn't have a mind filled with memories of death and killing nor a broken, incomplete body. But Lord Devereaux didn't need her the way Stanley did. Devereaux couldn't possibly need her that much. Stanley had to go back. If Marjie was with him, he could feel whole and peaceful and good, even in the midst of violence.

The moment of soul-deep longing came to an abrupt end. *In the midst of violence.* How could he even think of taking her back there with him? Had she not just finished telling him of her suffering under her father's cruelty? What he had seen in France, even just since the official end of the war, far outweighed the torment from which she had pleaded to heaven for escape.

Marjie would be unhappy in the life he could offer her. The senseless death and suffering would eat away at her sensitive spirit. She would ache for every person she saw in pain. She would be bewildered, burdened by the hatred that still permeated so much of the Continent on both sides of the conflict.

He could not do that to her.

But neither did he think he could endure that life without her.

Stanley heard Marjie sigh.

"I promised Mater I would help her sort through fabric swatches. She is redecorating the Dower House. I think she is hoping to move in and clear the way for Philip and Sorrel to fill the house with little Jonquils." Marjie sat straighter and broke the contact between them. It was probably for the best, but Stanley regretted the loss immediately. "No one in the family discusses it, but I know everyone wonders if Sorrel is even able to carry a child, considering the extent of her injuries."

Stanley had wondered the same thing, though he had never voiced the concern.

Marjie rose slowly to her feet, as if reluctant to leave. Hope stirred in Stanley's heart, but he pushed it back.

"Why must life be so complicated?" Though Marjie whispered, Stanley heard.

"It seems to be the way of things," he said.

Marjie looked back at him, her smile once again evident, though perhaps a touch less lighthearted than it had been. "I will see you later, Stanley."

He nodded and watched as she left what was swiftly becoming his favorite room at Lampton Park. He knew the conservatory would forever remind him of her.

When he was once again alone, he rubbed his face with his more cooperative hand. He pushed out a difficult and audible breath. He desperately needed Marjie. He acknowledged the dependence he had on her brightness and goodness. Her faith in him, though given without full knowledge of his guilt and deterioration, gave him faith in himself. But she was not meant to live the harsh and often unforgiving life of a soldier's wife.

He straightened his posture. He'd allowed himself to slacken, to lower his guard.

"Always a soldier." The command had kept him alive many times. A soldier found the strength to endure and did what was best for the group as a whole. Marjie deserved better than he could give her. He would simply have to find another way to survive.

CHAPTER ELEVEN

MARJIE SAW STANLEY ONLY THREE times in the three days following their conversation in the conservatory. He made an appearance at dinner each night but retired to his rooms immediately thereafter. From what she could ascertain from the comments of the staff, he had been out and about. Mater could boast an abbreviated conversation. Everyone had seen at least a glimpse of him—except for Marjie.

He'd gone all the way to Nottingham just that morning without a single word of good-bye. She had spent the day lost in her own uncertainty.

The manor house was a classic example of a rambling country residence. Its corridors seemed to twist and turn endlessly. Yet it was not imposing or intimidating. One almost felt invited to wander its expanse and become hopelessly and comfortably lost within its walls. Marjie found herself doing precisely that as she passed the time between tea and dinner.

She hardly noted her surroundings nor attempted to orient herself as her mind focused exclusively on her time in the conservatory. Speaking of Father and her guilt over his death had been relieving in a way she could not have imagined. She understood in her mind that she could not possibly be considered responsible for her father's passing, yet in her heart, she felt a twinge of uncertainty.

Sorrel, she knew, would have dismissed her concerns with quick and inarguable logic—she was extremely sensible in a way Marjie could never be. Fennel would have probed deeper into her worries and concerns and, no doubt, left her feeling even more emotionally spent than she already did. Mother would have refused to listen.

Stanley had allowed her to voice her concerns. He had comforted her with a simple touch. He had neither belittled nor dismissed her feelings. He had been precisely what she had needed in the years since her father's death.

She stopped her aimless walking and closed her eyes as a moment recreated itself in her mind. Only two days after they had first met, Stanley had walked with her through the formal gardens at Kinnley. She had expressed concern that Sorrel was growing ill again, and somehow, during the course of their slow wanderings, she had admitted to the constant fear that lurked in the back of her mind that Sorrel would yet succumb to the fevers that plagued her. Marjie had not admitted that to anyone else.

"I feel so very helpless," Marjie had confessed, blinking back the tears that had threatened.

"I understand that feeling well," Stanley had said. "After my father died, I felt very much the same way watching Mater so obviously suffering from her loss."

"What did you do?"

"I found a way to help. I saw to those little needs of hers that Father had always been so attuned to: a shawl when she was chilled, an embrace when she was troubled, companionship when she appeared lonely. It was the one way in which I could help. There were aspects of her burden I could not shoulder nor relieve."

"So you devoted yourself to those things you were capable of addressing?"

"Precisely."

"And that was enough?" She had never felt like her efforts were sufficient. "You didn't feel frustrated or lacking somehow?"

Marjie could still feel the warmth of his hand as it had rested on hers lying on his arm.

"Of course I wished I could have done more. I believe we all feel that way at times. But I realized I was doing all I could, and no person can be expected to do more than that."

In that moment, pondering his words, she had felt some of her worries ease. Doing what she could to help had never felt like enough until Stanley had assured her that it was. No one else had ever bothered to tell her her efforts were important or necessary or helpful. Was it any wonder she loved him so entirely?

The distance she felt growing between them hurt and confused her. What had she done to push him away? Had he found, during their separation, that he did not care for her the way he had seemed to? Had she merely been a diversion while he'd passed the time waiting to be recalled to the army?

"Ah, Marjie. Precisely the person I was looking for."

Though she recognized her brother-in-law's voice without needing to look at his face for verification, she opened her eyes. Philip stood directly in front of her, a look of amusement lurking in his eyes.

"I hope I am not interrupting anything," he said, his gaze darting around the deserted corridor with such a theatrical look of expectation that Marjie grinned at seeing it.

"I believe my moment of communion with the corridor is quite at an end, thank you," she said.

"Excellent. Might I convince you to accompany me into the library?" Philip motioned to the door directly beside Marjie. Had she spent her moment of reflection in full view of the room? She could feel heat sneak into her face. At least he could not possibly know what she'd been pondering as she'd stood there. That would truly have been mortifying.

She stepped inside the library and, at another gesture from her brother-in-law, sat in a chair near the fireplace.

"If you will forgive me, I will forgo the usual pleasantries and simply delve directly into the heart of the matter." At Marjie's nod, Philip continued. "I am worried about Sorrel."

Her sudden alarm must have shown.

"She is relatively well, I assure you. It is, actually, the fact that she seems well that concerns me. I realize that sounds very contradictory. I am not as familiar with the history of her ailments as you most likely are, and I am hoping you can set my mind at ease."

"I will do my best."

"The fever we were anticipating when we left London has not come to fruition." Philip's brows were drawn together, his forehead lined in thought. "Though she was a touch warm the evening of Lord and Lady Techney's ball, she never became truly feverish. Her limp has become more pronounced, and though she goes to tremendous lengths to hide her discomfort"—he gave Marjie a knowing and commiserating look, to which she nodded her understanding. Sorrel was remarkably determined never to allow others to see what she saw as a weakness in herself—"I can see that she is in more pain than usual. The brace Mr. Johns created for her had seemed to be working relatively well up until these last couple weeks."

"Perhaps she simply pushed herself too hard," Marjie suggested. "She is not accustomed to the rigorous demands of the *ton*, even if it was not the dizzying whirl of the Season."

"I have thought of that possibility." Philip's shoulders sagged ever so slightly. Marjie did not often see the impeccable Earl of Lampton with anything less than perfect posture. Only Stanley's rigidity of late rivaled Philip's very proper bearing. "I forget sometimes that she will not admit when she is worn to a thread, and I fear I did not always consider her difficulties when planning our schedule. Come spring, I will insist on curtailing our activities when the Season descends. I think, however, that is not the culprit in her current circumstances. Not the *only* culprit, at least."

"What is it you suspect?"

"Let me tell you rather what I have observed. I am hoping you may have suspicions or, at the very least, thoughts on what may be behind the state of her health." Marjie nodded, and Philip continued. "As I said, she is in more pain than before, but more than that, she seems to be struggling to walk, relying more on her cane than she has been in recent months. It is as if her balance is off, as if her hip has once again, despite her brace, become prone to misbehaving. 'Slipping from joint' was the phrase the surgeon, MacAslon, had used when explaining why he was unable to fix her hip as he had the rest of her leg. The hip was shattered enough to prevent it from fitting together as precisely as it ought but not so badly that it is unusable."

Marjie had heard as much when she had first come to live with Philip and Sorrel not more than a month after Sorrel's corrective surgery. A fleeting thought that perhaps Stanley had suffered a similar injury moved swiftly through her mind.

"As if to negate my assumption that she had simply overused her weak leg, she seems to be ill."

"But you said she was not—"

"Not *feverish*," Philip said. "But in all other respects, ill. She has virtually no energy. I have never known her to sleep so late in the day, nor to appear so entirely unrested upon awaking."

"Perhaps she is tired from the journey?" They had made the long trip from Town only a few days before.

"We have traveled distances before, and though I could see she was tired, she never allowed that to stop her from rising at her usual hour and pushing through her day. Especially not several days later."

That was true enough. Though Marjie loved her sister dearly, she had to admit Sorrel was remarkably stubborn.

"What is more, she returned her breakfast tray this morning entirely untouched. She did little more than pick at her luncheon and took only the slightest bit of nourishment at tea before insisting she had no appetite."

Marjie had never known Sorrel to be a poor eater. She was by no means gluttonous but had never been one to skip meals. The only time Sorrel ever chose not to eat was in the midst of her fevers, when she was too ill to do so.

"Has this happened before?" Philip asked. "If she were feverish, not that I wish for that, this would make a great deal more sense.

She insists she is fine and has even become irritated with me over my concerns. She told me to stop being a 'fussy nursemaid.'"

"Then she isn't terribly ill." When Sorrel was truly ailing, she was far more accepting of the help she required. If she was objecting so vocally, she was far less unwell than her symptoms would indicate. "I cannot say this has happened in the past; her illnesses have always followed a very predictable pattern. Were this her usual ailment, she would have been quite feverish already and would now be on the road to recovery."

Philip pushed out a breath that could either have been relief or frustration. "Perhaps I should send for Dr. Habbersham."

"I wouldn't advise it," Marjie said. When Philip looked ready to object, she hastily explained. "If you subject her to doctors when she has no real need of them, she is far less likely to submit to their care when she does."

Philip offered a small nod as if to acknowledge the wisdom of her words. "Do you think she has any idea how much I worry about her?"

"Yes." Marjie was certain of it. "And I imagine she wishes you didn't have to."

"True." They sat a moment in silence before Philip spoke again, his forehead still creased with lines of worry. "Have you made any progress with Stanley?"

Marjie's heart ached further simply hearing his name. "No."

"I have attempted to talk with him about his experiences, hoping he would reveal something that would explain the change in him, but he was entirely unwilling."

Marjie nodded. Stanley had been very closed off about his experiences when they had spoken about her letters. "I cannot help but suspect that he does not talk about his time away because he does not wish to think about it."

"I have heard former soldiers speak of their army days," Philip said. "To be sure, they focus on the more lighthearted moments as opposed to the battles and suffering, but I cannot say I have any experience with someone who avoids speaking of it entirely."

“He told me he did not write to anyone because he did not want us to worry.”

Philip laughed but without an ounce of humor. “Because six months of silence would convince us all that everything was fine.” He shook his head. “If he had merely wished us not to worry, he would have written the sort of things soldiers write to their families, speaking only of friends and the weather and the places he was seeing. He would have made it sound as though he were on an extended holiday. Not writing at all doesn’t make sense. Stanley was never the secretive type. There had to have been more of a reason than that.”

Marjie thought so as well. Stanley hadn’t written to anyone. She could understand his concern that she or Mater would have worried if he’d shared the more difficult experiences he’d had, whatever they were, but surely he didn’t think Philip or any of his other brothers would have wallowed in concern over him. They were made of sterner stuff.

“Beggin’ yer pardon, Yer High and Mighty Lordship.”

Marjie turned toward the sound of the voice. Stanley’s valet stood just inside the door. He was a young man, probably close to her own age, who always looked just a touch cocky.

“Yes, Pluck?” Philip had already transformed into the picture of dandified elegance he always presented to the world. He swung his quizzing glass on its ribbon, looking bored and utterly carefree.

“I was told to post these here letters fer Cap’n Jonquil, but I’m thinkin’ iffen yer High and Mighty Lordship would frank ’em, it would be a great help to them that’s getting the letters. ’Twould save them the cost of paying for ’em when they arrive.”

“Of course. I will frank any and all of Captain Jonquil’s correspondence.” Philip’s eyes had narrowed. Marjie let her gaze jump between Philip and Pluck. Had she heard correctly? Stanley was writing to someone?

“There’re two letters,” Pluck said, holding them up.

Philip gave Marjie a look of confusion as he rose and took the missives. It took but a moment to frank them in preparation for posting. Marjie had long thought it an odd quirk of the postal system that the recipient was required to cover the cost of sending a letter. It had always seemed to her it ought to be the other way around. Philip, whose status as a member of Parliament gave him the right to send mail that did not have to be paid for on the receiving end, had franked all of her letters to Stanley, as well as those she sent to Fennel. Her younger brother, no doubt, appreciated not having to spend his pocket money on letters from his sister.

Marjie came and stood near Philip's desk, looking across at the letters lying there. One was addressed to a Mrs. Goodwin and the other to a Mrs. Hammil.

"I am certain there is an explanation," Philip said.

Marjie blinked back a tear. If he was writing to these women, why had he never written to her?

"I'll jus' give these to the butler," Pluck said, reaching for the letters.

"No." The suddenness of her response surprised even Marjie. She grabbed the letters off Philip's desk. "I'll give them to him after I finish the letter I am writing to Fennel."

She was nearly to the other side of the house before she finally admitted to herself the reason for her insistence on keeping Stanley's letters, even temporarily. She had wanted a letter from him so desperately for nearly half a year that to finally hold one, even one not addressed to her, was a temptation she hadn't been able to resist. Those two sealed missives, addressed to women she had never even heard of, represented months of dreams that had never come true. She clutched the folded parchment even as she felt her heart crack painfully inside.

CHAPTER TWELVE

An hour remained until dinner. Stanley wasn't overly hungry, but he waited impatiently for mealtime. Only during dinner did he allow himself Marjie's company. The temptation to throw all his convictions aside and make a push to win her affections, regardless of the impact on her or anyone else other than himself, had nearly proven far too great. Avoiding her had seemed the best option.

Pluck disagreed. Stanley had lost count of the number of times his batman had used the phrase "rush the wall" during their journey to and from Nottingham that day. By the time they'd returned to Lampton Park, Stanley had informed him in language one learned only in the army just what he could do with that wall. And Pluck, being Pluck, had laughed.

Stanley had denied himself the luxury of lying down, knowing he was tired enough to simply sleep through the night. He would not miss dinner. He had to see Marjie at least once that day.

So he was wandering the halls, passing the hour before his favorite time of day. He had regained some of his stamina. The commissariat couldn't compete with the Lampton Park chef, nor could the constant tension of life in the aftermath of war offer even a hint of the solace found in the peaceful English countryside. Being home again, Stanley could almost believe in the divine reparation his brother Harry and so many of his fellow clergymen preached of. He almost felt hopeful that the familiar words of Ecclesiastes were more than the empty poetry of the ignorant—maybe there was indeed both a time to kill and a time to heal.

Stanley walked to the conservatory without thought. He had spent a great deal of time there the past three days. He sought Marjie's company vicariously, hoping he could find in the walls of glass a tiny bit of her comforting presence.

He took in the moist, earthy air of the indoor garden in such an enormous quantity that his entire chest swelled with the influx of breath. The air held the very smell of life. Odd that in all the years he had lived at Lampton Park he had never realized the significance of that aroma. Five and a half years of becoming nauseatingly familiar with the smell of death had given him an appreciation for its opposite.

Before the lungful of air had a chance to dissipate into his spent and broken limbs, all the air was pressed from him in a whoosh of surprise. Marjie stood near the iron bench that he had occupied day after day. She did not look at him but rather watched the dimming light of day outside. The blazing hues of sunset gave her golden curls a hint of fire. He, like a moth to a candle, felt himself drawn to her.

He moved closer. Either she was very distracted, or she was ignoring his arrival. He knew he didn't move quietly; his walking stick tapped loudly against the stone floor of the conservatory. Yet Marjie didn't look at him as he approached.

As he drew nearer, he could see she wore a very pensive expression. What was worrying her? He had heard through Pluck, who had obtained the information from the bevy of servants below stairs, that Sorrel remained unwell. Perhaps her sister's health weighed on her.

"Good evening, Marjie."

That she didn't seem at all startled by his sudden words told Stanley she had, in fact, noted his arrival. She still didn't look at him.

Marjie wrapped one arm around her middle; the other appeared to be pressed to her heart.

"Marjie?"

She didn't respond, which was not at all like her. Was she hurt? Ill?

He moved with more speed than grace to where she stood. "Marjie, what—?" The question died on his lips. A tear sat in the corner of her eye, seemingly ready to drop. He searched her face for some clue, some indication as to the source of her suffering. That tear hovered only a moment longer before slowly slipping down her cheek.

Stanley's heart seized painfully in his chest. He stood, frozen, watching the tear fall. Nothing should ever make his Marjie cry.

"You have been writing letters." Her whisper shattered the silence that surrounded them.

"Yes. I sent two today." The admission seemed to upset her. "I was a little late in doing so." The letters ought to have been sent from France, but being ordered back to England had interfered with his plans. "I am hoping the recipients will forgive the delay." He had no idea how those letters were received. It was entirely possible they were resented.

"How late were the letters?" Something very odd colored her tone—it was flat, very nearly emotionless.

"A fortnight."

Marjie looked up at him then. The anguish in her eyes cut through Stanley with all the searing pain of the bullet he'd taken at Orthez. "*I* waited for six months." Her voice broke on the words. Mingled with her look of pain was a flash of anger Stanley hadn't been expecting. "But my letter was not merely delayed, was it? You never had any intention of writing to me."

"Marjie—"

"I am certain those women will forgive you a fortnight's delay."

Enough accusation hung in that sentence that it set Stanley's back up a little. Getting those letters written and posted had taken a great deal of effort, considering he absolutely hated the undertaking.

He did not need further proof that he would never be entirely free of the blasted war. It followed him all the way back to England, back to his place of solace. Was even his time with Marjie to be tainted by it?

"I am certain you had something very important to write to them about." She seemed to doubt it, as if it had been a letter filled with the idle gossip of two aged dowagers.

Tension rippled through Stanley's body. *Something important to write about?* He felt his jaw clench. Was he now to be criticized for attempting to redeem what little remained of his soul? "I had the immense privilege of informing 'those women' that their sons are dead." The words snapped out of him. Lud, he hated the army sometimes.

"Dead?"

Somewhere in the back of his mind, Stanley registered the suddenly fragile quality of Marjie's voice. "Two of my men. They were killed in France just before I left."

"But I thought the war was over."

"It will never be over," he grumbled. He turned away, ready to leave. He needed to push all thoughts of war and death and fighting out of his mind. He needed to remain in control of himself. Again, his oft-repeated survival strategy echoed in his mind. "Always a soldier." He needed to clear his thoughts, to step behind his shield of neutrality once more.

He felt the light pressure of Marjie's hand on his a split second before the flash of pain that followed. He winced, pulling air in through his clenched teeth. He could feel his hand shake, and he struggled to keep hold of his walking stick. As suddenly as her touch had come, it disappeared.

He waited for the questions, for the words of pity and worry. She would fret; she always fretted. He did not want to be the invalid to her nursemaid. She was supposed to be an angel, untouched by violence and suffering, and he was meant to be a source of only happiness for her. That had always been what he'd imagined. Before Napoleon's return and the resurgence of war, he'd dreamed of that both literally and figuratively. Marjie was always meant to be his escape from the slow, deteriorating death of guilt and regret born of years spent in the business of warfare.

But Marjie didn't ask any questions. When her silence stretched longer than Stanley could endure, he turned his head back to look at her once more. No pity registered in her face. Though there was a hint of worry, she mostly looked heartbroken.

"I am sorry I was short with you," she said, her chin quivering as she spoke. "I was just so . . . so—" Marjie dropped her eyes, and her cheeks pinked with what looked like embarrassment. "Jealous."

Jealous?

"All I ever wanted was a letter, Stanley. A single note. I know you said you didn't want me to worry, but not hearing from you, not knowing . . . It was horrible." Again she wrapped her arms, both this time, around her middle, almost a self-offered embrace. "At first, I simply told myself you were busy, that you had more important things to do." Stanley heard her implied words. Marjie saw herself as unimportant to him. "But after Waterloo"—Stanley winced at the name, just as he always did—"I was desperate. We all were. Every day the lists grew longer, and every day I was more afraid to read them."

"What lists?"

She looked up at him again. Her eyes were bleak, haunted. Without thought, Stanley reached for her, cupping her face in his left hand. She closed her eyes just as she had that night by his fireside. "The casualty lists," she whispered. "We read them every day. I felt so relieved when your name didn't appear, but I could never be certain. Names were added all the time. I died a little every day as I searched, so afraid your name would appear there."

Here was yet another reason to feel guilty. By not sending word that he was alive, he had added to their distress. His family would have recognized that whatever he sent had not been written in his own handwriting, he not having a usable right hand. That would have piqued their suspicions that all was not well, and they would have worried anyway. Nothing he did seemed to truly help them.

"What a coldhearted person I must be to be jealous of these women you have written to, who have lost so very much when I have you here safe with me." Another lone tear slid silently down her face. "I only wanted a letter. I wanted it so desperately."

His throat constricted. She needed to understand, at least a little. But explaining any part of this meant thinking about the horrors he'd barely survived, reliving the pain and the sounds and smells of the battlefield. It meant admitting he'd come home disfigured and broken. He couldn't admit all. But she ought to know enough to ease her own pain.

He brushed the track of moisture from her cheek with his thumb. He lightly caressed a wispy gold ringlet before allowing his gloved hand to slide down her arm and clasp her hand. He needed the strength of her touch. "I didn't write the letters to those two women."

"But you said—"

"I dictated them." He was determined to conclude his confession before his memories overpowered him. "I have sent letters to the families of every soldier in my squadron who has been killed in the more than five years since I joined the army. Most families receive no notice or regrets from the army beyond what few personal effects can be returned to them. It is cold and unfeeling, but that is the nature of war."

Marjie pulled on his hand—his left, thankfully—and he followed automatically to the bench and sat awkwardly. She sat beside him. He could feel her eyes on his face but couldn't bring himself to look at her when speaking of dark times he'd rather forget.

"So I started sending letters. I'd try to think of something to say, a memory of that family's loved one, something the other men admired about him. Little things I thought would help." Stanley swallowed against the narrowing of his throat. "It sounds pretty arrogant, I suppose, thinking that anything I wrote would help." He couldn't stop the groan deep in his throat as the next thought formed the instant before he spoke. "There were so many after Waterloo. But I couldn't write the letters."

"Was it too difficult?" Marjie asked, and he knew she referred to the emotional toll. That certainly had been a factor but not what he'd meant.

"I couldn't *write* them," Stanley repeated. "I wasn't physically able to." He looked into her eyes for the first time since beginning his rather unspecific explanation. "Though I thought of writing to you, I *couldn't*."

He watched as Marjie's eyes dropped to his right hand, gloved and resting on his lap.

"I have noticed you do not use your right hand," Marjie said. "It seems to pain you."

"I was injured." *Please do not ask more. Let that be enough.*

She didn't press. She didn't speak at all. Marjie took his right hand in hers, holding it so gently she might very well have been the angel he'd always thought her to be. Stanley stiffened as she tugged lightly on the smallest finger of his glove.

"Marjie, please don't." He knew what she would see.

She looked up at him, and to Stanley's surprise, some of the anguish had left her eyes. She touched his face and smiled ever so slightly before returning to his glove. Slowly, gently, she pulled it off.

As his hand slipped free, the feeling of relief he looked forward to every night rushed through him. With his glove removed, the leather and sweat and rubbing no longer irritated his wounds. But the sight of his gnarled hand required it remain covered during the day and that he endure the discomfort of doing so.

Marjie's eyes hadn't lifted from his hand. The splotches of deep black were still there, and the melted, twisted skin and puffy red sores had not miraculously healed nor grown even more horrendous. As always, he could smell the battlefield again, could see the horror on Pluck's face as the fire drew closer to him. He swallowed against a surge of bile. He tried to pull his hand away, but Marjie had a surprisingly firm grip.

"Is it a burn?" She spoke as calmly as one would when inquiring whether he cared for sugar in his tea.

"Yes." He couldn't manage more than the single syllable. He fought every moment against the memories that flooded over him. In his mind, he could hear the sounds of men crying out in agony and guns pounding the air.

"It continues beyond your cuff." Marjie was unexpectedly calm. She did not fuss, nor sob inconsolably, nor run from the room in horror.

The sound of her voice tugged at him, pulling him momentarily from his thoughts, freeing him for an instant from the memories he could never seem to escape on his own. He nodded in response to her observation. The burn reached nearly to his elbow.

"Your glove irritates it, Stanley. You simply must allow it relief from the constant rubbing. Sorrel had to do that while her leg was healing the first time. Absolutely nothing touching it but air and a very soothing salve."

Stanley sat silently for a moment. She had not asked for a detailed explanation or insisted she be told the difficult details. The assault of unwanted memory eased, and her face refocused.

She looked up at him. "Thank you for telling me."

She was thanking him for exposing her to this? A gently bred young lady was meant to be sheltered from the grotesqueness and unpleasantness found in the world.

"When you didn't write, I worried that you had forgotten all about me."

Stanley shook his head. "Never that."

"I think I will go give Cook the recipe for that salve." Marjie rose to her feet. "Perhaps it will help."

"Perhaps."

She smiled at him, and much of the tension drained from his body. Memories of that smile had, at times, been his only grip on his sanity.

In a movement so quick and so fluid he hardly realized what she was doing, Marjie leaned toward him and placed a brief, featherlight kiss on his cheek. It was precisely the sort of kiss one received from one's mother while still in leading strings, and yet it set his heart to pounding once more.

She flitted from the room with her characteristic cheer. He smiled. He had just ungloved his mangled hand and, to a degree he usually avoided, relived a piece of Waterloo, and still he smiled.

His angel, it seemed, was a miracle worker.

CHAPTER THIRTEEN

Mr. Harold Jonquil, the next-to-youngest Jonquil brother, had joined the family for dinner at Lampton Park that night. With a man of the church in the house, Marjie ought to have felt more guilty about slipping from the drawing room in order to undertake a series of petty thefts. "Holy Harry," as Marjie had heard the older Jonquils refer to their very clerical brother, would likely not approve. He could be overwhelmingly pious.

Marjie, however, was determined. The idea had occurred to her only moments into the evening meal as she'd watched Stanley eat. She doubted she would ever forget how painful his hand had looked earlier that evening in the conservatory. She could not even imagine the circumstances under which it could have been so horribly burned but had sensed immediately that he was not at a point where he could talk about the experience.

She had made up her mind and firmed up her plan by the time Sorrel had indicated the ladies were to withdraw and leave the gentlemen to their customary after-dinner port. Not ten minutes later, Marjie had reached her intended destination. She would have to add "being in a gentleman's bedchamber" to that evening's list of broken rules. It was one she had broken before—recently, in fact—with Stanley present and no one else to lend a degree of propriety. Though she entered the bedchamber alone this time, she had come with the sole purpose of making off with a few of his personal items, which made her presence almost as unacceptable.

She glanced around the room, trying to decide the most likely place Stanley might keep what she was attempting to pilfer. A drawer seemed the most fitting location. She crossed to a chestnut tallboy and began pulling the drawers open one at a time. Three drawers into the endeavor, she was absolutely certain she had turned a deep, telling shade of red from hairline to toes. She ought to have realized his more personal items of clothing would be kept in the chest of drawers.

"Up to yer elbows in the Cap'n's smallclothes, are ye?"

Marjie spun at the unexpected voice, her heart thudding in her throat. Stanley's valet stood just inside the door, watching her with a cheeky grin. Her face burned with embarrassment. How had she overlooked the possibility that a servant might wander in? She had thought only of the fact that the family would be occupied.

"I can tell ye where he keeps his handkerchiefs iffen ye're after a keepsake. I hear ladies like that sorta thing."

A keepsake? Her mission was far more essential than that! Marjie squared her shoulders. "I've come to rob him." She spoke with what she felt was admirable conviction.

Pluck's eyes lit with laughter. "A regular sneakthief, are ye? What would ye be makin' off with, then?"

"Couldn't you just pretend you didn't see me in here and leave for a few minutes until I'm done?"

"C'mon now, Miss Kendrick." Pluck moved closer. "A hardened criminal cain't be beggin' and lookin' all mournful. If ye're gonna pull the slip on some nob, ye gotta be unrepentant. And, laws a mercy, ye gotta be quick about it."

"Well, I am new at this."

"So what is it ye're trying to slip off with?" He seemed far too comfortable with the situation.

"Do you usually assist people who are stealing things from Captain Jonquil?"

Pluck's grin grew positively mischievous. "I've a feeling he wouldn't begrudge ye anything ye wanted to carry off."

Marjie wasn't so certain. "Actually, I think he may be quite upset."

Pluck lifted an eyebrow, looking curious but disbelieving.

"Are you willing to aid and abet a criminal, Pluck?" She needed an accomplice. Otherwise, she'd be mortified by the time she finished digging through drawer upon drawer of Stanley's most private belongings.

"I could give it a go."

Marjie faced him with all the determination she could muster. "I have come to steal his gloves."

"His gloves?" Pluck clearly hadn't been expecting that.

"Only the right ones. But the right glove from every pair he has. I am also planning to slip off with"—she thought that was the phrase Pluck had used—"several of his buttons."

"Which buttons?" Pluck spoke as though he had a firm idea.

"From the cuffs of all of his sleeves and jackets."

"Would those be the right cuffs, Miss Kendrick?"

Marjie nodded.

"Ye know about his hand, then?"

She nodded again. "He showed me."

Pluck's eyes flew wide open, a look of absolute shock on his face. "He let ye see his hand? All uncovered and laid bare?"

"It needs a chance to heal without being rubbed raw day after day. I realize he cannot walk around without a shirt on." An embarrassing blush slid across her features. Again. Marjie pressed on. "But having his sleeves a little looser would have to help, I would think. I told him so this afternoon, but I noticed he had his gloves on again at dinner, and his sleeves very tightly buttoned."

"Aye." Pluck nodded. "He don't like people seeing his wounds. Sorta embarrassed, I think. He also don't like talking about 'em or thinking about 'em. Don't like the reminder."

Would she be causing Stanley more suffering by forcing him to expose at least one of his injuries to the eyes of the world? She simply had to. It would never get well if he didn't. Infection had been Sorrel's greatest enemy after her accident. She knew that until Stanley's burn healed more fully, he remained at very high risk of losing his hand, or worse.

"That is why he must have no choice. I am stealing his gloves." Would Pluck assist her? She likely could not manage the trick if he intended to thwart her efforts.

"If I give ye his shirts and jackets, can ye get the buttons off?" Pluck asked. His eager agreement set Marjie's mind at ease.

She pulled out of her reticule the small sewing scissors she had retrieved from her room on her way to Stanley's bedchamber.

"And while ye pocket his buttons, I'll grab his gloves."

She had a sizable stack of shirtsleeves and jackets in a very short amount of time. Marjie sat in the armchair she'd occupied on several occasions while Stanley had been on the Continent. Pluck knelt in front of the tallboy, pulling a pile of gloves from a low drawer Marjie had not yet checked.

She snipped threads and removed buttons quickly and efficiently. "He did not say specifically how he injured his hand," she said to Pluck as they went about their ethically questionable task, "but I believe it occurred at Waterloo."

She glanced at Pluck, where he sat sorting through gloves. He looked even younger than usual, sprawled on the floor that way.

"Ay. An' he'd prob'bly skin me alive fer tellin' ye, but iffen he's showing ye his hand, I figure ye've a right to know how it happened. 'Specially seeing as how ye seem determined to help him."

"I would do anything to help Stanley," Marjie insisted.

"Laws, don't stop snippin'," he said. "We ain't got a lot of time."

Marjie set back to work, and Pluck talked while he placed one half of each pair of gloves into a pile.

"I fought with the artillery at Waterloo," he said. "It's where no-accounts like me get put when we run off to the army. Artillery or infantry. There was a fire. Enemy guns hit a little too close. We was trying to save the ammunition before it exploded."

"Exploded?"

"Took out two of the horses and three of our men. Fire just kept spreadin'. We got the balls moved, but the fire was too big, and I couldn't get out."

Merciful heavens. "You were trapped?"

"Figured I was gonna die there." He spoke with a dismissal that didn't ring at all true. "Then in comes this Blue on horseback; keeps his big gray under control in the madness. He holds his hand out, right into the flames, and yells, 'Grab hold.' Pulled me out, he did, and rides off with me, dropping me at the rear of an infantry square. Didn't realize till later he'd spent the ride trying to put out the fire what was burning up his arm and hand."

Marjie closed her eyes, trying to push out the sudden vision of Stanley on fire. "He saved your life."

"Aye," Pluck said, his voice gruff and quiet. "A regular Good Samaritan, he was. There were others who rode past the fire, shoutin' they was sorry but couldn't help."

"But he stopped." She would have expected nothing less from Stanley. His compassion had drawn her to him when they'd first met.

"He don't like to talk about it, but I asked him once why he did it." Pluck stuffed a handful of gloves back in their drawer and rose, holding the remaining half of each pair. "Cap'n just said he didn't want to see anyone die without hope again."

"Again?"

Pluck dropped the gloves on the table next to Marjie and grabbed a couple of jackets. Between sentences, he pulled buttons off the right cuffs. "Do ye know what a forlorn hope is, Miss Kendrick?"

She shook her head. "It has a very poetic name though."

"That's what ye fancy folks would call 'ironic.' A forlorn hope is the first wave of men who attack an enemy stronghold. They are the first group to rush the enemy line. Ain't no defenses, no smoke cover. They make deuced good targets, actually."

"How in the world could anyone survive such a thing?" Marjie's stomach dropped at the thought.

"Most of 'em don't." Pluck's eyes remained focused on his task. His posture had lost its casualness. "It's always volunteers that take on the forlorn hope—men that need the prize money or are lookin' for a promotion. 'Course, they have to live through it first."

Marjie shuddered. A person would have to be very brave or very foolish to undertake such a thing. A soldier volunteering for such a mission would have to be reconciled to the very real possibility of death.

"Cap'n—he was a lieutenant then—went in with the forlorn hope at Orthez."

"He did what?" Stanley had volunteered for the forlorn hope, for a suicide mission?

"The men what volunteer for that don't have much of a chance of coming out alive. I guess Cap'n thought I deserved more of a chance than those soldiers had."

"Philip never said anything about Stanley being part of a forlorn hope." Marjie searched her memory but knew nothing of the sort had ever been mentioned. Stanley certainly hadn't related that experience.

"His High and Mighty Lordship prob'bly don't know." Pluck shook his collection of buttons in his closed hand. "Cap'n lived through it but took a shot in the shoulder."

Marjie nodded. She knew Stanley had returned to England after Orthez to recover from a wound.

"Army made him a cap'n after that."

"A promotion for surviving," Marjie said.

"Aye, but it weren't what he wanted from the forlorn hope."

"Isn't that the reason for volunteering?"

"It's one reason," Pluck said.

What else had Pluck said? "He wanted the money, then."

"Cap'n comes from a well-to-do family," Pluck said. "Don't think he needed the money."

"What other reason could there be?"

Pluck shook his head and started hanging up Stanley's jackets—those with removed buttons—in the armoire.

"That is part of the puzzle, isn't it?" Marjie snipped off the last button.

"Puzzle?" Pluck offered that same faux innocence he'd used before.

"He has changed, Pluck. He is unhappy, and it is torturous to see. Please help me help him."

"There're some things I was told in confidence, Miss Kendrick," Pluck said. "That man saved my worthless, miserable life. I'll not break my word to him."

"Can you at least tell me what happened to his leg? He won't discuss it with anyone."

"No." He spoke firmly, instantly, forcefully.

Whatever had happened to Stanley's leg, then, was crucial to discovering why he was suffering so much.

"Did the doctors say whether or not they think his hand will heal?" she asked.

"They wasn't exactly thinking so far down the road," Pluck said. "After everything that happened to him at Waterloo, they didn't really figure he'd live long."

His words robbed her of breath, almost of thought. "They expected him to die?"

"It was a near-run thing. In the end, though, I think he wanted to see his loved ones again more than he wanted to die."

"But he does not seem very happy to be here among his loved ones."

"It's hard for men like him who are just good, ye know—the kinda men who, if they weren't fighting a war, would be living quiet lives, helping people, and doin' good works, and bein' regular saints, and all—to do and see the kind of things soldiers have to do and see." Pluck rubbed at the back of his neck. "It eats at 'em, makes 'em question what kinda person they really are. Their lives get too dark, and there ain't no . . . no . . ."

"Hope," Marjie finished for him.

"Give him a reason to hope again, Miss Kendrick," Pluck said. "I'm beginning to think ye're the only chance he's got."

J

CHAPTER FOURTEEN

"This is insubordination." Stanley glared at Pluck with an intensity that had on more than one occasion pulled confessions from the soldiers under his command.

Pluck did nothing more than tweak an eyebrow. "Ye gonna have me court-martialed, Cap'n?"

"My brother and his family will arrive in a matter of minutes," Stanley said. "I cannot greet them looking like this." He raised his bare right hand, motioning to it with his left as the sleeves of both his uniform jacket and shirtsleeves drooped lamely away from his elevated wrist. "You produce my glove and buttons, or I will have your neck."

"Nah, ye don't mean that."

"Chance it. I dare you to." Stanley pressed the words through his locked jaw.

He had been dreading the dinner party already. Layton, the second-oldest Jonquil brother, could be horrifically insightful.

Layton's wife had lost a brother to the war, a soldier Stanley had known—another name on the long list of friends and colleagues who hadn't lived through the battles that still plagued him. Would she ask about her brother? She wouldn't have to do so directly for the horrors to plague him. Just knowing she would be there had already pushed memories of Lieutenant Linwood into his mind.

The thought of seeing Caroline, Layton's daughter, plagued him most. Caroline had been born not long after Stanley had first joined the army. She had, in his mind, represented the reason he had fought as hard as he had. Visions of the kind of world she would grow up in if they did not emerge triumphant had haunted him, pressing him on when the weight of it all threatened to crush him.

"I cain't give ye your gloves nor your buttons 'cause I didn't finger 'em," Pluck said. "Now be a good cap'n and march on downstairs."

"Captains do not take orders from privates."

"But they do take them from countesses." A new voice entered the debate.

Stanley snapped his head in the direction of his door. Sorrel stood there, watching him with a look he found even more daunting than the one he'd used on Pluck only moments earlier. She had a way of making him feel like a raw recruit being called to account by an uncompromising general.

"I understand you intend to insult me by refusing to join the dinner party I have organized," she said.

How did he answer that without either indicating his intention to be uncivil or committing himself to attending?

Sorrel advanced toward him. She moved with the determination and confidence of Wellington and Napoleon combined. The thump of her walking stick and the noticeable limp in her gait did nothing to diminish the air of control she exuded in each and every situation. Stanley's limp, on the other hand, made him look pathetic.

As Sorrel drew near, Stanley slipped his right hand slightly behind his back. No point starting the staring before completely necessary.

"Layton will be here in a moment," she said. "I expect you to be in the drawing room to greet him and his family."

"I am having something of a wardrobe difficulty." He very nearly added a firm "sir" and a salute. The army could have used someone like his sister-in-law.

Sorrel looked him up and down. "Nothing essential appears to be missing."

"Half of my gloves have disappeared." He stood at full attention while speaking to her, not that his soldier's posture ever completely slipped.

"We will not hold you to the formality of being gloved," Sorrel said.

"I hold myself to that formality."

"Do not waste my time with half-truths," Sorrel said. "You are hiding your injuries, as always. I have seen how you keep yourself apart from everyone, and all on account of your relatively minor limp."

"Minor?" Was the woman blind?

"The moment your limp is as obvious as mine"—Sorrel practically spat out the words—"I will allow you a more drastic word than *minor*."

He had to concede that her limp was more pronounced than his. The limp didn't bother him most anyway. He could endure the sight of his mangled hand and the memories that inevitably followed; however, he hated knowing that a piece of him had been hacked off and tossed aside. It made a person feel very disposable.

"Now, do you plan to join your family for dinner, or am I to assume that the victorious British Army consisted entirely of cowardly, sniveling infants?"

Pluck's snicker did not help. "He'll be there, m'lady." He bowed to her. "Cap'n Jonquil ain't never been a coward."

"Very good." Sorrel turned swiftly, though not smoothly, and walked toward the door. She stopped a few steps short and turned back. "A word of advice, Stanley—"

He waited as silently as he had when receiving orders from his commanding officers.

"Use the walking stick in your left hand."

"But it is my right leg that is injured," he said.

"A common mistake amongst amateurs." The slightest hint of amusement tugged at her lips. "Your walking stick will be far more effective when used on your uninjured side."

That didn't make a great deal of sense.

"Trust me." Apparently his doubt showed. "Time the use of the cane to match your injured leg but held in the opposite hand. You'll notice an improvement."

He acknowledged her advice with a nod of his head. His right hand would hurt less if not forced to constantly grip the head of his walking stick. He could at least try.

"One more thing." Her expression grew quite somber once more. "Wipe that glare off your face before you head downstairs. I swear to you, if you make my sister cry one more time, I will skin you alive." She looked like she meant it.

"I would never make her cry, not intentionally." He felt ill at the very thought of causing Marjie pain.

"Then forgive her," Sorrel said, "and be kind."

"Forgive her?"

Sorrel's eyes sparkled quite suddenly, and Stanley had a feeling she was inwardly laughing at him. "For stealing your gloves and buttons."

Marjie! The idea that she had stolen those things had never entered his mind.

"Five minutes, Stanley," Sorrel said. The words were obviously a command. She walked out with all her usual resoluteness.

"Makes a fella feel like salutin', don't she?" Pluck said.

"Yes, the countess has that effect on a person."

A little less than five minutes later, his walking stick in his left hand and his right kept as near his side and inconspicuous as possible, Stanley stepped into the drawing room. He did not see Marjie, but a quick scan of the room proved that nearly everyone else was accounted for. Mater sat on a sofa talking with Marion, Layton's wife, and Sorrel. Harold had arrived as well, his usual look of pious contemplation firmly in place.

Layton and Philip, who stood beside each other near a far window, looked over at Stanley as he came inside. They made an interesting picture: Philip's taller, leaner frame bedecked in his usual flamboyant attire contrasted with Layton's brawny build and subdued choice of clothing. Their grins, however, were identical.

"Stanley!" Layton crossed the room. He'd been so achingly unhappy in the years following the death of his first wife. Marion's arrival in his life had changed him for the better.

Layton looked Stanley over. "You look horrible."

Stanley was startled into a chuckle. "Thank you."

"Be nice to your brother." Marion rose and walked toward them. Stanley required a moment to acclimate himself to the change in her appearance. She still had unfathomably red hair and an infectious smile, but she was more rounded in the middle than she had been the last time he'd seen her some six months earlier.

Mater had mentioned Layton and Marion were expecting new arrivals toward the beginning of the next year. Corbin and his wife, Clara, were anticipating an addition to their family in the spring. Thus far, Jason and Mariposa, who had been married for only a couple months, had not made any announcement. The country would soon be overrun with Jonquils. Everyone remained entirely silent on the topic of Philip and Sorrel and their future family, however.

"A few extra meals," Marion said to Stanley, "and a bit of rest and you'll be quite your old self again." Marion tended to be unrealistically optimistic.

"Where did Caroline wander off to?" Layton looked around the room.

"She'll be back in a moment, dear." Marion smiled up at her husband. "Marjie insisted on straightening the girl's ribbon."

"Those two have become thick as thieves," Layton said.

Thieves. An interesting choice of words considering Marjie's recent nefarious activities.

Something quite suddenly collided with his legs. Stanley clung to his walking stick and managed to keep his balance. He glanced down and found that Caroline had flung herself against him, wrapping her arms around his left leg.

"Stanby!" she said, her face pressed against him. Caroline was rather famous amongst the Jonquils for her inability to pronounce anyone's name correctly.

"Sit down, Stanley," Marion gently instructed, "before she knocks you right off your feet."

Recognizing the wisdom in her words, Stanley moved with some difficulty—Caroline did not release her hold on his leg—to a nearby armchair. He dropped into it, and Caroline climbed onto his lap. Stanley leaned his walking stick against the side of his chair and wound his left arm behind Caroline to prevent her from tumbling off.

Before Marjie, it had been Caroline's face he had pictured when trying to push the horrible images of war from his mind. He'd spent many nights lying on his cot, listening to the eerie stillness that always descended on the camp the night before a battle and, in his mind, escaped it all. He would think of home and the tiny child in the miniature Philip had sent him. He would picture her growing up in a world free from the icy grip of war.

"You walk like Aunt Swirl now," Caroline said.

"Yes, I believe she has been copying me," Stanley said, managing a light response. Leave it to a child to jump right to the heart of the matter.

"Marching fixed my grown-up ribbon." *Marching* was Caroline's version of Marjie's name. "See?" Caroline tipped her head so he could see the bow tied quite saucily just above her left ear.

Such unspoiled joy over something as simple as a ribbon. He had pictured her life that way. She would never wear the expressions of fear and exhaustion he had seen on the faces of children her age and younger scattered across the ravaged Peninsula. All the death and loss had given her that.

"Marching said I look elegant." Caroline lowered her voice to a conspiratorial whisper. "It is my very most favorite ribbon."

"Is it?"

"Touch it, Stanby." She smiled up at him. "It is sooo"—she dragged out the *so* to a very dramatic length—"soft."

He reached up and ran the tip of his finger along the smooth edge of the satin ribbon in her golden curls. Marjie's children would someday look precisely like Caroline, and they would be every bit as angelic. Out of the corner of his eye, he saw her there, watching him. A smile lit her face, and warmth spread through Stanley at the sight of it. He would buy every one of her daughters yards and yards of ribbon if only to bring just such a look to her face. Except . . . her husband would most certainly object.

"Oh, Stanby." Caroline wrapped her hands around his outstretched arm. "You have a hurt."

Too late, he realized he'd touched her ribbon with his right hand, his left being occupied with holding her on his lap. Stanley's eyes darted around the room. For a fraction of a moment, they were all staring at the mutilated remains of his hand that had, before Marjie's interference, remained tucked out of sight. Then, in perfect unison, every pair of eyes looked away and conversations began with an abnormal abruptness that spoke volumes of everyone's mutual discomfort. Even Marjie diverted her eyes.

"Stanby?" Caroline hadn't released his wrist yet, though her touch was light enough that it didn't really hurt.

"Yes, Poppet?"

"I have a hurt too," she whispered, and her enormous blue eyes instantly turned shimmery with unshed tears. Caroline laid his hand ever so gently across her legs, as if it were made of the most fragile porcelain. She raised her left hand, only her pinkie extended. Tied around the end of her tiny finger was a scrap of fabric. "I cut it on a rock by the river because I fell in. Papa said I was very, very brave, even though I was scared. Were you scared when you got your hurt, Stanby?" Caroline's eyes had dropped to his hand once more. She ran her hand softly down his jacket sleeve, as if soothing the pain she sensed there. "I think you would have to be very brave with such a big hurt."

A big hurt. Was that the term one used when a man traded his soul for a little girl's future?

Caroline continued to stroke his arm. "Do you get to stay here now? Now that Badpoleon is gone?"

He wanted to. He wanted to stay and never go back. "No, Poppet. I have to return to the other soldiers."

Caroline sat up a little, just enough to look into his face. Her eyes had grown wide, her mouth set in a quivering pout. "But I don't want you to go," she said. "I want you to stay here with me. We can ride your big gray horse like we did before."

The big gray horse was dead, blown out from under him at Waterloo.

"When it is time for me to go back, I will have to do so," Stanley said, his throat narrowing at hearing the thought spoken out loud. He'd been away from it all for less than a month, and already the thought of returning felt like walking into a prison cell after the briefest glimpse of freedom.

"If you go back, who will kiss your hurt and make it better?" Caroline asked.

Nothing would make it better. A man who had been through all he had could never be whole again.

"Mama kissed my hurt." Caroline had begun calling Marion "Mama" in recent weeks, according to Mater's very detailed account of the family's recent history. "It didn't make it stop hurting, but it made *me* feel better."

"I am glad your hurt is better," Stanley whispered. He breathed through a sudden surge of emotion. He had made very certain that her hurt would never amount to his.

"Mama loved it all better," Caroline said. "If you stay, Stanby, your hurt will get better too." His vision blurred with the sting of tears he refused to shed. He wanted to believe it, wanted to believe there was a cure. "I can love you bigger than the biggest hurt."

"That is a great deal of love, Poppet." Stanley tightened his grip on her.

"Do you have a lot of hurts?" Caroline asked.

Stanley tried to clear his suddenly constricted throat, blinking against the pooling moisture in his eyes. "Yes, I do." The words were barely audible. Where had the soldier gone? Where was his self-control?

She lifted both her little hands to his face, touching his cheeks. "There are so very many of us," Caroline whispered, leaning in close to his face. "We can love you all better." She ran her palm along his cheek, wiping away a tear that had escaped his eye. She wrapped her arms around his neck and leaned into him.

He closed his arms around her, pulling her into a tight embrace, his hand pressed against her golden ringlets. He leaned his head against the top of hers and closed his eyes to hold back the remaining tears. One tiny girl had managed, in a matter of moments, to bring years of silent despair perilously close to the surface.

J

CHAPTER FIFTEEN

STANLEY COULDN'T REMEMBER A THING that had been said at dinner. The conversations had swirled around him as he'd struggled with his composure. He had never managed the all-encompassing numbness that so many of his comrades had, so he had learned to focus on being a soldier, forcing the thoughts and memories that haunted him far enough into the back of his mind that he could function. At some point, he felt certain he would lose the battle and everything would rush out. He'd come far too close in the drawing room.

No one mentioned the tears he'd fought while Caroline had sat on his lap, but awareness lurked in everyone's eyes. Marjie had been unusually wary. Whether she was upset to have seen him so nearly unmanned or was, as Sorrel had hinted, feeling guilty at having made off with his gloves and buttons, Stanley couldn't say. Neither could he decide how he felt about the growing distance between the two of them. He might very well break down entirely if she was near him.

He excused himself the moment the ladies left the dining room on the pretense that he felt unwell. His brothers accepted the excuse, and he hobbled from the room like a coward.

Layton had been sporting that contemplative look that had, in their childhood, always preceded a very thorough interrogation in which one's secrets and most private thoughts were unearthed and examined entirely against one's will. Harold had, as always, looked far too saintly to be a flawed human like the rest of his family, and Stanley had no desire to serve as the obvious contrast to that display.

"I ain't even finished my dinner yet, Cap," Pluck said as he laid out Stanley's nightclothes. "Had to give up my seat right next to Jane, Miss Kendrick's abigail. Fine bit o' femininity there."

"My apologies that your duties have interfered with your romantic aspirations." Stanley fumbled with the buttons on his jacket. He was wound so tightly from the upheaval of the evening that his one good hand refused to cooperate. "If I could get out of this blasted uniform on my own, I would." He dropped his hand in frustration. "Fiend seize it, I'm so deuced helpless all the time."

"Here, Cap'n."

Stanley looked up, knowing his expression was probably mutinous. He needed a seventeen-year-old boy to help him take off his uniform. Pluck stood in front of Stanley's chair, no look of pity or amusement on his face, holding out to him a pair of scissors.

"What—?"

"Fer yer buttons," Pluck said.

"You want me to cut them off?" He couldn't be serious.

"Seems like a good solution to me."

"What am I supposed to do tomorrow night when I dress for dinner? Am I to present myself with my jacket flapping about me like a deuced, blasted, scraggly bird?"

"I'll sew the buttons back on," Pluck answered.

"Do you sew?" Stanley doubted it. Pluck didn't have any of the other necessary accomplishments to be a useful valet.

A smile more mischievous than amused spread across Pluck's face. "Jane can sew."

"I will not give any of the servants more work to do simply because you are feeling like being a troublemaker."

Pluck sobered in an instant. "Ye ain't never been one for spoutin' strong words without provocation, Cap'n," he said. "But ye ain't hardly said one sentence since I came in here that didn't have at least one word ye likely wouldn't say in front of yer mum. I was just thinkin' that cutting off them frustratin' buttons would do ye some good."

"It would be cathartic, you decided?"

Pluck's brow furrowed a little. "Is that one of them highbrow profanities?"

A short, low burst of a chuckle escaped Stanley's throat. "No, Pluck. It means something that makes a person feel better."

"Why didn't ye just say that?" Pluck shook his head. "Ye nobs sure know how to talk and talk and never say anything simple."

Stanley smiled at that.

"So are ye gonna cut them big, shiny buttons off, or should I help ye push 'em through them itty-bitty button holes?" Pluck's choice of childlike adjectives and his suddenly overly sweet tone did it. Stanley held out his hands for the scissors. He wasn't entirely adept at using them in his left hand. Careful to cut only the threads and not the uniform itself, Stanley snipped off the first button. He watched it roll down his chest and off his lap, spinning on the floor like a top before coming to a rest near his feet.

He lifted his eyes to Pluck's grinning face. Oddly enough, the unorthodox approach to undressing *was* remarkably cathartic. Pluck picked up each button as it fell to the floor and shook the collection in his hand while Stanley cut.

"Daddy Hill would have our hides if he could see this," Stanley said as he cut the last button off. "He is rather stiff about uniforms, you know."

"Aye," Pluck said. "But iffen he can overlook yer not wearing yer sword, I figure he wouldn't raise too much fuss 'bout cuttin' yerself outta that blasted uniform."

Stanley pulled his arms free of his shirt—the task made infinitely easier by the lack of buttons down the front closure and on the usually difficult right cuff. Lud, it felt good to be able do something that simple without needing assistance.

"Not like the jacket won't be right as a rivet come tomorrow night," Pluck said, dropping his handful of brass buttons on the dressing table. "We ain't cut off nothin' that can't be put back on."

That, Stanley knew, was not always the case. He pushed out a breath. His hand was already ungloved. The leg came off next.

"You ready?" Those two words from Pluck in that exact detached tone always started the ritual.

"Take the blasted thing off, and get it over with."

Pluck's head jerked in his direction. Stanley understood why. He'd deviated from the established protocol. But he felt too raw for the false casualty of their normal routine.

"Are ye well, Cap'n?" Once in a great while, Pluck actually looked his age. The unnatural aging effect of war would slip away, and one could see the kid he still was underneath. Stanley almost couldn't bear to look at him in those moments. Too many other young soldiers flashed through his mind—children, really—whom he'd led into battles they didn't survive.

"I'm tired, Pluck," Stanley said, pushing the memories back once more. "Help me out of this . . . thing. I want to go to bed."

Pluck knelt on the floor in front of his chair, and Stanley avoided looking at him as he tugged Stanley's boots off and set them aside. The steps were mechanical, entirely memorized. Stanley pulled the leg of his trousers up to his knee, where the straps and buckles kept everything held together. Pluck had to help with the buckles, as Stanley hadn't mastered it one-handed. He hadn't particularly wanted to, preferring to look the other way while he relived a painless version of the worst day of his entire life.

"Stanley?" A knock on his door accompanied the sound of Marjie's voice.

His heart immediately flew to his throat. His eyes met Pluck's. "Rebuckle it," Stanley urgently whispered. The leg hadn't been completely detached.

"Wanna put yer boots back on too?" Pluck asked, quickly refastening the buckles.

But the door creaked open.

"Blast it," Stanley muttered under his breath. What was she doing, coming to his room? Granted, she'd done so before, but that had been pushing propriety to its breaking point. To come again, and so late, was too high a risk, and not merely to her reputation. What if she'd been only a minute later? His leg would have been off already. He wasn't ready for her to see that—not yet. Not ever.

Pluck tugged the leg of Stanley's trousers back down over his wooden leg just as Marjie peered inside the doorway.

"Stanley?" Marjie said.

He pulled himself to his feet, hoping the lack of movement in what appeared to be his stockinged right foot would be less noticeable if he was standing. His heart thudded painfully as she stepped inside. It wouldn't take long, if she was paying any attention, for her to notice that something was wrong with his foot.

"I've brought the salve I told you about. Cook made it up from the recipe I gave her." She crossed toward him, holding out a jar with a slightly green concoction inside.

He inched back. Distance was key—the deception worked only if one wasn't afforded a good look.

"Pluck." Stanley relayed his orders in one syllable, and Pluck, being army trained, understood precisely what was expected of him. He took the jar from Marjie and stepped back out of the way again but remained in the room.

Marjie's gaze darted between Pluck and Stanley. "I am hoping it will help."

"Yes, perhaps." If he gave her short enough answers, she might leave more quickly.

"How is your hand today?" she asked.

So much for a speedy exit. "As well as can be expected," he said with little emotion. She needed to be discouraged from remaining.

Marjie stepped closer. Stanley stepped back. His leg wasn't fastened as snugly as usual, and he had to grasp the back of the chair he'd been sitting in to keep from toppling over. She needed to go before he completely disgraced himself.

"Marjie—" he began, but she cut him off.

"Your gloves have been off; I think that will have helped." Marjie reached out, obviously intending to take hold of his hand and examine it for herself.

"Marjie," Stanley objected. She needed to go.

"And the salve will be soothing, I am certain of it," she continued, her fingers brushing against his.

"Miss Kendrick." The words snapped out much as they had when amongst his men.

Marjie's hands dropped instantly back to her side, and her eyes flew to his face.

"It is time for you to return to your own rooms." Stanley kept his tone firm, although a little less sharp.

"But your hand—"

"I am perfectly capable of seeing to my own welfare, and Pluck is here to provide whatever assistance I might wish for."

Spots of color crept across Marjie's cheeks. "I only wanted to help," she said in a small voice.

Stanley fortified himself against the urge to reach out for her, to soothe away the look of embarrassment on her face. If he gave in to the impulse, she would not leave. "I do not require your help," he said tightly.

Marjie shrugged, tipping her head to one side. On the surface, she was the very picture of indifference, but her lips quivered. She opened her mouth as if to say something but seemed to change her mind. In a flurry of skirts, she spun and practically ran from the room.

Stanley stood frozen, his eyes glued to his empty doorway. Marjie had said she had shrugged just like that when her father said something hurtful to her.

"Ye was a little harsh, Cap'n," Pluck said. "She was just trying to help."

He had very nearly made her cry.

He grabbed his walking stick and moved as quickly as he could toward the door. The corridor was empty. He stopped a few feet from the doorway to Marjie's room. He could hear Philip's voice coming from his own room. To be seen entering Marjie's rooms at night in only his shirtsleeves and pantaloons would be unacceptable.

"You were a bit harsh on your sister, dear," Philip said, his voice seemingly floating out from the sitting room that joined the master suites. "She was only trying to help."

That sounded alarmingly familiar.

"So she said," Sorrel answered. "But she needs to learn that her interference is not always welcome. The girl drives people absolutely mad."

"Was it entirely necessary to tell her so?"

Marjie had been rebuffed by Sorrel as well? Stanley knew how sensitive she was. The double rejection would hurt deeply, and he had contributed to it.

He leaned heavily against the wall. He hadn't intended to hurt her. The harder he tried to do what was right, the worse everything seemed to become.

J

CHAPTER SIXTEEN

Marjie knew she looked horrendous. A night spent weeping had left her with red, puffy eyes accented by dark circles of fatigue.

"I do not require your help."

"You are enough to drive a person to insanity."

Stanley's and Sorrel's words had not quieted overnight. Each reverberation cut at her. Father had said the same sort of things again and again. Sorrel could be impatient when she felt unwell; Marjie knew as much and tried not to let it bother her. But she had never expected Stanley to push her away so coldly.

She had spent the morning in her room, working indifferently at her embroidery. Avoiding everyone had proven a good strategy in the past, as she could not make a nuisance of herself that way. The hours of unchanged scenery had begun to wear on her, however, and she opted to take a turn in the gardens.

Despite the nearness of November, the weather had not become overly chilly. Her gloves and spencer kept her relatively warm as she wandered amongst the hedges. In the quiet of the gardens, she could think.

Stanley apparently didn't welcome her efforts on his behalf. She would have to impose upon herself the same distance and detachment she had adopted with Sorrel after Philip had suggested she not fuss so much. Stanley had insisted he could see to his own welfare. He had the salve and had not, she'd noticed with satisfaction, worn a glove over his burnt hand. She did not yet know what injury he had suffered to his leg but would trust Pluck to see to it.

If only she knew of an unobtrusive way to help.

She pulled herself from her all-consuming thoughts in time to realize Stanley was approaching from the house. His limp seemed to be improving a little. He still held his foot stiffly as he walked and seemed slightly unsure of his balance, but he appeared less dependent on his walking stick. That had to be a good sign. Marjie tucked the observation away, unsure if voicing her happiness aloud would be unwelcome.

"Good afternoon, Stanley," she offered when he came near enough to hear. She held back the inquiry into his health that automatically formed in her mouth. *He does not wish for your help*, she reminded herself.

"I—" He stopped short, his eyes narrowing as he focused on her face. "You've been crying."

"It is the cold air," Marjie lied haltingly. "It irritates my eyes."

He stood silently watching her. Marjie could feel warmth spread across her face under his scrutiny.

"I don't like when you cry." Stanley spoke so softly Marjie barely heard him, his sadness evident.

Marjie swallowed against the sudden lump in her throat. This was the Stanley she had fallen in love with. He was compassionate and tender and gentle. Yet she couldn't dismiss the version of him she'd been confronted with the night before. He'd spoken sharply. He'd shown no desire for her to remain, no joy in her company.

"I am fine, I assure you." She attempted to summon a believably content expression. "Have you tried the salve yet?" She wished the words unspoken the moment they'd left her mouth. The question sounded far too much like her usual fretting, and he wouldn't like that.

But he didn't look upset. Perhaps she hadn't annoyed him with her inquiry after all.

"You did not exaggerate its effectiveness. I shall be certain to take a great deal of it with me when I am called back into duty." A momentary flash of pain appeared in his eyes. Marjie had seen the look before, always when Stanley spoke of returning to his post with the army.

"I will write out the recipe." She kept her hands at her side through sheer willpower. How she wished to smooth the lines of worry that had appeared on his face. "Then you can have more made if need be."

"Thank you," Stanley said, his voice and mannerisms oddly detached from the moment.

"Perhaps some of your men could benefit from the ointment as well."

Stanley nodded, the same distant look still in his eyes. "It would be the only good thing I did for any of them," he muttered.

As a nonfusser, Marjie was a complete failure. She pressed her hand atop his walking stick without a single thought for her earlier vow to keep her distance. His eyes returned to her face. The deep misery in his expression reverberated as an ache in her heart. If only she knew how to help. Such an intrusion would probably be unwelcome, but she desperately needed to do something.

Marjie reached out and gently cupped his face. Stanley closed his eyes, his expression seeming to grow even more pained.

All those long weeks of wishing he were near and imagining touching him, holding him, feeling his arms around her again came rushing back. Nothing had gone as she'd expected since his return. There had been no joyous reunion, no furthering of the connection she had felt with him from the moment they'd first met. She had, instead, found herself walking a fine line, never knowing if he appreciated or resented her presence in his life.

Just as she decided she ought to pull her hand back, Stanley turned his head and lightly kissed her palm.

Her heart skipped a beat before lurching back into rhythm.

Stanley shifted again so his lips lightly brushed the very tips of her fingers. "Marjie," he whispered.

She stepped closer to him, each breath requiring effort. The warmth of him penetrated the chilled air, and the familiar scent of his soap enveloped her senses. The tension in her eased in that instant.

This was home.

Her hand slid from his face to rest on his chest. His free arm wrapped around her. At the contact, she saw him wince—his *right* arm had pulled her closer.

"Your hand," she whispered in concern.

He shook his head, his eyes still closed. Marjie rested her head against his shoulder and felt him rest his cheek against the top of her head. He had held her in precisely that way in the very same garden on the day he'd left to rejoin his regiment. That tender moment had been marred by worry and uncertainty. In this embrace, she felt hope.

"I am sorry I snapped at you last night," he said. "It was unpardonable of me. I was weary and concerned at the risk you were taking with your reputation and—" She felt him sigh. "I am sorry. I ought to have been kinder."

"You are entirely forgiven," she said. "I should try harder not to be fussy. I realize how very unwelcome—"

"Marjie." Stanley interrupted her confession.

She pulled back enough to look up at him.

"Do not belittle your compassionate nature. This world needs more humanity, not less. It is in far too short supply."

"I think you have seen too much inhumanity, Stanley. You have lost faith in mankind."

"But not in you," he whispered. "Never in you."

He leaned closer to her, just a breath nearer, but Marjie's heart responded loudly. Her hand, almost of its own accord, shifted from his chest to his neck as he continued to close the distance between them.

His mouth brushed hers so lightly it might have been nothing more than the touch of a breeze. He didn't loosen his embrace. Her heart thudded erratically in her chest.

At the sudden sound of footsteps on the graveled garden walk, Marjie froze. She could feel Stanley tense. Her eyes flew open. His expression registered a moment's regret before he stepped deliberately away from her. That he seemed as reluctant as she went a long way toward easing her disappointment at the loss of his touch.

She turned toward the approaching footsteps and hoped her countenance was not too tellingly flushed.

An upstairs maid hurriedly walked to where Marjie stood and bobbed a curtsy. "Pardon me," she said. "There's a visitor to see you, Miss Kendrick."

"A visitor?" Who could possibly have come to visit her? Mother had, in a letter to Sorrel, declared her intention to remain in Tunbridge Wells through at least the remainder of the year, necessitating that both Marjie and Fennel be accepted as guests at Lampton Park during the holy season.

"Yes, Miss Kendrick. 'Tis Lord Devereaux."

Lord Devereaux. His arrival was unexpected but not unwelcome. She had wondered since leaving Town how he was. She knew he did not look forward to the approach of Christmas, as that had been his late wife's favorite time of year. It had held a special significance in their courtship, which simply added to his discomfort.

"Tell him I shall be there directly."

The maid curtsied once more and quickly returned in the direction of the house.

Lord Devereaux had wanted to get to know Stanley, and Marjie wished for Stanley to get to know him. They were both good and kind gentlemen, and she simply knew the two would like each other. The fact that making the reintroductions would also allow her more time in Stanley's company certainly contributed to her eagerness.

Marjie turned back around. "Stanley—"

She saw nothing more than the back of him as he made his way down the garden path. He hadn't offered so much as a farewell. He had simply left her standing there. In light of the embrace and all-too-brief kiss of only a moment before, Marjie had not expected abandonment.

She stood watching him a moment, unsure of what she ought to do. She could easily catch up to him; he did not yet move swiftly. Dare she risk being seen as cloying and fretful? Suppose he left because he once again wished to be alone. He had apologized for being short with her the night before but had not indicated that he had not meant his words of rebuke.

"I do not require your help." He had spoken clearly and precisely. There could have been no mistaking his meaning.

Marjie took a deep breath. She could give him space. Just as Philip had said, she needed to learn when to be attentive and when to back away. And Stanley *had* kissed her. Heavens, he had kissed her. That was reason enough for hope and optimism.

When she arrived in the drawing room, Mater and Lord Devereaux were speaking. They acknowledged her entrance, greeting her as she moved to sit nearby. After a moment, Mater drifted to a chair a little distance from them.

"I was passing through the general area and couldn't resist coming by to see you," Lord Devereaux said. He looked happier than Marjie remembered seeing him before. "I have come to a decision of which I think you will approve, though I am beginning to wonder if I am destined to regret it."

"And what decision is that, my lord?" Marjie smiled in return. Lord Devereaux, despite his continued grief, was an easy conversationalist. Should he ever decide to marry again, he would make some lady a very fine husband.

"I have thrown the Duchess of Hartley into a full fit of hysterics by accepting her invitation to join her annual Christmas house party after three consecutive years of refusing."

"You have not." As near as Marjie could gather from their conversations at various *ton* events, Lord Devereaux had not intended to accept. The annual gathering of his closest friends had begun early in his marriage, and the month-long festivities reminded him a great deal too much of his wife.

"I have, indeed."

She laughed at the dramatic expression of shock Lord Devereaux managed to produce.

"I am so happy that you will not be spending Christmastime alone," Marjie said.

"Something I would never have even considered doing without your gentle but persistent prodding." His gratitude held not a hint of censure at her interference in his affairs. "I have decided that you are correct on one very vital point."

"Only one?"

He laughed lightly. "One very vital point," he repeated, emphasizing the word *vital.* "It is time and past I rejoin Society, and though I suspect I shall always miss my dear Miranda, I believe I will be happier spending some time in the company of others."

"The society of true friends will always be welcome," Marjie said.

"You seem to have quite a full house here."

"We do. With so many of the Jonquils living nearby, there is never any shortage of people."

Lord Devereaux glanced quickly at Mater before returning his gaze to Marjie and lowering his voice. "How is your young captain?"

"His injuries are more extensive than I at first realized." Marjie kept her voice low as well. "And I fear he is unhappy. His experiences with Wellington's forces weigh very heavily on him."

"He joined the army at a young age," Lord Devereaux said. "The violence of war can be scarring at such an impressionable time of life. Waterloo was, as I understand it, especially horrific."

Marjie nodded, remembering the story Pluck had shared of Stanley rescuing him from an explosive and dangerous fire. That haunted Marjie. She could see in her mind the terrifying image of Stanley literally on fire.

"I do not know how to help him," Marjie said.

Lord Devereaux had long since taken on the role of older brother. She felt at ease sharing her worries with him. He would neither laugh nor dismiss her concerns.

"I had hoped to see him, actually," Lord Devereaux said.

"I was going to ask him to join us, but he—" How did she explain without completely disgracing herself? She had been on the verge of, she hoped, being quite thoroughly kissed when word of his arrival had reached her and Stanley had subsequently left.

"I assume Captain Jonquil was less than enthusiastic about my arrival." A single corner of Lord Devereaux's mouth twitched upward.

"I am not certain your presence is the reason he . . . disappeared."

"I suspect it is precisely the reason. Most gentlemen dislike the idea of a rival."

"A rival? You do not think he believes you and I—that we—"

Lord Devereaux chuckled. "Are romantically attached to one another?" he finished for her. "That is exactly what I suspect."

"But that is absurd. You are—"

"Too old?" Lord Devereaux raised an eyebrow.

"That is not at all what I was going to say."

"Too homely? Too prosy? Too boring?"

Marjie shook her head. "Now you are teasing me again."

"Then what is your objection?" His expression was not entirely jesting, she noticed. "There are some who would still consider me eligible despite my advanced years and hermit-like tendencies."

"I had meant to imply only that you are not interested in a wife."

Lord Devereaux began to fidget a bit, shifting about on his chair. "I have considered the possibility of late." He steepled his hands in front of him, something Marjie had noticed he did when he felt contemplative. "I have been lonely and find myself thinking that I would like the companionship one enjoys in marriage."

His words surprised her. She hadn't realized he might contemplate marrying again. She had known from their very first meeting that he was painfully lonely. She recognized that in him, for she had been lonely as well. While she hoped he found far more than mere companionship in marriage, she knew that to have someone with whom he might talk would be beneficial. The emptiness of his home would not pain him so acutely, and he could begin to find some pleasure in life again.

"Is this why you are joining Their Graces' house party?" Marjie asked. "So that you might find a wife?"

Lord Devereaux's expression lightened once more. "No. I am merely *considering* the possibility, not actively pursuing it. The house party is little more than a step toward rejoining Society."

"When do you plan to arrive there?"

"Tomorrow," he said. "I am to arrive a full three weeks in advance of the remaining guests. I think Her Grace is afraid I will back out if she does not have me under lock and key."

He would have company, and that, Marjie knew, would alleviate a great deal of his loneliness.

"I hope you have a splendid sojourn," she said.

"And I wish you luck with your thick-headed captain. If he has not yet realized how entirely devoted you are to him, I begin to think he does not deserve your affections after all."

"I wish you could have talked with him finally," she said. "You would like him better if you knew him."

"I had wanted, if nothing else, to convey a message to him," Lord Devereaux said. "A tenant family of mine had a son who fought in the war. The boy was killed at Albuera when he was only eighteen years old. A fortnight later or so, they received a letter from a young Lieutenant Jonquil."

Marjie listened raptly. This was one of Stanley's letters, the ones he wrote to the families of men who were killed, the letters he had said probably made no difference at all.

"He was not their son's commanding officer," Lord Devereaux continued, "but he took the time to send them a brief note expressing his condolences and sharing a few small memories of the boy. They still speak about that unlooked-for kindness whenever their son's name is mentioned."

If only Stanley knew. His letters had indeed touched those who received them.

"I had hoped to thank him on their behalf," Lord Devereaux said. "But I did not wish to embarrass him by doing so in company. These tenants of mine are not literate—the local curate read the letter to them—and so they could not pen their own note of gratitude. I must say, Captain Jonquil's thoughtfulness impressed me."

"He has sent other letters as well," Marjie said. "He has written to the family of every man in his squadron who has fallen."

"I imagine that is a lot of letters."

Marjie nodded. Stanley had said as much.

"I do not know any of the other recipients," Lord Devereaux said, "but I am certain that those letters are as treasured by them as they are by the Wells family."

Those words remained in Marjie's head long after Lord Devereaux's departure. Stanley was so certain his letters were unappreciated and unwanted. He had said in the gardens that he never did any good by his men. Here was another piece of the puzzle. Stanley doubted his impact, his influence for good. He felt himself something of a failure. Marjie truly believed there were people throughout England who would disagree, and not just Stanley's family. In her heart, she knew Stanley needed to know that.

CHAPTER SEVENTEEN

Ever since Lord Devereaux's brief, unexpected, and, as far as Stanley was concerned, entirely unwelcome visit, Marjie had spent a great deal of each day in Philip's library bent over the desk, writing letters. She had an air of anticipation and purpose about her that had Stanley worried. That something of significance was in the planning, he had no doubt. Further, that this occurrence related somehow to Lord Devereaux's interview with Marjie, Stanley was absolutely certain. The conclusion that had nagged at Stanley since the not-nearly-elderly-enough widower's departure a week earlier was that Lord Devereaux, blast him, had advanced his suit, perhaps to the point of being accepted.

Stanley tortured himself with unanswerable questions. Ought he not to have kissed Marjie? If he were being perfectly honest with himself, compared to how he would have liked to have kissed her, that brief interlude hardly counted. Had he alarmed her or trespassed upon her good nature? On the other hand, perhaps he should have put more fervor into his efforts and, as Pluck would say, stolen a bit more of her heart. Except, that would not have been honorable, knowing as he did that she was as good as engaged even before Lord Devereaux had descended upon them.

His hand was healing to the extent it ever would. There were fewer points of irritation and cracking, thanks to both the absence of constant chafing and the soothing nature of Marjie's salve. Sorrel's advice about his walking stick had proven beneficial, and though the shift of weight it created had led to some blisters on the stub of his leg, his limp was improving. Just out of curiosity, he'd attempted to cross his room to the washstand that morning without his walking stick and had, to his complete surprise, managed it without falling on his face. He probably could have gone farther if the leg had been secured more tightly and if Pluck hadn't performed one of his annoyingly hilarious dances of joy. The boy really did need to work at being a properly subdued servant. How was a one-legged man supposed to enjoy any of his accomplishments when he was laughing too hard to maintain his balance?

Stanley smiled briefly at the memory before the weight of reality sank in. He welcomed the improvement in his health but found it horribly ill-timed. Just the day before, he had received a missive from Horse Guards informing him that a Colonel Fallwell, representing Lord Hill, would be arriving at Lampton Park in three weeks' time to ascertain Stanley's fitness to return to his duties.

"Although the wars are officially at an end, peace is not yet established," Lord Hill's letter said. Stanley had read it multiple times, his spirits lowering with each repetition. "Experienced officers are thin on the ground just now, so many having sold their commissions and returned to civilian life, and His Majesty's Army is in need of your organizational and leadership skills."

Lord Hill seemed to know the precise words that would negate all the arguments Stanley had built up over the weeks of his furlough. The army did not expect him to fight or march into battle, something he could not remotely do. He was needed to organize those who would undertake the minor skirmishes still occurring. He would be required once again to decide which of his men were sent into a fight and which remained out of harm's way.

Stanley understood the thinly veiled reference to the large number of officers who'd left the army following Waterloo. Many of those who had volunteered to fight for their country had done so with every intention of returning home once Napoleon had been defeated. Stanley, however, had seen his oath of service as just that—an oath, a promise to his country and King. So long as he was needed, he would serve.

"The difference between a gentleman and a blackguard is honor," Father had said to Stanley when he was still quite young. He'd never forgotten those words, and indeed, had spent his life attempting to live up to them.

Life in the army had simply solidified his determination. Honor meant everything to a British soldier. No accomplishment, no matter how vast, was praiseworthy if accomplished dishonorably. On the field of battle, when the fighting was fiercest and most horrifying, those officers who led their men, who fought despite injury and threat to their own safety, were the ones who earned the respect of their fellow soldiers.

Honor was the very fiber and soul of a man. Stanley had given his word to serve his country, and he would not break that commitment, regardless of what it cost him. To do so would sound the death knell to his integrity. Thus, his improved health robbed him of the only honorable means of escaping, if temporarily, his return to the field.

He would be sent back to France, where his regiment was. Stanley could sit a horse, though not at a full gallop and certainly not with any degree of grace. But that had little bearing on his situation now. The cavalry charges he had participated in again and again were no longer necessary. He would be doing precisely what he'd been doing before Lord Hill had sent him home temporarily: organizing patrols and guard rotations, helping suppress uprising among the citizenry. The lingering bitterness in Napoleon's former troops had increasingly led to attacks on British soldiers. Stanley would be handed the task once again of arranging for the burial of his men who were unfortunate enough to cross paths with those bent on revenge. There would be more letters to send to grieving families. There would always be letters.

And there would always be another war. Sometimes, there was more than one. They'd been at war with the former colonies in the midst of the war with Napoleon. Things were never entirely peaceful in India. No matter that England liked to think of itself as having reached a period of peace, another war always lurked in the shadows.

Stanley swung around, having covered a good portion of the garden. November had come in as cold as he ever remembered it being. No doubt the warmer temperatures of the Continent had confused his inner thermometer. He welcomed the bite of the air, however, and he understood the necessity of exercise. He needed to build his strength and endurance before returning to his post.

Marjie would be married soon enough, and her letters would stop. He could never prevent her from entering his thoughts, but she would be lost to him so entirely that thinking of her would not be comforting as it had once been. He would have her twenty-five letters and nothing else.

He could have almost borne the thought of returning to the army if there had been any chance Marjie would be there with him. Her faith in him would have sustained him through the darkness of descending back into that abyss. Her presence would have soothed him when the inevitable weight of death and suffering bent him under its load.

"Selfish coxcomb," he muttered at himself. She would be in agony living that life, and he knew it. Lord Devereaux offered her safety and security and a shield from the horrors of the world. She belonged at home in England, living happily in peace and comfort.

Stanley made his sorry ascent of the front steps. Stairs were still difficult. He took them slowly and slightly sideways. The morning mist had only just begun to dissipate, and memories of his childhood enveloped him. The manor house at Lampton Park had always stood as a beacon of sorts. He would lean out the window of the traveling coach whenever returning home from Town or school. The house would come into view, and every care and worry would simply melt away. He missed that simpler time.

Beck, the butler, held the door open as Stanley stepped inside, the warm air caressing his wind-bitten face. By the time he had limped his way to the base of the front staircase, even his foot had begun to thaw. One benefit of a wooden leg was its imperviousness to the weather. He smiled wryly at the thought.

"More letters for the post, Miss Kendrick?" Beck asked in his always correct way.

Stanley's eyes, as always, refused to shift at all from the sudden sight of Marjie. She should always wear blue, he had long ago decided, though perhaps without that one golden curl hanging over her shoulder. A man could endure only so much temptation before tossing his best intentions out the window.

"Yes, please." She handed a stack of sealed missives to the butler.

A stack? Stanley hadn't ever received multiple letters from her at one time. Certainly they weren't all for Lord Devereaux. His less-than-charitable side hoped the pile contained not a single letter for his lordship.

He could tell the exact moment Marjie realized he stood there. She grew suddenly very still, and a look of something like guilt crossed her face. Her color deepened by more than one shade. Odd, that. Why would she be so entirely uncomfortable over something as commonplace as sending letters? It wasn't as if he didn't know she was a faithful correspondent.

Unless she felt guilty being so closely in company with a gentleman she had embraced and by whom she'd been kissed within moments of her apparent engagement to another gentleman entirely.

If her embarrassment hadn't been almost immediately followed by a very friendly smile, Stanley would have worried that those moments he cherished every bit as much as her letters had seriously undermined their friendship.

"Good morning, Stanley." She spoke with every indication of sincerity, and yet, the slightest hint of uneasiness lurked.

"Good morning. You appear to have been busy." He indicated the letters Beck was even then walking away with.

"Yes, that—I—" Why was she so nervous? "I do like to write letters."

"Yes, I know."

The familiar tap and drag rhythm of a walking stick and limp drew their attention before another word was spoken between them. Sorrel stood at the first-floor landing. Her descent was more awkward than his own had been earlier that morning.

"She looks pale," Marjie whispered.

Sorrel looked more than merely pale. She looked exhausted and in a significant amount of pain.

Marjie moved to the foot of the stairs and looked up as her sister made her way down. "Are you feeling well?" she asked her sister.

"Yes." Sorrel's monosyllabic response would have been sharp had she managed more than a minimal amount of volume. "I am hungry."

"I am certain a tray could have been brought to your room," Marjie said.

"I am not an invalid." The desperation in her response was not difficult to decipher. Sorrel was attempting to convince herself that she spoke the truth.

Marjie's gaze turned to Stanley. "What should I do?" She mouthed the words, but Stanley understood. Marjie worried about fussing, thanks to Philip's hints and Sorrel's very direct complaints, and had to fight her natural inclination to help.

He returned his attention to Sorrel, trying to decide how they might help without raising her hackles. She lowered herself to the next step just as the last drops of color drained from her face.

"Marjie!" Stanley called out, knowing he would never get to Sorrel in time. Unfortunately, his instructions were either too late in coming or too vague.

Sorrel hit the step hard with her right hip before Marjie realized what was happening and grabbed hold of her sister. A moan of pain indicated Sorrel had not, thankfully, lost consciousness. Stanley moved closer as quickly as he could. Sorrel, of all people, could be counted on to shake off any offer of assistance, even if doing so meant being left in an undignified heap on the stairwell. Instead, she lay in Marjie's arms without the slightest resistance.

"Stanley," Marjie whispered. "What should I do?"

He straightened, issuing a whistle he knew would bring the staff faster than he could reach the nearest bell pull. That whistle had successfully caught the attention of his men during the chaos of battle.

Beck appeared first. His barely concealed confusion at the unusual summons slipped into concern as his gaze fell on the sight of the countess, apparently helpless in her sister's arms. But Stanley had no time for sympathies, no matter how appropriate.

"Have Will report here at once," Stanley instructed, naming the largest of the Lampton Park footmen. He could easily carry Sorrel back up to her room, something Stanley knew himself incapable of. "And send one of the groomsmen to Dr. Habbersham. Lady Lampton is in need of him."

"Yes, Captain Jonquil." Beck turned, about to undertake the task.

"Philip should be found," Marjie said. "He will wish to know."

Of course. Leave it to Marjie to understand what Sorrel needed most. "Beck."

The butler turned back.

"Send word to the stables to have a horse saddled." Philip had gone riding with Layton. Stanley could track them down, knowing all too well the usual Jonquil brother riding paths, some of which were difficult to explain. He would find them faster if he went personally.

A nod and the butler exited the room entirely.

"Any particular message you wish me to deliver to your husband, Sorrel?" Stanley asked, fully expecting a stinging reply. Truth be known, he *hoped* for one. Anything less would be indicative of greater illness than she had let on.

Sorrel lifted her eyes to where Stanley stood watching her. Frustration mingled with pain in her gaze. She opened her mouth as if to answer him, but no words escaped. Then something happened that Stanley had never seen before. Sorrel's chin quivered, and tears gathered very suddenly at the corners of her eyes.

"I will see that he is here as swiftly as possible."

He moved as quickly as his battered body would allow. He passed Will on his way out. The rather burly footman would see to it Sorrel was returned to her bedchamber without incident. Not until Stanley actually arrived at the stables did he remember that riding was not as easy for him as it had once been.

If he was soon to be recalled to the Peninsula, as Hill's letter indicated, he'd best grow accustomed to riding despite the lingering awkwardness of it. He hoped only that neither Philip nor Layton noticed the odd set of his leg and the utter ridiculousness of his struggle to mount and dismount. While he may have been forced to lay bare his mutilated hand, he had no intention of confessing to everything.

CHAPTER EIGHTEEN

THE SOUND OF LAUGHTER GAVE them away. Stanley had guessed his brothers' location correctly on the second try. They were on the back acres, following the property line between Lampton Park and Layton's estate, Farland Meadows, just past a copse of trees they'd more than once pretended was Sherwood Forest when they were children.

"Halloo!" Stanley called out as he rode toward them.

Both blond heads turned in his direction. "Halloo yourself, you sluggard!" Philip called back. "About time you got a little exercise."

Layton chuckled, and Philip grinned.

"What convinced you to finally join us?" Layton asked when Stanley came within conversational range.

"Philip, you have to return to the house." Stanley locked his gaze with Philip's, who grew instantly grave. "Sorrel's had a fall"—Philip drew in a sharp breath—"on the stairs." Stanley saw the panic in his brother's face. "She appears to be well enough. Habbersham's been sent for."

Philip didn't pause for even a moment. His powerful black horse sprang at his command and flew across the grounds toward the manor house.

Stanley followed, surprised that he maintained his seat with less effort than he would have expected at a fast canter. He didn't dare try a full gallop, however.

Layton matched his horse's gait to Stanley's. "Was Sorrel badly hurt?" he asked.

"She was conscious, and though she seemed to be in some pain, I do not believe she was badly injured. I'm more concerned that she seemed ill."

"Philip said she's been unwell."

Stanley nodded. "How is Marion feeling?"

No hints of concern entered Layton's expression. "She is still running us all into the ground. She is a force of nature, my wife."

She was also precisely what Layton had needed to breathe life back into his home and family. All of Stanley's older brothers had found women who brought them joy and made their lives whole. They, lucky dogs that they were, actually got to keep their beloveds with them.

Beck informed Stanley and Layton upon their arrival at the house that Lady Lampton was safely in her chambers with the dowager countess at her side, along with Lord Lampton, who had only just arrived. Where, then, was Marjie?

"And the doctor has been sent for?" Layton pressed.

Beck managed to look haughtily offended without undermining his demeanor of servitude one iota. "Captain Jonquil's orders were carried out to the letter, I assure you, Mr. Jonquil," he said with palpable dignity.

"I'm in the suds now," Layton muttered under his breath, turning back toward the front steps, where a groom held his horse in anticipation of his departure. "No one questions Beck's competency with impunity."

Stanley smiled a little at that. All the Jonquil boys had at one time or another felt the steely stare of their butler's disapproval.

"Send word to the Meadows if there is anything I can do." Layton mounted his horse with a fluid grace that had once marked all the brothers' equestrian endeavors. Stanley had made a quick and exceedingly awkward dismount when they'd reached the house, doing so at precisely the moment Layton was most occupied with his own dismount.

Stanley didn't watch him ride off. He recognized the stirrings of jealousy and bitterness and preferred not to wallow in them. He, thankfully, had regained his ability to sit a horse and reminded himself of that fact several times as he crossed to the stairwell and slowly made his way up.

For months, people had been spouting lists of all the things he had to be grateful for. As he'd been faced with the army sawbones amidst the cries of his fellow mutilated soldiers, he'd been told to be grateful the amputation was to be below the knee and not above. While he'd screamed in agony as his uniform had been ripped free of the oozing burn that covered his lower arm and hand, he'd been told to be grateful the burn wasn't larger. As the infectious fever he'd fought afterward raged, he'd been assured he was lucky he was still alive. Except, if he'd been dead, there would have been no pain.

Such maudlin sentiments generally indicated he was in need of rest. He walked slowly toward his room, moving a little awkwardly, the ride having jostled his artificial leg slightly out of position. He really needed to figure out how to improve the fit, preferably before being recalled.

Marjie sat in a chair in the corridor, head hung, hands clasped in her lap. Was Sorrel worse off than he'd thought?

"Marjie?"

She looked up, and his heart felt as though it had stopped. Tears coursed down her cheeks. "Oh, Stanley!" The way she said that exact phrase tugged at him every time. Her voice held the oddest mixture of sadness and budding hope—as though she were entirely certain that he alone had the ability to soothe and comfort her.

Did she feel that way about Lord Devereaux? Before he had time to determine if that thought arose more out of triumphant satisfaction or pure and simple jealousy, Marjie rose from her chair and essentially flung herself into his arms. In an instant, his uncertainty and frustration melted away. Holding his angel was all the salve he ever needed.

He put a hand out to the wall to steady himself. He needed a place to sit before he fell over. "Let's find a quiet room," he suggested.

She didn't object but stayed tucked against his side, his arm wrapped about her as they stepped out into the corridor and began a quick search. A small sewing room not far distant sat empty. He left the door quite appropriately open as he guided her inside and helped her onto one side of the small sofa before sitting beside her. She needed comforting, and he needed her presence to ward off the last remnants of his own heavy mood.

She leaned her head against his shoulder, turning her face in toward his chest—an unforeseen but much appreciated arrangement. He carefully shifted his right arm and wrapped it around her shoulders.

"What has happened, dearest?" he said.

"Sorrel threw me out of her room." The sobs she attempted to hold inside shook against him. "She told me I had turned into a fussy old dragon, and the moment Mater came inside, Sorrel ordered me to 'take myself off.'"

"My sweet Marjie," Stanley whispered. How desperately she wished to help her sister. How much she worried over her. If Sorrel weren't so determinedly independent, Marjie's sometimes overly solicitous ministrations would not rub her so entirely the wrong way.

"I tried so very hard not to fuss," Marjie said. "I only said that I hoped she had not hurt herself badly."

"Your words were quite thoughtful and not at all fussy."

"Do you really think so?" she asked with a hint of relief.

"I really do," he said. "You must remember that Sorrel dislikes feeling dependent upon people, so she would have taken exception to your words regardless of how innocuous they were."

Marjie raised her head and looked at him. How was it possible that even with a reddened nose and tear-streaked face, she was still the most beautiful woman Stanley had ever seen?

"She did not complain when Mater asked her essentially the same thing." Her eyes were positively pleading with him for a reassuring explanation.

"I suspect she feels her dependency even more acutely when she requires assistance from or is a source of concern to you because you are her *younger* sister. As the elder, she likely believes she ought to be the one doing the worrying and assisting."

Marjie's brow furrowed in obvious contemplation. "Mater *is* rather like a mother to her."

"Yes. And one does not feel awkward being assisted and coddled by one's mother."

"I suppose not." Another tear leaked from her eyes. Stanley wiped it away with a gentle swipe of his thumb. Marjie covered his hand with hers where it rested against her cheek. She closed her eyes and leaned into the caress.

It was not, he thought with a jolt of sudden hope, the action of a lady engaged to someone else. Perhaps she had not as yet accepted Lord Devereaux's proposal. Perhaps he had not lost her as entirely as he'd feared.

He didn't allow the idea to remain. He had only that moment and perhaps a handful of others before he returned to his duties. With an effort of Herculean proportions, Stanley broke the contact between them. He kept a soft smile on his face to take any sting out of his pulling away.

Marjie returned his smile with a slightly tremulous one of her own. She leaned her head against him once more. Heaven help him, he didn't have the strength to pull away. "Thank you, Stanley."

"Thank you?"

"I always feel better, happier, when you are with me."

"As do I," Stanley whispered, hardly believing he had made the admission.

They sat in silence as the minutes passed. Stanley kept his arm around her shoulders, breathing in the sweet scent of her and forcing thoughts of his departure out of his mind.

"Please do not take this amiss," she said after a moment, "but I hope the army does not wish for you to return anytime soon."

Stanley smiled. How could he possibly take that statement as anything other than a sentiment in complete accord with his own feelings on the matter?

"I *do* hope to see you recovered, but I will miss you when you are gone. Things will not be the same with you away. I have been hoping, at the very least, you will be here for Christmas. That is only seven weeks from now. Certainly you will be allotted that much time."

"Actually—" The words seemed to catch in Stanley's throat. He hadn't admitted to anyone that his time was swiftly coming to an end.

Marjie must have sensed his sudden tension. She pulled away from him and twisted enough to look directly into his face, her expression quite noticeably worried.

"I have received word from Horse Guards that a representative is being sent in three weeks." Stanley pushed the words out quickly.

"Only three weeks?" Her face paled as she spoke.

Stanley nodded.

"Do you think—" She blinked rapidly. "Do you think you will be recalled to your regiment?"

"I do."

Her eyes locked with his, a question lurking in her gaze, though Stanley couldn't say what that question could be. "In France?"

Stanley nodded.

Her look had not grown any less questioning. She watched him with an air of expectation. "When do you think you will return to England?"

Stanley dropped his gaze to her hands clasped together on her lap. Tension radiated from her posture. "I do not anticipate returning anytime soon," he said. There was no predictable schedule in the army.

When she did not respond after several long moments, Stanley lifted his eyes to her face. Still she wore that expression of uncertain anticipation. "Will you miss . . . England when you are gone?"

That slight pause caught Stanley's attention. He did not think she had asked about potential homesickness. "I *will* miss England," he said. "And I will miss you."

To his surprise, she didn't look reassured or relieved at his admission. If anything, her countenance seemed to fall further. She gave a tiny nod, her eyes dropping away from his face.

"I—I should—" She rose from the sofa and glanced only briefly back at him before hurrying from the room.

He knew he'd said something wrong but had no idea what it might be.

J

CHAPTER NINETEEN

Marjie sobbed into her pillow.

"I will miss you." Those words had felt very much like a slap in the face.

He was leaving her behind. Apparently, there would be no declaration of love, no wedding ceremony, no happily ever after. For weeks, Marjie had hovered between resignation in the face of Stanley's initial indifference and hope at his increasing warmth. She'd read love into every tender moment they'd shared.

"Would you still help him if he didn't love you?" Philip had asked.

How confidently she'd answered! So certain had she been that Stanley did indeed care for her that she'd brushed aside the possibility that he did not. He might not have loved her as she'd hoped, she had told herself, but his regard would grow. How foolish her conviction seemed now.

Sobs tore through her body. She ought to stop investing so much of herself in the people she cared about. There would be far less disappointment in her life.

"Miss Kendrick?" She recognized her abigail's voice. "Lord Lampton has asked for you to come to the drawing room."

Marjie took a shaky breath but did not lift her head from her pillow.

"He is there waiting for you," Jane said.

"Thank you. Tell him I will be there directly." Marjie's voice wavered rather drastically as she spoke, a fact Jane could not have missed.

As soon as Jane's footsteps faded into silence, Marjie pulled herself to a seated position. She forced several trembling breaths before she felt steady enough to walk across the room to her wash table. She splashed and scrubbed her face with the cold water. It seemed that all she did of late was cry.

A quick glance in the mirror showed her efforts had only minimally restored her appearance. She offered the shrug she'd so nearly perfected during her years with her father. That would be her strategy moving forward, to simply pretend she wasn't carrying more pain than she felt capable of enduring.

She reached the drawing room only ten minutes after Jane delivered Philip's message. She had thought his request had been addressed exclusively to herself, but the room was far from empty. Philip stood leaning against the fireplace mantel. Mater sat on the sofa nearby. Stanley occupied an arm chair.

Marjie dropped her gaze the moment she found Stanley. She kept her head lowered and quickly took a seat beside Mater.

"On with it, Philip," Mater said. "What did Dr. Habbersham say?"

Philip pushed out a breath. "Other than a few bruises, Sorrel wasn't hurt by her fall."

Marjie kept her eyes lowered but listened intently.

"What did he say regarding her poor health of late?" Mater asked.

Philip hesitated.

Marjie took only shallow breaths, the tension building inside allowing nothing more.

"Dr. Habbersham believes that both her recent bout of unexplained illness and the difficulty she has had with her balance and the increased pain in her hip are all consequences of—are the results of . . . er—"

Marjie looked up at him, unnerved by his uncharacteristic fumbling. But then the slightest hint of a smile touched his somber expression.

Philip made a noise that sounded to Marjie like a chuckle of disbelief. "It seems Sorrel is increasing."

Marjie felt her eyes widen in utter disbelief.

Mater sputtered a moment as she attempted to speak. "Good heavens. I had hoped that someday—" Mater shook her head in apparent amazement. "This is the reason for her pain of late?"

Philip nodded. "The doctor says it is not uncommon for women in Sorrel's condition to experience some discomfort in the joints. With the state of Sorrel's hip being what it is, he feels this is simply an exaggerated and early version of that complaint."

"Will she be able to carry a child to full term?" Marjie knew it was rather too intimate a question for an unmarried lady to be posing, but it was the worry that had nagged at her ever since Sorrel's wedding.

Philip's face immediately registered his own concern. "That we do not know. The fact that she already struggles to stand and walk is not a good sign. Dr. Habbersham has suggested that she spend the remainder of her time off her feet."

"She will never agree to that." Marjie shook her head.

"Sorrel was remarkably accepting of the suggestion," Philip said. "The doctor did not, thankfully, feel she must remain abed at all times. She will dislike being carried about but will prefer it to being entirely confined."

"Will doing so increase the chances of a good outcome for the baby?" Mater asked.

"I don't know," Philip said. "Dr. Habbersham said it is not only the baby whose fate is uncertain in all of this. He has no way of predicting the impact on Sorrel."

"But there is some hope of a good outcome." Mater sounded very guarded in her declaration.

"A glimmer at least."

Marjie understood what Philip had not said outright. He was not reassured enough to allow himself to feel more than minimally hopeful.

"How is Sorrel reacting to the news?" Stanley spoke for the first time.

"She is very quiet," Philip said.

Marjie's stomach dropped. Sorrel was almost never quiet.

"Go sit with your wife, Philip," Mater said. "These next few months will be difficult for the both of you, and I daresay she could use a little comfort just now."

Philip nodded and silently left the room. Under normal circumstances, his announcement would have been received with well-wishes and joy. Instead, they were all worried and burdened, unable to allow themselves the slightest bit of excitement.

Quite as if she hadn't cried her very heart out earlier, Marjie felt hot tears sting the back of her eyes.

"To be overly hopeful is to invite the punishments of God," Father had so often said. A person was meant to be uncertain and unhappy in life—that was his interpretation of things. Too often he had proven correct. She could not bear it any longer.

She jumped to her feet. "Why must every bit of hope be tinged with loss?"

"Marjie—" Mater's gentle voice barely penetrated.

"Sorrel does not deserve this, and neither does Philip. They should be celebrating, not—" The words caught on a sob she ruthlessly pressed down. "I cannot bear it."

Nearly blinded by her tears, Marjie fled from the room. Another blow, she was certain, would break her heart entirely.

Philip rarely left Sorrel's rooms over the next two days. Marjie slipped inside a couple times, though she was careful not to make any inquiries or look the least bit concerned. Sorrel's coloring was still off, and her appetite had not entirely returned. Under normal circumstances,

Sorrel would not have tolerated two days confined to her bed. She, oddly enough, seemed almost content.

"Do we need to reschedule The Gathering?" Marjie asked Philip on the third day after Sorrel's fall. They, along with Layton and Mater, were closeted in the library, writing letters and sorting through correspondence. They were in the midst of a plot of monumental proportions, which Philip had insisted on dubbing "The Gathering."

All three of her fellow conspirators looked at her with that expression of surprise everyone around her had worn the past three days whenever she spoke, which had grown increasingly infrequent. She simply felt too heavy for chatter and conversation.

"Sorrel won't hear of it," Philip answered. "She insists she'll keep to the chaise longue Mater suggested be placed with the other chairs under the tents that will be erected for The Gathering."

Marjie nodded and turned her attention back to the letters she was sorting through and checking against the master list they had created.

"This is a great deal to plan for in a fortnight," Mater said. "Though I suppose if we waited any longer, the weather would be too cold for this particular style of gathering."

"And Stanley wouldn't be here," Marjie said with a sigh.

All six eyes were trained on her again.

"Why wouldn't Stanley be here?" Mater asked.

Stanley hadn't told them?

"What have you heard?" Philip looked concerned and confused. They all did.

"Stanley has received a letter from the army," Marjie said. "A representative is coming to check on him in less than three weeks."

Silence followed her revelation.

"Is he well enough that they will call him back?" Mater whispered as though she feared the answer. Thankfully, she had asked Philip—Marjie did not feel equal to the task of responding.

"Physically, I think he would be considered fit enough," Philip answered. "He certainly is not up for a march, but I saw him ride only three days ago. His seat is not as firm and sure as it once was, but he can manage well enough for the demands of the occupation."

"But he still seems so unhappy," Mater said. "Not nearly as much as at first, but—" She shook her head, her eyes focusing somewhere in the distance.

"Why doesn't Stanley sell his commission?" Layton asked no one in particular. "I feel certain he has no desire to continue with an army career."

"Do you think he could be convinced to sell out?" Mater asked with the tiniest bit of desperation.

"That would depend on his reasons for not doing so thus far," Philip said.

Determining Stanley's reasons for his actions had become a regular undertaking for Marjie. Why hadn't he left the army? Why had he returned after Napoleon's exile when so many others had not? Why didn't he wish her to be with him when he returned?

"One has to wonder," Layton said, "if Stanley can be trusted not to push himself into something that would do him more harm than is justified."

Any man willing to rush into almost certain death could not be counted on to consider his own safety.

"Why do you shake your head, Marjie?" Philip asked.

She looked up from her ignored letters.

"Do you not think Stanley will be careful of his well-being?"

"His history does not give me confidence," Marjie answered quietly.

"Most men were injured at Waterloo," Philip said. "We can hardly blame him for that."

"Not Waterloo," Marjie whispered.

Philip's gaze became too pointed for comfort. Marjie lowered her eyes again. "Not Waterloo? Orthez, then?"

"Another injury from battle," Layton insisted.

Marjie shook her head again.

"You do not think he was injured in battle?" Philip sounded entirely confused.

"Not injured in the battle, precisely," Marjie said. "Stanley volunteered for the forlorn hope. He was injured while undertaking a suicide mission—one that was not required of him, one he actively and willingly volunteered to undertake. A man who would volunteer to die is not one I would consider careful with his own welfare."

A single beat of silence followed. Then all at once, Mater broke into tears, Layton muttered, "Good heavens," and Philip snapped to a stand, his chair scraping the ground behind him.

"If you will excuse me," Philip said through tight lips.

"You are going to seek out our brother?" Layton asked.

Philip nodded.

"I'll join you." Layton stood as well.

Philip moved stiffly toward the library door. "What the deuce is going through that boy's head?" he muttered as both brothers stepped out of the room in search of Stanley.

A very good question—one Marjie could not answer.

J

CHAPTER TWENTY

A QUICK SUCCESSION OF KNOCKS sounded at the closed door of Stanley's room. "One moment," he called out, pulling himself to his feet. He was getting better at rising.

He crossed to the door, relying less on his walking stick than he once had. He wasn't sure whom he expected to see on the other side, but Philip's valet was certainly not on his list of possibilities.

Wilson stood quite still, perfectly silent, and entirely on his dignity. Stanley solved the mystery of Wilson's presence the instant he saw the battered black rod he held in his right hand.

"Ah, lud." Stanley slammed the door shut, as he knew he was expected to do. He was a grown man, for heaven's sake. He hadn't had to undertake this ritual in years.

Right on cue, Wilson administered three solid blows against the door with, if he was doing the thing properly, the black rod. Whose idea had this been originally, anyway? It was not only absurd, but it probably also bordered on treason. A person simply didn't mock the Crown and Parliament.

Stanley shook his head and opened the door once more.

Wilson cleared his throat. "Captain Jonquil, you are hereby commanded to remove immediately to the House of Peers."

It was a horrifically flawed recitation of Black Rod's summons to the House of Commons at the State Opening of Parliament. Philip had first fashioned the altered version of that very traditional passage before Stanley could even remember. Layton had whittled the rod. Jason had pointed out that it absolutely had to be black.

Why in the world were they still doing this? They were no longer boys to be entertained by such things.

Wilson handed the rod over to Stanley before bowing and walking away. If they had undertaken the exact ceremony, Stanley would have followed Philip's valet with all the casual disinterest he could muster to the gatehouse, which had served as the House of Lords in the Jonquil parliament for decades. The House of Commons had been assigned the boathouse. Jason had always found that insulting; the boathouse was small and drafty but had been required to accommodate all the brothers except for Philip and Layton; they had claimed the rights of Peers, being heirs to the Lampton titles and the Farland title, respectively. Whichever servant was talked into playing the role of Black Rod was instructed to hand the rod over to the brother he summoned last.

Stanley shook his head but couldn't help a bit of a smile. They had rather enjoyed their overly complicated approach to calling one another to a council or discussion away from the ears and eyes of their parents. Again, if they had possessed the slightest desire to be accurate, their parents would have been present, playing the roles of monarch and consort. The brothers had been adamant about overlooking that particular technicality.

Stanley made his way across the grounds. Had he chosen to walk, he would certainly have managed the unhurried swagger expected of those representing Commons when adhering to the summons to appear in the Upper House. He, however, did not think falling on one's face was part of the ceremony and, therefore, chose to make his way to the gatehouse on horseback.

The door had been left open in anticipation of his arrival.

"This is so ridiculous," he said to himself, and yet, he was enjoying himself.

He dismounted, pleased that he could do so without feeling quite so certain he would stumble in the undertaking and, wrapping his horse's reins around a nearby branch, stepped inside the cozy gatehouse. Any similarity to the true opening of Parliament ended at that point in the ceremony. There would be no separation of houses, no formality, no pomp. Stanley dropped into an unoccupied chair and watched Philip and Layton lounging quite at their ease in chairs of their own.

Stanley tossed the black rod onto a bench pushed up against the wall nearest the door. The stick was kept in the gatehouse unless being used for a summons.

"Marjie says you've heard from Horse Guards." Philip spoke with a casual air, but both he and Layton watched Stanley intently.

Stanley nodded.

"Were you planning to mention this to any of us before you were recalled to your regiment?" Philip asked. "Or were we simply to wonder one evening why none of us had seen you about for a while?"

"As if anything could be kept a secret around here." Stanley meant the reply to be cheeky, but he felt the near desperation that accompanied the declaration. He was attempting to keep a great many secrets, and they weighed more on him every day.

"How many secrets do you have, Stanley?" Layton possessed an uncanny ability to seemingly read thoughts. He had done so often when they were all children.

"Not nearly as many secrets as I'd like," Stanley muttered.

Philip's mouth pulled into a frustrated line. "How is it that I nursed you for weeks last year and you never thought to tell me the true nature of your injury?"

Last year? "I was injured at Orthez," Stanley said. "You knew as much."

"But there is more to the story than that, isn't there?"

Stanley resisted the urge to squirm. They were tiptoeing too close to the line. "Men are injured in battle all the time."

"Cut line, Stanley." It was almost a sigh put to words. Philip rubbed his face with both his palms, a mannerism that had once belonged to their father. Stanley looked away, the pang of loss too acute in that moment. "There is a vast difference between the dangers inherent in a battle and the almost guaranteed death of a forlorn hope."

"Pluck told you." Stanley was going to absolutely strangle him.

Philip shook his head. "Marjie."

"Marjie? How did—? I didn't tell—"

"Anyone," Philip finished.

Layton took over the inquisition. "Why would you volunteer for such a thing? Did you wish for a captaincy so much?"

Stanley slumped in his chair. This was why he never told anyone. They always wanted to talk about it, to hash out the details and motivations and outcomes. He preferred to forget the entire thing. "I didn't do it for the promotion." Career advancement had been the last thing on his mind.

"Was your income from the estate insufficient?" Layton's voice asked one question, but his eyes were digging for something else entirely.

Stanley shifted his gaze to the crackling fire in the fireplace. There were no secrets in their family—it was frustrating as the devil.

"A person doesn't risk death for money," Stanley said quietly.

"Were you trying to prove something, then?" Philip didn't keep his voice as calm as Layton's, frustration encasing every word. "To be heroic and dashing?"

Stanley cleared his throat against the lump forming there. He didn't want to think about any of this, about the desperation he'd felt leading up to Orthez. Only Waterloo had been harder than Orthez. He wanted to put it all behind him, to not allow any of it to poison him until he returned and couldn't avoid doing so. Couldn't they give him a few weeks' respite?

"One would think you were trying to get yourself killed," Philip said.

Stanley pressed his eyelids closed, tears squeezing from the corners. His lungs caught and pulled against each breath he took.

"Stanley," Layton said quietly. "What happened?"

"It had always been just a game." The whispered words broke as they escaped his mouth, like glass dropped against a hardwood floor. "That was all war ever was—a game we played as children by the river. We'd stage heroic battles and fight bravely, and when it was over, we all got up and walked home together."

His entire body shook as he pushed out another breath. He could feel everything pressing free, all the thoughts and worries and pain he'd hidden inside. With his eyes closed, he could see them, the Jonquil brothers, as children. Then those laughing faces transformed to those of other boys who'd fought battles and paid with their lives.

"No one gets up in war. They lie where they fall. Everyone else marches on, looking around and wondering who isn't going to survive the next battle. It was supposed to be simple, like the game. If one was brave and followed the battle plan, everything was fine. Just a game where no one died and no one got hurt and . . ." He dropped his head into his upturned hands, leaning forward in his chair. He couldn't push back the memories and the pain.

"But it wasn't like that at all. Three hundred sixty-one." The number was tattooed in Stanley's memory. "That's how many people I knew, knew personally, who died between the time I reached the Continent and the Battle of Orthez." Too many faces swam through his mind. "They weren't even all soldiers." Tears coursed more quickly down his face, some pooling in his hands. "There were women and families who followed the drum, marched alongside us with their husbands and fathers, and they didn't always survive. They weren't even there to fight, and they died." He lifted his head, but his eyes couldn't focus enough to see anything but the fuzzy light of the fire. "There were thousands of others—people we passed in the villages—who were starving to death, casualties of a war they didn't ask for and couldn't end, conquered people who were desperate. I helped carry soldiers off the battlefields only to have them die before I could get them help. Some were so mangled and ripped apart that we couldn't even tell who they were.

"I can still see every one of them, a constant stream of faces. There are days when I close my eyes and the faces won't go away.

And mixed in with all the rest are the men I—" *Killed.* But he couldn't say it out loud. "I couldn't bear it anymore."

The silence between them dragged out. He tried to stop the memories but couldn't hold back the onslaught.

Layton didn't let the subject rest. "And the forlorn hope?"

Stanley felt himself droop further. "I just wanted to go home."

"Were you that desperate?" Layton asked. "You would only be sent home if you were horribly injured, but you were far, far more likely to be killed."

"Either way, I would have been done." The words were barely audible, and Stanley wasn't entirely certain either of his brothers had actually heard him.

Philip stood, crossed the room, and sat in the chair nearest Stanley's. "If things were so bad, why didn't you tell me? We could have arranged for you to sell your commission."

Stanley shook his head.

"Why not?" Layton asked. "If you dislike the army so much—"

"I gave my word," Stanley said. "My solemn oath to the army and the Crown that I would serve. There was no predetermined allotment of time. It wasn't a promise to be loyal and fight for the Kingdom only until I no longer enjoyed the work or it became inconvenient. It was a commitment. A gentleman does not break his word."

"The buying and selling of commissions is part and parcel of the armed services," Philip said.

"Which is part of the reason so many incompetent officers botched so many things." Stanley shook his head. He'd seen what happened when men tossed aside their promise to serve and left holes in command. Inexperience became the ruling force in the engagements that followed. Lives had been lost that would not have been. "I do not hold my honor so cheaply."

"But to be willing to die—"

"Everyone who fights a war must be willing to die." Stanley could hear his sudden sharpness. He would get up and pace if he weren't absolutely certain he'd topple over.

Philip sighed rather loudly and with noticeable heaviness. Stanley kept his gaze focused on the fire.

"Would you never consider selling your commission?" Layton asked.

"So long as they need me and I am able, I will go where I am sent." Could they hear the resignation he felt?

"Are you fit enough to return?" Philip asked.

Stanley nodded slowly. "Since W"—he cleared his throat and forced the dreaded word—"Waterloo, I've done more organizing than fighting."

"That should be easier to endure." Layton sounded reluctantly optimistic.

Stanley very nearly snorted out loud. "Certainly. I still get to decide who marches to their death; I simply don't have to watch them do it. Won't that be so much better?"

"There should be fewer deaths now that the war is over," Philip said.

"Fewer deaths." Stanley sneered at the coldness of that phrase. "Only in the army would *fewer* deaths be such an improvement. Would you feel better if someone told you after an epidemic had decimated your family that you ought to put your mind at ease because there should be *fewer deaths* in the future?" He shook his head again and again.

"Did you never find any satisfaction from your service?" Philip sounded nearly as weary as Stanley felt.

"I know it is what Father always said I would be good at, so, in that sense, I suppose there is some satisfaction. But I do wonder why he thought I would excel at killing people and watching half-grown boys die." Boys like Pluck, a frightened face behind a wall of flames. In that moment, he had looked closer to seven than seventeen.

"Father knew you were happiest when you were helping people," Philip said. "He thought you might find the opportunity to do that in the army."

"Help people?" Every muscle quivered with the growing tension seizing through him. "I have shot men dead. Tell me, Philip, how much did I help them?" Stanley glared at his eldest brother, daring him to turn those years of survival into something noble. Philip paled. Perhaps reality had finally penetrated. "I chose which of my men were at the front of a battle charge, knowing those on the front lines were the least likely to survive. I sent boys and men with families out to their deaths. How did I help them? Tens of thousands of men died at Waterloo. What good did my fighting do any of them?"

"The victory at Waterloo saved us all from another dozen years of war," Philip said. "Everyone who fought there did good. *Everyone.* For the first time in the history of the Kingdom, the Crown is awarding a medal to every one of our soldiers who fought in that battle."

Stanley's hackles instantly rose. "A medal?"

"As a means of expressing the gratitude of the entire Kingdom."

"It is essentially saying, 'Here's a hunk of metal with Prinny's ugly phiz stamped on it. Thank you for spending five years of your life having your soul ripped to shreds. We're ever so grateful.' I don't want it."

"I don't think the medal is intended to be equal in any way to the sacrifices made," Layton said. He always had been the brother who tried to soothe tempers. At the moment, it was decidedly annoying. "It is simply an acknowledgment."

"I don't want it." Stanley pronounced each word with tremendous precision.

"Then what do you want, Stanley?" Philip was not the peacemaker Layton was. "You don't want to sell out. You don't want to be in the army. You don't want the medal you earned. What *do* you want?"

Too many things he would never have.

"When I accept your medal from the Prince Regent on your behalf, since you obviously will not be doing so yourself, what would you like me to tell him you want instead?"

Philip's sarcasm was the final push that sent Stanley past his usual barrier of self-protection. "Tell him I want my leg back."

CHAPTER TWENTY-ONE

Stanley muttered an oath under his breath at the look of shocked understanding that crossed his brothers' faces. He hadn't intended to confess to any of this. Blast the House of Lords. He had always been more likely to spill his secrets to Philip and Layton than to any of his other brothers.

"You lost your leg?" Philip asked after the uncomfortable silence had stretched out overly long.

"I hate that expression." There would be no avoiding an explanation now. He felt too weary to even attempt it. "It sounds as if I misplaced the deuced thing. 'Now, where did I put my leg? I was so certain it was right here.'" He would have rolled his eyes if he'd been one for such a theatrical expression. "I didn't lose it. I know exactly where it is."

"Where is it?" Again, Layton's tone indicated he was searching for answers to more than just the question he'd asked out loud.

"My men buried it under a tree in Belgium." He refused to break into tears again. "Pluck turned it into an overblown ceremony. They eulogized the devil out of that stupid leg and wept like it was their mothers they were burying."

More like every fellow soldier they'd lost and mourned for. Only sixty-five of the 260 men in the Thirteenth who had gone into battle the morning of Waterloo had returned at the end of that single, horrific day of battle. Some were dead, some wounded. Some were simply never found. Stanley knew the men who'd buried his leg hadn't been weeping over the lifeless hunk of flesh. They were simply crying out as human beings puzzled and pained at the inhumanity of war. Though they all understood the necessity of the fight, the aftermath was difficult to endure.

"It was even given a headstone—not everyone who died at Waterloo was granted that. It was just a rock with a poem scratched onto it.

'Here lies our dear captain's leg.

'It didn't stand a chance.

'Turns out his leg was luckiest.

'The rest of him's in France.'"

At Philip's crack of laughter, Stanley felt a smile tug at his mouth. It *was* a rather witty inscription. None of them had been too keen on the idea of marching to Paris.

"Pluck said they spent an entire night composing the epitaph. As I understand it, they were thoroughly foxed by the time they finished their little poem."

Philip's grin tipped lopsidedly. "Oh, I am certain spirits played a vital role in that composition."

"Where was your leg amputated?" Layton asked. "And don't say 'Belgium,'" he quickly added in the instant before Stanley opened his mouth to say precisely that. "I mean, where on your leg?"

"Just below the knee," Stanley said. The subject was proving less horrific to discuss than he'd anticipated. At least Layton and Philip didn't look disgusted or disturbed. He had yet to see a look remotely resembling pity.

"You have acquired some kind of prosthesis, then."

Stanley acknowledged Layton's statement with a nod of his head.

"How did it happen?"

Stanley looked at Philip, though Layton had asked the question. Philip had grown strangely quiet. He watched Stanley closely but didn't say a word.

"Cannon shot." The familiar sounds and smells echoed in Stanley's memory, but he pushed on. "Took Shadow right out from under me."

"I wondered what happened to your horse," Layton said.

"Most of my leg came off right there on the field, stripped down to fractured bone and some scraps of flesh. Only one of the lower leg bones remained entirely intact, though my foot was entirely whole. War is like that. Some things are destroyed completely while others are left untouched." He could feel his mood slipping once more. Talk of warfare always dragged him back there.

"I think I will commission Pluck to write a poem in honor of my chest," Philip said quite suddenly.

Layton laughed in obvious surprise. "Your chest?"

"Certainly." Philip once again wore his remarkably thorough mask of featherheaded carelessness. "The perfection of my chest was quite irrevocably flawed, you know. I have a battle scar." His pomposity was so overblown, Stanley didn't for an instant take his assertion seriously.

"You mean that little scratch you got at Kinnley?" Layton drawled.

Stanley very nearly laughed at Philip's theatrical look of shock. "Scratch? I was shot."

"Well, hand me a handkerchief before I'm soaked with tears," Stanley said dryly. "*I* have been shot hundreds of times." The actual number was seven, but he was enjoying the air of exaggeration that had descended on their conversation. His spirits were certainly rallying, something he found difficult to do on his own.

"I can see you have absolutely no appreciation for what has become of me." With that mock-offended declaration, Philip stood and began tugging at his cravat, his jacket having been off since before Stanley's arrival.

"What are you doing, Flip?" Layton asked.

Philip tossed his cravat onto his chair and began unbuttoning his waistcoat. "I will have my poem if we have to write it here in the House of Lords. Find a pen and paper, Stanley." Philip worked at the buttons of his shirtsleeves.

"No one needs to see this." But Layton was laughing. "We want Stanley to fill out, not lose weight because you've made him retch."

Philip had begun untucking. "I believe *best* would be an appropriate rhyme for *chest.* Write that down."

Stanley laughed out loud. "With what? There are no writing implements at hand, and I refuse to hobble around looking for one."

"*Impressed* would work as well."

"How about *obsessed*?" Layton suggested. "That rhymes."

"You, my brother, are not a poet." Philip pulled his shirt over his head and tossed it on top of his abandoned cravat. "Now," he dramatically indicated the very obvious scar high on the left side of his chest, "does this not inspire a composition?"

"As a matter of fact," Layton said, "I feel a verse coming on." He cleared his throat.

"My brother Flip went searching 'round

"For what he could not find.

"For the more he looked and searched and sought,

"The more he lost his mind." Layton ended with an exaggerated smirk.

"Well done, Layton," Stanley said.

"Atrocious!" Philip's entire face twisted in disapproval. "You did not spare a single syllable for the spoiled splendor of my chest. Try again."

"'Spoiled splendor?' That's taking things a bit far, don't you think?" Layton shook his head. "It looks like you simply spilled something on yourself and haven't bothered to clean it up. The scar isn't even that interesting."

"I suppose you are in possession of a very 'interesting' scar?" Philip's look of condescension pulled another laugh from Stanley.

"Yes, on my left leg," Layton said.

"If you take your trousers off, I really will start retching," Stanley said.

"*Lower* leg." Layton propped his left foot on the footstool in front of his chair and began rolling back his pant leg. A thin, zigzagging scar ran nearly six inches down the side of Layton's calf.

"Oh, please," Philip said. "That is hardly noticeable."

"It may be lighter than yours, Philip, but what it lacks in pigment it makes up for in character."

"And what do you propose we rhyme with *leg*?" Philip asked with a flamboyant gesture of annoyance.

"Poached egg," Stanley offered.

All three brothers burst out laughing.

"I had no idea the House of Lords conducted its business half naked."

Stanley recognized that voice. Based on the looks of barely concealed amusement, so did Philip and Layton.

"Holy Harry," Philip said under his breath.

"Great, Flip," Layton muttered back. "Now we're going to get preached to."

Stanley glanced toward the door and had to bite his lips against another wave of laughter. Holy Harry was in fine form, his right eyebrow raised to precisely the correct level of clerical disapproval.

"We stand before you," Philip said with the air of one making a very difficult confession, "guilty of the very great transgression of coveting our brother's injury-inspired poem. We were attempting to compose poetry of our own in order to relieve the weight of envy upon our souls."

Harold swept them with *the look*—the one he'd perfected not long after taking his first steps—the look that had clearly indicated he was destined to be a very devoted servant of the church. "And your penance involves removing various articles of clothing?"

"Of course," Philip answered in all seriousness. "Inspiration, you scc."

"I am absolutely certain Byron composes his works in varying states of undress." The mischief in Layton's eyes very nearly broke Stanley's rigid hold on his laughter. Holy Harry would certainly not approve of the infamous Lord Byron.

"These are all poems written to your scars?" Harold still hadn't moved from his perch in the doorway. His gaze shifted to each of them in turn.

"Except Layton's. His doesn't really count."

Harold didn't acknowledge Philip's jab at their brother. Stanley seemed to be Harold's focus at the moment. For perhaps the first time in Harold's life, Stanley saw a remarkable resemblance between Harold and Layton. He had that same soul-searching look on his face but with such a mixture of vicarly concern that Stanley couldn't help fidgeting under the scrutiny.

"I have a scar." Harold stepped farther into the room.

"Please let it be someplace hard to get to." Philip actually steepled his hands as if directing the wish heavenward.

Layton attempted to cover his laughter with a cough. Stanley held back a smile.

Harold, having joined the rest of them near the fireplace, pushed back his collar a bit and tipped his head so his jaw on the left side was more visible. A line of white ran along it, probably two inches in length.

"What happened?" Philip examined the old scar.

"I was shoved into the stream on the north end of the Park. I cut my jaw on a rock at the bottom."

"What did you do to provoke your attacker?" Layton asked.

Stanley could think of any number of times Harold had annoyed every one of his brothers enough to warrant a dunking.

"I—" Harold was suddenly terribly red and stammering. He cleared his throat. "I kissed her."

Philip's eyes and mouth made three wide Os on his face. Layton's expression wasn't any less astonished.

"Whom did you kiss?" Philip's eyes were glued to Harold.

Their usually somber brother grew even redder.

"If you don't tell us, we'll simply speculate," Layton warned.

"And go about asking everyone until we find the poor female," Philip added.

Harold tugged a bit at his cravat. In a voice that sounded rather strangled, he said, "Sarah Sarvol."

"Bridget's cousin?" Layton looked stuck between baffled surprise and outright amusement. For many years, Layton hadn't been able to speak of his late wife with anything other than tremendous sadness. He'd healed enough to speak of her family without noticeable pain. "They haven't visited from America in years."

"I know," Harold muttered.

Stanley and his brothers exchanged looks of shock. Harold cleared his throat again, shifting about and eyeing the door.

Philip grinned at Layton. "So when are these Yankee relations of yours returning for another visit?"

"I would wager they will make the journey in another year or so."

At Layton's words, Harold paled beneath the blotchiness of his very uncharacteristic blush.

So Harold had had an unsuccessful flirtation, had he? It was unexpected, for sure.

"That is, unless they decide to come sooner, which I have heard from Mr. Sarvol is entirely possible."

Again Harold's coloring grew worse.

"Sarah's brother, Scott, is Sarvol's heir," Layton said. "There is talk of him and his sister returning rather permanently so the boy can be taught to run the estate before Sarvol sticks his spoon in the wall."

Harold spoke so abruptly he very nearly cut off Layton's words. "I came only to tell you that Mater wishes you to know that dinner is to be served in less than an hour. Marjie said she saw Stanley riding off with an enormous black stick, and I was certain you'd called Parliament into session again."

"Sorry you weren't summoned, Harold," Philip said with a grin. "With you in the clergy now, we weren't entirely certain which House to place you in, you having great ambitions and all. The archbishops sit with the Lords, as I am sure you are aware."

"And, as I am sure you are aware, in actuality I am only the curate of this parish." Harold stood very much on his dignity. "I work harder than any vicar, certainly harder than the one I technically work for now, and though I have heard you explain to people that I am a vicar, you know perfectly well I am not. Not yet. I am too young. So I work, and I wait."

"Patience *is* a virtue." Philip spoke as though he was informing Harold of a great truth.

"As is"—Harold pointedly looked at Philip's unclothed chest—"modesty."

"And let us not underestimate the beneficial nature of a quick dip in a cold stream." Philip wiggled an eyebrow at Harold.

Their very staid brother turned on his heel and left the gatehouse without a backward glance. The exaggerated rigidness of his posture told Stanley Harold wasn't nearly as composed nor as indignant as he wished to let on. Talk of Miss Sarah Sarvol had thoroughly discomposed him.

"I, for one, am shocked." Philip pulled on his shirt. "Harold, kissing a female in such a manner."

"I'm surprised Holy Harry knew how to kiss a female in any manner whatsoever," Layton said, unrolling his pant leg. "I fully expected him to court some hapless lady by reading sermons to her."

"Perhaps there is some Jonquil in him after all," Philip said.

"Because he attempted to woo a young lady?" *Why am I smiling so much all of a sudden?* Stanley didn't think his smile had lapsed from the moment Philip pulled off his cravat.

"No, because he mucked it up so badly," Layton answered.

Philip nodded sagely. "The mark of a true Jonquil is the ability to do anything and everything possible, and a few things slightly impossible, to make a fool of himself in front of the fairer sex. I am certain that is part of the family motto."

Fortitudo per Fidem. That was the family motto. *Strength through Loyalty.* The Jonquils were nothing if not loyal—to one another, to causes they believed in, to all that was honorable and right. It was the reason Stanley could never leave the army. It was the reason his family would never truly expect him to.

"We should head back before Mater decides to send us to the nursery without our dinner," Philip said, having finished dressing.

Stanley pulled himself to his feet and retrieved his walking stick.

Layton stood beside him. "Thank you for telling us what you've been enduring," he said quietly. "We have been imagining some vastly horrific reasons for your unhappiness."

"It was surprisingly relieving to talk about," Stanley admitted. "Not that I want to go on a circuit of speaking engagements."

Philip smiled at him. "You might have to anyway. Mater ought to know."

"Would you tell her?" Stanley asked, knowing he was being a coward. He did not, however, wish to cry in front of his mother, and he knew the moment she grew teary, he would lose his own composure again.

Philip nodded. "We'll talk to Mater." He looked to Layton for confirmation and received it. "Under one condition."

"What's that?" Stanley was instantly wary.

"*You* have to tell Marjie."

J

CHAPTER TWENTY-TWO

MARJIE WAS LONELY.

All stood in readiness for The Gathering only a week hence. She felt decidedly unneeded in matters pertaining to Sorrel's welfare. Mater and Marion had become her sister's confidantes, and Philip's attentiveness ensured that not a single need of his wife's went unmet.

Marjie had been doing her best to maintain a distance from Stanley, both physically and emotionally. Doing otherwise simply hurt too much. Over the past few days, he'd seemed to almost be seeking her out, and avoiding him had become more difficult, due partly to the fact that she truly missed his company. Her heart, however, could not bear to be bruised again.

Luncheon would be served soon, but Marjie had no desire to partake. Philip wasn't expected to leave his library, having some pressing estate matters to see to. Stanley had been conspicuously absent since breakfast, and that would leave Marjie exclusively in the company of the three women and their talk of children and confinements.

She had decided to spend the afternoon in her bedchamber, more likely than not gazing out of her window, wondering what it was about her that eventually convinced the people she loved to keep her at arm's length.

The air of indifference she clung to in company dropped the moment she stepped inside her personal, private bit of the house. There was no reason to pretend that her heart wasn't breaking when there was no one to see it. She'd taken to shrugging so often that her shoulders felt tense at the end of each day.

She sighed and sat on the edge of her bed, her gaze settling on the window, as always. It was a pleasing prospect, the bare trees dancing in the late-autumn breeze. Her thoughts wandered.

Stanley had seemed happier. He hadn't been brimming with joy by any means, but a degree of contentment had settled over him. What had brought about the change? She hoped it would last, that returning to his regiment would not destroy his happiness again. Were she going with him, she might be able to help. He would have someone to talk to at least.

Reminding herself once again that Stanley had been most clear on the matter of her place in his future, she pulled her thoughts back to the present. She needed a distraction. Where had she put that book she'd been pretending to read?

Her gaze fell on a single white rose lying on her bedside table. It had been cut and dethorned. As she stepped closer, she saw a folded bit of parchment beside it.

Her name was printed on the front in letters so shaky and ill-formed that she immediately suspected the note had come from Caroline, though she could not think of a reason for the young girl to be writing to her. Marjie unfolded the small sheet of paper. In the same blocky lettering were two simple sentences.

Please come sit with me. I am waiting in your favorite room.

It was inexpertly signed "Stanley."

Marjie sucked in a trembling breath as everything fell into place. He had to have written with his left hand, hence the uncertain penmanship. He had sent the rose, knowing somehow that white roses were her favorite. He was waiting in the conservatory; she had told him that was her favorite room.

She pressed her hand to her pounding heart. "He wrote to me." After all her months of anguished waiting, her Stanley had written to her.

She pulled open the drawer where she'd faithfully kept the ribbon she'd intended to tie around his letters. With shaking fingers, she wrapped it around that single missive and tied it in a bow in the front.

She had a letter!

She very nearly ran from her room, ignoring the startled look she received as she flew past an upstairs maid. In her mind, she kept repeating, "He wrote to me!"

Stanley was in the conservatory when she arrived, his back to her, his focus on the view outside. He turned as she approached, no doubt hearing the sound of her swift footfalls. He smiled at her, and Marjie melted.

Here was the reunion she had envisioned: a letter from him, a token of affection, and a smile of welcome when they met again.

She felt tears well up in her eyes but did not pause a single moment to halt their fall. She rushed to where he stood and threw herself into his arms, wrapping hers around his neck.

"Oh, Stanley," she whispered.

Gently bred young ladies did not kiss gentlemen. But she did, fervently and affectionately. Every ounce of her heart took part as she pressed her lips to his. She felt his arms wrap more tightly around her as he returned her kiss.

He whispered her name as he gently pulled back, his breathing as ragged as hers. One hand brushed tears from her face. His other arm still held her to him.

"That was quite a 'how do you do' you just offered. I am not sure Lord Devereaux would approve."

"He would tease me mercilessly." She felt remarkably content standing there in Stanley's embrace. With a silent sigh, she laid her head on his shoulder, grateful she was tall enough to do so, even if barely. "Between him and Philip, I have quite had my share of surrogate older brothers."

"Older bro—?" Stanley's shocked question ended abruptly. She truly wished she could see his face, though she was unwilling to move a single inch from the circle of his arms. "Yes, older brothers can be a trifle annoying at times." There was actually joy in his tone.

Marjie breathed deep the smell of him. How she had missed being close enough for that familiar scent to comfort her as it always had.

"Might I ask what warranted such an unforeseen greeting?" Stanley asked, not releasing her in the tiniest bit.

"You wrote to me." She had to fight back the tears that threatened to spill over again.

"All this over a note?"

"I wished daily for a simple note from you while you were away."

Stanley's hand lightly caressed her hair. "I confess I didn't realize until just now how truly important that was to you."

"Without a letter, I couldn't be entirely certain you hadn't forgotten me."

Stanley's hands shifted to Marjie's shoulders, and he set her back from him a little. His gaze captured and held hers. "I never once forgot you, Marjie. I thought of you every day. Even in my moments of delirium you didn't leave my thoughts."

"Delirium from the fevers?"

Stanley nodded.

"Because of the injury to your hand?" She could well imagine the infections that had set in from such a severe burn.

"And to my leg." His expression clouded a little. "Can we sit?" he asked. "I am not certain my balance will last much longer."

"Of course." Marjie slipped her hand into his undamaged left and walked with him the few steps to the iron bench she'd so often occupied.

Stanley sat silently a moment, his face growing more somber. Marjie didn't at all trust the change. She grasped his hand, holding it in both of hers.

"My leg was very badly injured at Waterloo." He said the name of the battle with less difficulty than he had those first few weeks.

Thank the heavens for that small improvement.

"It was—" Stanley cleared his throat awkwardly. Marjie squeezed his hand. "It was not salvageable."

Marjie thought on that for a moment, trying to decipher his meaning. For the second time that afternoon, she felt a mishmash of clues suddenly rearranging themselves: the stiffness of his right leg but the lack of pain. It had been badly injured and considered "not salvageable." "Your leg was amputated." She made the connection out loud.

Stanley nodded but did not look at her. He sat awkwardly, uncomfortably.

Marjie had no trouble identifying the emotions flitting across his face. "Now you are expecting me to be disgusted or pitying or horrified."

"Aren't you?"

Marjie reached up and gently touched his cheek. "What would have happened if your leg had been left as it was after the battle?"

Stanley dropped his gaze to the hand she was still holding. "It would have grown putrid."

"And in war, is not infection a greater threat than any enemy?"

Stanley nodded, still not looking at her. Obviously, he found this hard to speak of. She had heard crippled soldiers express frustration and loss at their injuries. Many felt themselves somehow less than the person they had been because of their loss of abilities.

"If Sorrel's leg had required amputation to save her life, I would not have cared for her any less than I did before," Marjie said. "She means more to me than the mere sum of her parts."

She brushed her fingers through the hair that fell across Stanley's forehead. She trailed her fingers down the side of his face, resting them beneath his jaw. He did not respond to the upward pressure she exerted. "Please look at me," she whispered.

He raised his head, and the pain in his eyes very nearly brought her to tears again. What a weight he carried. He had obviously decided that what he had endured, that the toll of battle on his body, would cost him her affection, perhaps even her respect.

"I love you, Stanley Jonquil." He could not possibly know the risk she felt admitting as much. "I love you for who you are inside." She moved her hand from his face to his heart, laying it there for emphasis. "I love your goodness and your kindness. Though I wish with all my heart I could take away the pain you have endured, I am selfish enough to be grateful that the surgeons kept you alive by what means they could." A tear rolled down her face. Heavens, she had spent a lot of time crying.

Stanley seemed to be holding back tears of his own.

"I prayed constantly for your return," Marjie said. "I simply wanted you here again. Perhaps it is my fault this happened."

"Mar—"

"I ought not to have been so unspecific or persistent. I will carry the blame for that on my soul if I must, just as I do with my father." Marjie leaned closer to him; she couldn't seem to help herself. Months of fearing for his life pressed against her still. "I could not have lived if you were gone."

She wasn't sure who initiated the kiss that followed—it was brief and gentle but poignant. She could feel a certain hopelessness in Stanley that tore at her heart. What was wrong still?

He wrapped his arm around her shoulders and pulled her to his side, her head once more resting against him. She felt him sigh, though he made no sound.

"If I were but a farmer," Stanley said, "would you be happy spending your life with me?"

"I would be happy with you if you were a highwayman," Marjie said.

Stanley chuckled a little, the sound almost sad.

It was his profession, then, that stood in the way? "If you weren't a soldier, would you marry me?" Marjie had no idea where her sudden forwardness came from. She was always more confident with Stanley than with anyone else but had never before been quite so bold.

She felt him kiss the top of her head. "If I weren't a soldier, I'd have married you at Kinnley the very day I met you."

Her heart soared. Not wishing to make him regret admitting so much, Marjie matched his light tone. "The very day?"

"Within the week, at least."

"You must have liked me very much." She closed her eyes, her heart pounding against the lingering possibility of rejection.

"I think I have loved you forever," Stanley said quietly.

"But as a soldier, you cannot marry me?"

"There is but one thing I wish for more than to have you with me," Stanley said. "I wish most for you to be happy. I have given this a great deal of thought. I know that life in the army would make you miserable." Marjie opened her mouth to object, but Stanley spoke before she could. "The war may be over, Marjie, but the suffering continues. People are still dying. There are those who yet view us as their enemy and treat us as such. Soldiers are still being killed. True peace will be a long time coming. I cannot ask you to endure that. As much as I wish you could be with me, as much as I need you by my side, I could not force you to share a life I know would make you unhappy."

Marjie shifted so she could look up into his face once more. "I could never be unhappy if I were with you." Didn't he understand that?

He lightly kissed her forehead before guiding her head back to his shoulder again. "You would be. You would come to know the soldiers only to have them die. Seeing the children of Paris suffering after years of neglect and hunger would tear at your heart. There are many people who are angry and unhappy and hateful. In time, the weight of it would pull you down."

She wanted to argue, to insist that she would be happy in any circumstances if only they were together, but his words held a great deal of truth. As she pondered the pain of losing people she had come to care about, of seeing children starving in the streets, of the pulsating hatred of former enemies forced into close confines, she knew such a situation would be difficult at best.

"You are certain, then, that you will be recalled?" she asked.

"Yes. And I have a duty to perform, one I have sworn to see through to the end."

He'd spoken of his career in those early days after they'd met as a matter of honor and loyalty to his country. Stanley did not intend to sell his commission and leave the army; his integrity would not allow it. His sense of honor was one of the things she loved most about him. She would never ask him to do something he would consider dishonorable.

They had another option though. "Not all army wives travel with their husbands." Being left behind would be hard, but knowing she was his wife would keep him closer to her.

Marjie felt Stanley shake his head before he even answered. Another crack split her heart. She'd expected him to refuse, but it hurt just the same. "You deserve better than a husband who would be absent for years at a time. That would make you nearly as unhappy as being in the midst of conflict."

"Then there is really no hope for us?" A moment more and she would be crying again.

"Hope is sometimes a fickle thing, my dear." The endearment felt painful when spoken as part of such a heartbreaking conversation. "We hang on to it because we need to, even when there really is no point."

"That is a very sad sort of hope," Marjie said.

Minutes passed. She didn't know how many. The sky outside darkened a bit as evening approached. She simply sat beside the man she loved and tried not to think about how much she had gained and lost in a few short sentences. He would be gone in a fortnight, and she would be alone again.

"Will you write to me?" Marjie asked, her voice not loud enough to reach beyond their little corner of the vast room.

He hesitated only a moment. "Until you are married and your husband objects."

How could he believe she would marry another when she loved him so deeply?

She refused to think on it, to even ponder the possibility of marrying simply to stave off her loneliness. She had two weeks left with Stanley, two weeks in which to convince him that being left behind with the reassurance of his ring on her finger was far better than being left behind with nothing. If she could not manage that, she would spend the fortnight building memories on which to lean when the weight of his absence grew too heavy.

Until he left, she refused to give up on what little hope she had, no matter how forlorn that hope proved to be.

J

CHAPTER TWENTY-THREE

SOMETHING WAS AFOOT. STANLEY watched the household staff slipping about furtively. Every time he came into a room, however, they stopped abruptly before scurrying away. More than once his appearance had stopped a conversation between various members of his family.

A moment earlier, he had stepped into the back sitting room only to have Mater insist that she, Sorrel—who was looking a little better than she had of late—and Marjie were in the midst of "female endeavors," whatever the deuce that was supposed to mean, and would he be so kind as to leave them in privacy.

Something was definitely afoot.

Knowing he was *de trop* amongst the ladies, he wandered in the direction of the library. Philip had been seeing to estate business all morning and would, most likely, welcome a diversion. Stanley certainly needed one.

Marjie had looked particularly devastating, and he'd been more than a little put out that he'd been sent away without a single moment to talk with her or, at the very least, simply sit beside her.

"Good afternoon, Stanley." Philip rubbed his face *a la Father*, as Stanley had seen him do many times before. Philip, it seemed, was under some stress. "How was your ride this morning?"

"Fine. Except that I had to listen to Layton bemoaning your absence. It was rather like listening to a debutante whose favored beau did not attend a ball. Pathetic."

"I'm afraid Layton's tender feelings for me get the better of him sometimes," Philip said with an exaggerated sigh.

"What kept you inside all morning?"

"Our father's unfortunate tendency to *not* gamble away his various properties." Philip smiled a little at his own quip. "One of the Lampton holdings, Fallowgill in Yorkshire, is proving to be an ongoing headache for me. Turns out the land agent was embezzling money. Now I am attempting to ascertain if that is the reason Fallowgill has been a drain on the Lampton coffers or if it, as an estate, is simply doomed to be unprofitable."

"You could sell it," Stanley said.

"If it weren't part of the entailment, I would."

"Do you think any of us truly realized when we were boys that Father might actually have had problems?" How ignorant they all had been of the worries and concerns of the world around them.

Philip rose from his seat behind the large mahogany desk, stretching his neck and back, then walked to a window. "Did you come in here to talk about my crooked land agent, or did you have another motivation?"

"The ladies of the house threw me out of the sitting room," he said. "They claim to be engrossed in some sort of female business, though I am convinced they are up to something."

Philip leaned against the window frame. "Didn't you quite recently say there are no secrets in this family?"

"Perhaps not among the men, but I am convinced the ladies are capable of leading us on a very merry chase."

Philip glanced past Stanley toward the door. "What do you think of Stanley's evaluation of his female relations?"

Stanley turned in his seat and saw Marjie standing in the doorway.

"I am not entirely sure if I am offended. A merry chase, indeed." She stepped into the room. Stanley watched her, a feeling of contentment settling over him at her mere presence. "Might I steal Stanley from you?"

"Certainly. Everyone else has been stealing from me lately. I should warn you though; he suspects you—and the rest of us, most likely—of being involved in secretive activities."

"What could we possibly have to be secretive about?" Marjie's eyes fairly danced with mirth.

What were they up to?

"Stanley always was of a suspicious nature." Philip actually winked at her. "Now go on and steal the boy if you're going to. I plan to find Sorrel and see if she has anything for me to do—I am sick to death of estate business."

Philip left the door ajar when he stepped out, as propriety demanded, but otherwise they were entirely isolated and alone.

"Everyone has refused to play backgammon with me," Marjie said, "and I had hoped you would agree to indulge me in a game."

That had been the first thing beyond "Pleased to make your acquaintance" that Stanley had ever said to Marjie.

Stanley stood. "Backgammon is a top priority of mine."

He had expected Marjie to smile or perhaps even laugh at his response. She did neither. Quickly and without warning, she reached up and took his face in her hands before pressing a light, brief kiss to his lips.

"What was that for?" he asked, because he wanted to know how to convince her to do it again, hopefully multiple times before his departure.

"Backgammon is a top priority of mine as well." Marjie slipped her arm through his. "The back sitting room, if you please."

Mater looked up from her embroidery and smiled when Stanley entered the sitting room with Marjie on his arm. Philip, Stanley was certain, muttered "backgammon" under his breath. Stanley had borne no end of goading from his eldest brother for his feeble attempts at wooing Marjie during that Christmas house party nearly a year ago.

"Be nice," Sorrel said to her husband. They were seated together on a sofa near the fireplace. She had been far less prickly with Stanley of late. Being off her feet had, it seemed, alleviated much of her pain and, as a result, restored her good spirits.

Stanley held out Marjie's seat for her before making his way around the table where a backgammon board had been set up already. He took his seat and glanced across the board at Marjie. "Have the three of you finished your 'female endeavors,' then?"

A hint of mischief lurked in her eyes. "For now."

"You are being decidedly mysterious."

"I know, and it is vastly enjoyable." Marjie laughed, her eyes dancing and sparkling.

The game began, though Marjie seemed to be paying as little attention to it as Stanley was. They talked on subjects ranging from the weather to the *ton* and every topic in between.

He would miss these moments after he returned to duty. She would be happier in England—that was his one consolation. He had every intention of enjoying what time remained, though he needed to find a way to keep something of a distance, else his departure would hurt them both far more than it had to.

As they set up the board for a second game, Beck approached with a silver salver and a single letter, which he held out for Marjie.

"Thank you," she said, taking the missive.

Marjie had received a great deal of mail in the past week or so. Stanley was certain it had something to do with the secret he had not been made privy to.

She could not have been more than a couple lines into the letter when she glanced up and turned ever so slightly in her chair to face the other occupants of the room. To Stanley's surprise, they were all watching her with looks of anticipation. "Lord Devereaux," she said.

Philip, Sorrel, and Mater all nodded. Glances were exchanged before everyone returned to whatever he or she had been doing before the arrival of the letter.

Stanley had stiffened at the mention of his erstwhile rival. At least he hoped Devereaux was a *former* rival. Better yet, he hoped Devereaux had never been vying for Marjie's affection in the first place.

"Is your honorary older brother well?" Stanley tried to sound casual and unconcerned. He wanted to believe Marjie had no deeper feelings for Lord Devereaux than familial ones. They obviously cared about each other, but there was a decided lack of passion.

"Quite well." Her eyes scanned the letter. "He is visiting with the Duke and Duchess of Hartley and is enjoying himself."

"You say that as if it were unusual for him."

She refolded the letter. "He has been very sad for a long time and far too closed off from the rest of the world."

"You worry about him." Marjie's compassion led her to worry for any person she saw in need, especially those close to her.

"I do, just as I worry over Sorrel and Fennel and—"

"And me?" He straightened the line of checkers nearest his left hand, avoiding looking at her. He wanted her feelings for him to be different, to be more than compassion.

She pulled his hand away from its distracted fumbling and intertwined her fingers with his. Stanley looked up. An almost shy look touched her face. "Not at all like you." Color stained her cheeks.

Stanley felt a smile tug at his lips. Marjie leaned over the table and closer to him. Stanley leaned toward her as well until a mere few inches separated them.

"I think, Captain Jonquil," Marjie whispered, "you do not comprehend how very much I love you."

"Even with no happy ending in sight?"

"Perhaps that is what is meant by 'hopelessly in love.'"

Lud, she smelled good. Having her deep-blue eyes so very near his was hypnotic. The slightest movement would allow him to kiss her once more. How soon such an opportunity would be lost to him.

He leaned the slightest bit forward. Marjie did as well. Stanley's heart rate increased instantly. Surely he couldn't be blamed for claiming a kiss even in light of their pending separation. Out of the corner of his eye, Stanley spotted Philip watching them quite pointedly. He raised an eyebrow in a look of mingled warning and curiosity. Stanley did not need an interpreter. A gentleman did not kiss a lady in full view of others.

Stanley contented himself with placing a very proper, if slightly lingering, kiss on Marjie's fingers. Her blush continued through their second and final game of backgammon. Shortly thereafter, Philip tossed out an invitation for Stanley to join him in the billiard room, an invitation he had obviously meant as more of a summons than a suggestion.

Philip closed the door after they arrived and halfheartedly undertook the game he had requested. How many times in one day, Stanley wondered, could a person play a game in which neither participant was truly interested? Stanley couldn't even use a billiard cue with his dominant hand so entirely mangled.

Philip lined up a pathetically easy shot. "As Marjie's only male relative, except for her school-age brother, and as her unofficial guardian, I suppose I ought to ask you what your intentions are."

"I have no dishonorable intentions." Could there possibly be a more awkward conversation to have with one's older brother?

"Do you intend to marry her before you are sent away again?" The thwack of two balls colliding echoed around the room. Philip straightened and leveled him a look that was nothing short of an interrogative father figure.

"I can't." The admission was no less difficult than it had been when he'd said as much to Marjie. Still, the reasons spilled from his lips, the same ones he had given Marjie.

Philip leaned against the edge of the billiard table, the game entirely forgotten. "She would not be suited to that life. *Either* version. You have already explained your reasons for remaining in the army, and I cannot say I fault you for that. Still, it seems a harsh sort of punishment for the both of you."

Stanley nodded. *Harsh* was a very apt word.

"At the risk of being a prosy, stuffy bore"—That was not a very promising preface. Philip pressed on—"I would offer you a little advice." If his expression hadn't been so empathetic, Stanley might have objected quite vocally. "As much as you must wish to have your fill of Marjie's affections before your departure, I would suggest you tread lightly. Holding her hand or going for a walk in the gardens would be unexceptional. But kissing the girl in the sitting room, or the gardens, for that matter, along with anything remotely resembling a torrid embrace would, I fear, leave her tender heart more bruised than need be."

"I am to act the platonic friend?" Stanley scoffed. "Could you have done so with Sorrel?"

"I did not say it would be easy, only that it would be best. Her attachment to you is as real as yours to her, but if you cannot offer her a future, Stanley, she must be allowed the emotional maneuvering room she will need to eventually move on."

Stanley had told himself precisely that for weeks, but it was still hard to hear. "I want her to be happy." Was he saying so for Philip's sake or simply to remind himself?

"I know. I've known that since you first met her."

"I was that obvious?"

Philip laughed. "Nothing indicates a Jonquil in love like rampant awkwardness."

Stanley smiled but couldn't sustain the effort. "You will take care of her, won't you?"

Philip dropped a hand onto Stanley's shoulder. "She will be fine. Only make sure that you write to us so we will know that you are fine as well."

Stanley nodded. In the moment Marjie had kissed him over the short note he'd sent her, he had decided that until a jealous fiancé or husband requested otherwise, he would write to Marjie. The letters would be short out of necessity, and they would be skewed recitations of his experiences out of deference to her sensitive nature, but he would write. And he would hold his breath waiting for her letters, the tiny piece of her he was permitted to keep.

J

CHAPTER TWENTY-FOUR

MARJIE HAD NO IDEA ON what pretext Philip had managed to take Stanley away from Lampton Park for the morning, but she blessed him for it. She cherished every moment of Stanley's company that remained to her—the army representative would arrive in only two days—but a great deal that day rested on Stanley's absence.

"The party from Havenworth has arrived, Miss Kendrick," a Lampton Park footman informed her as he passed by with yet another basket of food.

Marjie nodded, grateful to hear that Corbin Jonquil and his family had arrived. All the brothers would be present that day, except for Charlie, the youngest, who could not leave Cambridge so near the end of term.

She looked over the grounds, inspecting and worrying. Tables sat pleasantly spaced with long benches lining the sides. All was in readiness for the bonfire planned for that evening. Those invited to The Gathering had been trickling in all morning and were busily and willingly helping with the ongoing preparations.

She took a deep, calming breath. All would be well, she assured herself for perhaps the hundredth time that morning. She steadfastly maintained that Stanley would not only appreciate her efforts but would also benefit from them.

Two men, obviously young but aged by experience, dressed in well-worn and faded uniforms embraced each other. Introductions were made amongst their loved ones, though at too far a distance for Marjie to hear the exact words exchanged. Smiles wreathed every face. She had seen the same scene play out multiple times over the past hour or so.

"This will be good for him." It would be. It had to be. Should the scheme prove disastrous, she had no one to blame but herself.

"Miss Kendrick." Marjie instantly recognized the enthusiastic voice as Pluck's.

Fortunately for all of them, Pluck had managed to be left behind. He knew most of the former soldiers who had arrived; if not personally, he at least recognized their names and when they had served with Stanley, who had apparently found a confidant in his young batman.

Pluck could quickly pair up the new arrivals with those they would most wish to see. Some guests had come on behalf of a father, brother, son, or husband who had fallen in the war, and Pluck, within a couple of questions, managed to identify whom they represented and did so with none of the awkwardness Marjie had worried about. Perhaps most importantly of all, he had a knack for putting at ease those guests who found themselves overawed at being invited to the grand country estate of an earl.

"This here's Lieutenant Greenberry," Pluck said, the closest to a formal introduction as he was likely to come. He indicated the young man next to him. The lieutenant stood with the confident, almost combative bearing of an army man but possessed the face of an angel. "This is Miss Kendrick."

"Miss Marjie Kendrick?" Lieutenant Greenberry's inflection transformed the question into a simple statement of fact. He was a study in contradictions. One expected his voice to be gruff and his tone implacable, yet he spoke with an inherent gentleness.

"Yes, Lieutenant Greenberry. I am."

"I am no longer in the army, Miss Kendrick. Mr. Greenberry will do fine."

Pluck would have none of it. "Ah, but for the day, we're all back in the army, Greenboy."

The Lieutenant slapped Pluck on the shoulder. "I see some of the boys have even pulled out their Continental togs." He pointedly eyed a few of the guests who were wearing their uniforms.

"A reg'lar collection of fashion plates we are 'round here." Pluck pulled out the cheeky grin he so often wore and tugged at the front of his own artillery uniform. His role as Stanley's valet attached him to the dragoons, but he still wore the regimentals of his former unit. "'Course, none of us can compete with the figure our captain cuts in his shako."

Lieutenant Greenberry smiled before his cherubic features turned more somber. "And when do we get to see our captain?"

Every person Marjie had spoken with that morning had referred to Stanley in just that way, "Our captain," and each person who had inquired after him had worn identical expressions of concern.

"He's off jollyfyin' with His High and Mighty Lordship," Pluck said.

"Captain Jonquil's eldest brother has taken him into Collingham for the morning so that we might have everything ready when he returns," Marjie explained.

One of the footmen called out to Pluck, motioning him over to help with more of the arrangements.

"This is to be a surprise, then?" Lieutenant Greenberry asked after Pluck had left. The lieutenant seemed uncertain of the wisdom of Stanley's not being warned.

"I thought it best." Hesitation gripped her mind. Perhaps she wasn't as certain of her idea as she'd been attempting to convince herself she was. "If he had known . . ."

"If our captain had known he would be confronted with an estate filled with his army comrades and the memories that linger around them, he might have objected." Lieutenant Greenberry nodded. "Or he might have outright refused to attend."

"Was I wrong to plan this?" She suddenly felt very unsure of herself. "Will I be doing him a disfavor instead of helping?"

"That I cannot tell you, Miss Kendrick." Lieutenant Greenery motioned for her to walk alongside him. His manners inarguably placed him at least amongst the gentry. "But this I do know: if anyone can bring our captain around to accepting what would otherwise overset him, you can."

"I?"

"You were known amongst the Thirteenth as our captain's angel." They continued to walk. Lieutenant Greenberry glanced in her direction occasionally, just as she did in his. "You saved his life, though I doubt you realize it."

She was too astonished to even speak. Only with effort did she manage to place one foot in front of the other.

"We read your letters to him after Waterloo," Lieutenant Greenberry said. "No one could say for certain if he would recover or succumb to the infection and pain and . . . and sorrow of it all. There were a great many who gave up the fight. Our captain had been through more than many who did not live."

The more she learned of Stanley's experiences during and after Waterloo, the more convinced she became that she had come perilously close to losing him.

"I can tell you the exact moment when our captain decided to fight to stay alive."

Marjie kept her eyes firmly focused ahead, only vaguely processing the buzz of activity around her. She noted somewhere in the recesses of her mind that Corbin Jonquil, the third of the brothers, stood but a short distance off, greeting Mater along with his small family.

"He had been fading alarmingly fast," Lieutenant Greenberry continued, "and the surgeons had declared his fate to be out of their hands. I was reading to him that night; we took it in turns, wanting someone to be with him all the time if we could manage it. The Thirteenth had been assigned to march on to Paris, but a few of us who were planning to sell out received permission to remain with him before returning home."

"You must have cared for him a great deal," Marjie said. Stanley never spoke of any of this.

"He was . . ." Lieutenant Greenberry's voice trailed off as though he was attempting to find a word just beyond his mental reach. "I can think of no other way to phrase it, but our captain was almost like a mother to all of us. I know that sounds ridiculous, but he—Being with our captain was like being home again. Does that even make sense?"

Marjie nodded. It made perfect sense. "He is a very calming and comforting person, and he cares a great deal for the people around him."

"Yes," Lieutenant Greenberry said. "But I think we all sensed that he had to fight hard for that peacefulness. He exuded hope but struggled to feel it. He offered reassurance but did not feel it himself. He offered to us what no one was able to offer him, and he did so despite the tremendous effort required. We loved him for that."

Again, the contradictions Lieutenant Greenberry presented. He had served in war. He walked with an air of action and decisiveness. Marjie sensed in him the ability to be almost ruthless when the situation warranted it, yet he spoke easily of love and did it with such kindness and compassion.

"He gave us what we needed because we needed it, without thought for himself." Lieutenant Greenberry stopped their aimless wandering and turned to face her. "Our entire company would stop midstep when our captain received one of your letters. I swear we held our breath, waiting for the change in him."

The intensity in his face made her breath catch.

"Those were the only moments he was actually as peaceful and optimistic as he strived to appear. We all fancied ourselves half in love with you for what you meant to him. That was why we read him your letters when he was feverish and dying."

Marjie winced at the blunt wording. She had somehow managed to convince herself he'd merely been ill, not truly in danger.

"I was reading one of your letters the night everyone expected him to die." He paused and swallowed with obvious difficulty. "He was quieter, just as he had been while others were reading to him. His coloring was horrid, and his breathing had grown more shallow. I've seen men die before, but it was different that time. I was desperate for him to pull through. You have no idea what losing him would have done for the morale of, gads, of the entire army just about. Not to mention I count him as a friend. So I read every letter he had ever received from you. Then one line—one single line—grabbed him. You wrote 'Do you think it is too much to ask that you return and hold me just once more?'"

Marjie felt her color rise, knowing that Stanley's men had read her very private yearnings. Lieutenant Greenberry's face held no hint of censure nor ridicule.

"Something crossed his face in that moment. I can't even explain exactly what it was, a look he wore sometimes when he realized someone needed something from him that he knew would be difficult to give. I had served with him before Orthez and again leading up to Waterloo. I know that look well." Lieutenant Greenberry met her eyes once more. "He decided you needed him to grant that request more than he needed relief from his suffering. He stayed alive because of you, because you needed him."

A warm tear dripped off her jaw.

"Though not one of them will say as much directly to you, every man here who served with him these past six months will be singing your praises throughout the day. And there are many more on the Continent still who do the same. We owe you our captain's life, and that is a debt we know we are unlikely to find the means of repaying."

Marjie shook her head, his words repeating in her mind, each repetition equally baffling.

"Though we have come here to express gratitude for our captain, a great many of us have come with the additional purpose of meeting you and seeing for ourselves what an angel of mercy looks like." He smiled as if sensing that his words embarrassed her but did not, nevertheless, wish them unspoken. "Ah. I see someone crossing this way, and if I am not mistaken, he appears intent on speaking with you."

Marjie followed the lieutenant's gaze to Lord Devereaux, who was moving decidedly in their direction.

"It was, indeed, an honor to meet you at last, Miss Kendrick," Lieutenant Greenberry said. "And I, on behalf of all our captain's men, thank you from the very depths of my heart for his life and for the hope you gave all of us through him."

He made a very elegant bow, one executed with such sincerity that Marjie felt even more tears gather in her eyes. She barely managed to hold them back as she watched Lieutenant Greenberry walk away. She had done nothing more than write letters to a man she desperately loved. It had been an act of selfish need more than anything, really. Those letters had been her connection to him.

"Are you accumulating admirers?" Lord Devereaux asked, having reached her side. The laugh that accompanied his question echoed Philip's on so many occasions. "That young fellow seemed remarkably smitten."

"Not at all." Marjie tried to summon a smile. "He was thanking me for"—she quickly adjusted her answer—"arranging this day for so many to renew old friendships."

"Has our guest of honor learned of his fate yet?"

"You are in a very light and teasing mood today, my lord." Indeed, he had not stopped smiling. "Are you so happy to be out of doors on this brisk November day, or are you suffering from some lingering illness that has rendered you a bit nonsensical?"

Lord Devereaux laughed as she had hoped he would. "I suppose I have been in better spirits of late."

"Are you enjoying Their Graces' house party, then?" She hoped so.

A look of contemplation crossed his uncharacteristically expressive face. "I am at that." He seemed almost surprised.

"Is there any reason in particular? Any person whose company you have found particularly agreeable?"

He didn't answer. He didn't need to. His face gave him away. Someone had struck his fancy or at least caught his interest. Marjie's heart warmed at the possibility. Lord Devereaux was far too lonely and in great need of companionship. More than that, he needed to love and be loved.

"I appreciate that you have torn yourself away to join our gathering," she said.

"My tenants, those I told you had received a letter from Captain Jonquil, could not possibly have made the trip from Sussex. I am here on their behalf."

"I wish to hear a great many details about your house party." She walked with him back toward the heart of the gathering crowd.

"You are being unforgivably nosy." His grin took any sting from his words. "Besides, I do believe the last of the Jonquil clan, save your dear captain, has arrived. You really ought to join them."

"You will be left alone." Above all else, she wished him not to be lonely.

He simply offered an indulgent smile. "Believe it or not, I do have something of a knack for making myself agreeable."

They parted ways, Marjie wondering at the change in him. A few short weeks earlier, he would never have ventured out amongst a crowd of acquaintances, let alone strangers.

"Oh, please," she silently pleaded, "let this lady be good for him."

The Jonquil family, minus the three brothers who were not present, had gathered around Sorrel's chaise longue. Marjie loved to watch the Jonquil brothers with their wives and children. Their personalities were in many ways vastly different, but they all treated their loved ones with a degree of tenderness Marjie had never imagined in all the years she'd lived with her father.

"I suppose this is the moment of reckoning," Jason, the barrister, said, motioning with his chin toward the stables.

Marjie turned. Stanley had arrived back at the Park, and the look on his face was not one of pleasure.

CHAPTER TWENTY-FIVE

"What is all this?" Stanley looked around in confusion. There had to have been upward of five dozen people meandering about the grounds, in addition to what appeared to be the entire Lampton Park staff and a few maids and footmen in Farland Meadows livery. Interspersed amongst them all were an alarming number of blue dragoon uniforms, too many to be mere coincidence.

"It appears we have stumbled upon a party. Shocking." Philip wore his mask of mindlessness, but a mischievous twitch at the corner of his mouth belied the impression.

Stanley gaped at the faces he quite suddenly and unexpectedly recognized: Private Sands, who had left the army after taking a bullet at Albuera; Private Smith, who had very nearly died of dysentery during Stanley's third year on the Continent; Private Black, who'd lost an arm, a leg, and an eye during the forlorn hope at Orthez; Lieutenant Greenberry, a deuced fine officer who'd sold out after Waterloo. Why were they all at Lampton Park?

"If I didn't know better," Philip said almost sarcastically, "I'd guess this was some sort of reunion."

Reunion? Stanley glanced from Philip to the gathered guests. It *was* a blasted army reunion. Stanley could feel his gaze grow mutinous. He turned sharply and walked in the direction of the house.

"Don't you dare." Philip's command stopped Stanley in his tracks. "Many of these people traveled long distances to be here, and the effort of arranging for their transportation and, in some cases, the financial means for them to do so deserves a moment of your time."

"Time?" Stanley spun to face him. "You think I object to the inconvenience?"

"I think you object to the idea of remembering any of the things these people stand for in your mind," Philip answered, his understanding uncanny. "But you will do so, for their sake and your own."

"*My* sake? Revisiting any of this will do me no good."

"I never knew you to be a coward," Philip said. "This will be difficult, I can appreciate that, but I honestly believe you will be better for the experience if you can find the fortitude to face it."

"Is that why you went behind my back and planned this . . . this ridiculous scheme?"

"I did not plan it, though I helped with its execution."

"Then who did?" Stanley suspected Pluck.

"You think I will simply give you a name so you can throttle the poor soul?" Philip raised an eyebrow. "I think not."

"I won't go over there without a name," Stanley warned.

"Good heavens," Philip muttered. "It is as if you were five years old again."

Philip grabbed Stanley by the back of his arm and forcibly propelled him in the direction of the gathered horde. Stanley could do nothing to prevent being dragged, and he would not appear so ridiculous.

"So this is why you gammoned me into wearing my best uniform," Stanley muttered.

"Couldn't have you disgracing yourself." Philip pulled him all the way to the nearest knot of people.

"Lieut—Cap'n Jonquil." Private Nielsen had known Stanley before his promotion. The man enthusiastically shook Stanley's hand. Someone must have warned him, for he reached without hesitation for Stanley's left. "Can't say how pleased I am to have been invited and to see you again."

Stanley was forthwith introduced to Nielsen's young wife, Minna. His little boy was pointed out as he ran about with a group of children. Nielsen had been so young when first they'd met and so afraid he'd not survive. Yet here he was, alive and well, with a family of his own.

Names were exchanged all around the remainder of the circle. Stanley found he knew every one. Among them were names he'd written on letters long ago, names burned into his memory. A mother, a sister, a father, a wife of a soldier who'd been lost.

Each group of people was the same. He saw faces he recognized and heard names he would never forget.

"My mother wouldn't stop cryin' after word of Jem reached us," a sister of one of Stanley's earliest losses said. Tears pooled in her eyes as she spoke, and Stanley felt himself grasping at his vastly fluctuating emotions. "Then she got yer letter, Cap'n Jonquil. An' ye had so much to say 'bout poor Jem that was kind and happy. Turned her around, it did. She still was sad and missed him something awful, but she could smile again. She had the vicar read that letter again and again till she could say it word for word."

"I am grateful that I could do something, however small." He had done little but write a letter, and the disproportionate amount of praise he was receiving made him decidedly uncomfortable.

"Oh, but it weren't small," the woman insisted. "It meant the world to her."

"You did a lot of good, Stanley." Marjie's voice at his side came as a surprise. "I don't think you realize how much." She slipped her arm through his, leading him toward another gathered group.

"But Jem Baker is dead." Stanley shook his head. "I merely wrote a letter. How can that possibly compare to his family's loss?"

"You are measuring wrong." Marjie squeezed his arm. "Rather than compare the impact of a letter to that of a lost loved one, compare it to the impact of losing that loved one without receiving a letter of comfort at all."

She walked with him through several more introductions and reunions. It was easier with her beside him. As the impact of each name struck and he attempted to push back the memories various faces conjured up, she would squeeze his arm or move closer to him, and he found he could endure it.

Marjie didn't leave his side until they came upon a face Stanley had always felt was impossibly out of place on a battlefield.

"Lieutenant Greenberry." She stepped to where the young lieutenant stood and offered her hands. Marjie pulled him closer to Stanley, and he found himself forcing down a surge of pure jealousy. Greenboy, as they'd all called him, had charmed each and every female he'd come across simply by looking at them. He had seen nearly as much action as Stanley himself but without coming away scarred and broken. "Captain Jonquil has arrived at last."

"Jonquil." Greenboy was no longer in the army and was out of uniform, and though many of the other former soldiers had reverted to old habits as they'd been introduced, the former lieutenant offered a bow rather than a salute.

"Greenberry," Stanley shot back. Mixed with a desire to pull Marjie back to his side and scuff up that cherubic face of Greenberry's was a wave of remembered battles and an afternoon spent with a soldier they had, between the two of them, tried and failed to save.

Greenboy smiled at Stanley's curt tone, those dimples that more than one camp follower had swooned over popping up on either side of his mouth.

Stanley found himself unexpectedly and unaccountably chuckling. "You angel-faced devil," he said, holding out his left hand and receiving a hardy handshake.

"How have you been, Jonquil?"

"I believe I will leave you two gentlemen to your reunion." Marjie moved to Stanley's side. She raised up on tiptoe and whispered, "I am so very happy to see you smile again." She kissed him on the cheek, much as one would a sibling, then gently touched his face before walking away.

Stanley watched her go, his heart hammering in his rib cage. He'd taken Philip's advice quite to heart and had kept his distance from Marjie. Though he thought often of pulling her into his arms and kissing her thoroughly, he hadn't done more than hold her hand. That simple salute on the cheek had nearly undone him.

"Our captain's angel," Greenboy said.

"She really is an angel." His men had given her that name without realizing how much it fit her.

"An angel who is quite obviously in love with you." Greenboy motioned with his head toward the tables of food where the assembled guests were gathering. Stanley followed the unspoken suggestion, grateful Greenboy adjusted his usually brisk pace to allow for Stanley's permanently slower one. "While we are all grateful for this chance to see so many friends again, none of us is so foolish as to think she arranged all this for our sakes."

"*She* arranged all this? Marjie?" Not Pluck? Not one of his brothers?

"Her letter was almost ridiculously convincing," Greenboy said. "Not to mention the fact that there were a lot of us who were so shocked at receiving a letter from our captain's angel that we would have done absolutely anything she asked of us just for the honor of being written to."

"Her letters." So much of what he'd seen the last few weeks began to make sense. All the mail Marjie had sent, all the secretive looks and aborted conversations had been related to this. *Ridiculously convincing?* "What did she say in her letter?"

Greenboy's grin spread wider. "That you were home for a short time and that she wished very much for you to see the men who had come to mean so much to you during your service, along with a few other things."

"What other things?" Stanley wasn't sure why he wanted so desperately to know precisely what she had written about him, how she had convinced such a large gathering of people to come during a difficult season for travel. For some in attendance, such a trip would be a hardship on many levels.

"Let's just say she made it clear that you needed us to be here, and seeing as how you are our captain, none of us would think of being anywhere else, now would we?"

"She made me out to be a charity case?" Embarrassment warred with indignation.

"Your angel?" Greenboy scoffed. "Would she do anything like that?"

"No. No, she wouldn't."

"C'mon." Greenboy waved him forward, toward a clump of former soldiers laughing over pints and plates at a nearby table. "Come give the boys a few minutes. They need this as much as you do. We may not have left the service with the injuries you did, but we all carry around the weight of it. We need a dose of captain comfort."

Stanley cringed at the despised nickname. "Our captain" was tolerable. "Captain Comfort" made him sound like a shot of hard liquor at a seedy tavern.

The table full of mangled, prematurely aged, and weather-bitten men hailed Stanley as he joined them. How different they would all have been without their shared experiences. He summoned one of his artificial smiles, the kind he'd become so adept at during the war, and accepted a cup from Private Smith, who looked far better than he had the last time Stanley had seen him.

Smith had always been the best storyteller in their regiment. "We were just rememberin' that time marchin' through the Pyrenees when Major Horace-Fulton's mount refused to go another step."

Greenboy exchanged an amused look with Stanley, who couldn't help the mirth that spread across his own face.

"Poor ol' Horseface couldn't get the beast to move so much as an inch."

Snickers sounded around the table. Horace-Fulton had not been a popular officer. The entire regiment had enjoyed the major's humiliation at his lack of control over his own mount.

"So Major struts to his horse's head"—Smith stood with his chest puffed out in a deuced good impression of the loathed, arrogant officer—"an' barks at the thing, 'You will move!' An' bless 'im, the horse moved. Moved its head enough to bite a button off Major's jacket."

Stanley laughed at the memory. Not a soul had intervened as the major's horse had grown more insubordinate; they'd simply glanced at one another, silently laughing at a moment they knew would be long remembered.

"'Give it back,' Major ordered."

"An' the lovely horse spit it at him," Private Black shouted out, pulling laughs from the entire table.

"So what does the high-steppin' major say?" Smith looked around at the men, who all knew the answer well enough.

Stanley rose to his feet, pitched his voice at the ear-grating height that had easily identified Horace-Fulton amongst a crowd, and said, "'*I* am a major!'"

They all laughed deep and full. What a ridiculous picture that conceited man had made. His foolish escapades had been nightly campfire fodder.

"Pulled rank on a horse, he did!" Smith wiped at a streaming eye as he continued laughing.

The stories flowed endlessly. Stanley had forgotten how funny some of their experiences had been. He lived with the constant reminders of loss and suffering but had needed a reminder of the things he had actually enjoyed about his years of service.

Some hours later, a bonfire was lit, adding warmth and light to the approaching night. The staff brought out yet more food. Strangers had become instant friends, while old friendships were firmed and renewed.

Stanley found he was even able to greet Lord Devereaux with some degree of equanimity. He saw in the viscount's treatment of Marjie precisely what she had described: the attentions and concerns of an older brother. Lord Devereaux shared yet another story of a family who had been touched by Stanley's letters. It was mind-boggling. He'd written out of a helplessness he couldn't seem to shake and had unknowingly managed to do some good after all.

He stood near enough to the bonfire to feel its warmth and watched the faces around him. They had all lost so much, and yet hope and joy filled their expressions. He wanted to think he had played a role in their happiness, that the past five years hadn't been entirely destructive.

Stanley sensed Marjie's approach before he saw her. She had floated around, overseeing all aspects of the gathering, checking on Sorrel, though unobtrusively, and had generally held the entire day together. He was beginning to realize Marjie was, somehow, even more amazing than he had realized.

She stopped beside him. "Are you terribly angry with me?"

Of all the things she might have said, Stanley had not expected that. "Why in heaven's name would I be angry with you?"

Her gaze shifted from his face to the fire and the people surrounding it. "You didn't look very pleased when you first arrived."

Good heavens, she thought he was angry with her. Stanley temporarily consigned Philip's advice to Hades and wrapped his arm around Marjie, pulling her up against him.

"I wanted you to see—to understand—" She didn't lean into him but didn't pull away. "You said once that you wondered if you ever did any good by the men you served with. I needed you to see that you have."

Stanley turned enough to draw her fully into an embrace. He felt her arms wrap around his waist.

"Please don't be angry," she whispered into his coat front.

He bent enough to whisper into her ear. "I love you."

Marjie turned her face up to look at him, a pleading light in her eyes. Stanley kissed the tip of her nose but allowed himself no other liberties.

"And I thank you for this day," he added. "You have done more good than I think you realize."

CHAPTER TWENTY-SIX

STANLEY STOOD STIFFLY IN HIS bedchamber. He had assumed the stance of a soldier, reminding himself that his time as a civilian had, for all intents and purposes, come to an end. Colonel Falwell had arrived at Lampton Park. Stanley was to present himself to the waiting officer in a quarter of an hour. He dreaded it.

"Always a soldier." He'd taken to speaking the words out loud. He had an obligation to serve, and he would not be disloyal.

Pluck had been completely silent since luncheon, a sure sign that he too felt the weight of the coming interview.

"You realize, of course, that just because I am returning, you are not obligated to do so as well." Stanley had reminded Pluck of that fact multiple times over the weeks since he'd first learned of the colonel's scheduled arrival.

Pluck usually threw back something cheeky and humorous. His expression in that moment, however, was nothing short of entirely offended. "I go where you go, Cap'n. Plain as that. Now shut yer mummer and finish gettin' dressed. There's a deuced colonel downstairs."

Stanley's heart froze in his chest. Blast the boy, Stanley couldn't convince Pluck to stay behind where he would be safe. He insisted on following Stanley back into the army. If Pluck was killed, Stanley would never forgive himself. There would be no one to send a letter to. Stanley knew, though Pluck had never said so outright, that the boy had come to think of Stanley as his family. In return, Stanley felt responsible for him.

A knock sounded at the door. Pluck opened it. Marjie stood framed by the opening. Stanley was supposed to be keeping a distance between them but, confound it all, he needed her to calm him down.

"Am I presentable?" He knew his words weren't as light as he'd hoped them to be.

She leaned her shoulder against the doorframe and tipped her head to one side, inspecting him. "The hat makes you seem seven feet tall."

"Imagine how tall we look on horseback."

"So it is a matter of intimidation?"

"Always." He strutted to where she stood.

Pluck muttered something under his breath about the fancy toffs in the cavalry being all flash. Lud, the boy really was nervous. Stanley had signed up with the intention of remaining in the army. Pluck had joined to escape the streets of London. Stanley might be able to talk him out of returning to duty.

"You are missing your sabre," Marjie said, "but I have not seen you wear it since you returned."

Stanley shook his head. Even Marjie's presence couldn't entirely release the tension building in him.

"Would it be unforgivably intrusive of me to ask why?"

Stanley could see his sword in his mind the way he always remembered it, a length of steel so covered in blood that none of the metal beneath showed through. It was the last thing he recalled seeing before Shadow, a horse he'd had for years, had suddenly jerked beneath him and fallen dead. For a moment, Stanley hadn't felt any pain, even as he'd looked at the mangled remains of his right leg. In agony, however, he struggled to pull himself away from the battlefield, knowing he would likely bleed to death there where he'd fallen. In that moment, certain he would die at the hands of the enemy, the irony of it struck him. He had often cursed the French for the losses they had inflicted, for killing so many, but he was no different. The evidence had dripped from his sword even as his own blood ran from his body.

When he'd awoken after the amputation and had emerged enough from the subsequent fevers to make sense of his surroundings, one of the first things he'd seen had been that sabre. Pluck had cleaned it meticulously, but the leather loop at the handle was stained a deep red Stanley knew would never come out entirely. He'd refused from that moment on to wear the sword. He did not need the reminder of the things he had done.

"Will Colonel Falwell be upset if you don't wear it?" Marjie asked.

Stanley opened his eyes at the sound of her voice. "He probably already knows." Lord Hill knew, after all.

Marjie smoothed the wrinkles on Stanley's left sleeve, her eyes focusing too keenly on the abstract gesture. She always had a hard time looking at him when she was worried or upset. "You've sewn the buttons back on the right sleeves."

"The colonel may be willing to overlook a missing sabre, but I doubt he will countenance flapping sleeves."

"And the gloves."

Stanley nodded.

"You must be certain to put the salve on your hand tonight." Marjie straightened his collar without raising her eyes to his face. "It will probably be very irritated."

"Please look at me, Marjie."

She lifted her face, and Stanley instantly wished he hadn't made the request. Tears hung in her eyes.

He was doing the right thing, blast it. He was honoring his obligations, keeping his word. So why the deuce did everything keep getting worse?

"I need to go downstairs for my interview." Stanley tightened every muscle, set his jaw. The right thing was not always easy, but it was what he always did. "Colonel Falwell is waiting."

"He is going to take you away from me." Marjie's whispered words were thick with anguish. "He has come to break my heart."

Stanley kept his arms firmly at his side. How he wanted to simply hold her, to give them both the comfort of an embrace in an impossible situation, but he needed to learn to live without her, and the sooner he began, the better off they would both be. "Perhaps it would have been better if we'd never known each other. This wouldn't—"

Marjie pressed her fingers to his lips. Stanley took in a sharp breath. How he needed her! He held himself very still, as if at full attention in a drill.

"There are things I regret in my life, Stanley, but I will never regret knowing you. You have changed who I am, changed me for the better. Do not wish that away."

"Time to go, Cap'n."

Stanley nodded to Pluck but never let his gaze stray from Marjie's face.

"Will you have to leave today?" A frantic tremor shook her voice.

"No. I will be given my marching orders, most likely for a couple days from now."

Her gaze grew intent. "You will not leave without saying goodbye?"

"I promise."

Marjie smoothed his sleeves once more. "You had best not keep the colonel waiting."

Stanley took a fortifying breath. He memorized the feel of her touch. After he received his orders, Stanley would keep his distance entirely. He would slip back into the role of soldier, where all emotions were pushed aside and he made do with what little hope he had. He straightened his shoulders and made his way down the corridor.

Colonel Falwell sat at Philip's desk when Stanley entered. Philip had apparently left. The colonel rose, his uniform impeccably clean, down to the high-polished medals that marked him as a man of vast experience. Stanley saluted as was expected, beginning the usual greeting ritual between two officers, one of whom far outranked the other.

"I hope I am not late, sir," he said.

"Not at all, Captain Jonquil. Am I correct that this is your batman?"

Stanley nodded, motioning Pluck forward. "This is Private Stone, Colonel Falwell."

The colonel acknowledged Pluck's salute. "Obviously you were artillery."

"Yes, sir." Pluck could be rigidly proper when required. He even looked almost respectable in his artillery uniform.

"Do you plan to return to duty when Captain Jonquil does?"

"Yes, sir."

"And if he chooses to sell his commission?"

Pluck hesitated a moment. Stanley understood, though he doubted Colonel Falwell did. Pluck knew Stanley wouldn't leave the army, so it was an answer he hadn't expected to have to give. "I'd've followed my cap'n right into Napoleon's drawing room iffen I'd had to," Pluck said. "An' I'll follow him wherever he goes now."

Colonel Falwell nodded. "You are dismissed, Stone. I will send for you if you are wanted again."

Pluck offered another salute and left the room, pulling the door closed behind him. The colonel retook his seat at the large desk, instructing Stanley to sit as well.

"If all our officers inspired the kind of loyalty in their men that you have," Colonel Falwell said, "we would have trounced Napoleon in one year instead of twelve."

Stanley sat rigidly in his chair. Pluck's loyalty might very well get him killed. "Private Stone's attachment stems from a sense of obligation, not—"

"I speak of more than just Private Stone." Colonel Falwell wove his fingers together, resting his intertwined hands and his forearms on the desk. "You have caused quite a stir at Horse Guards."

"I don't understand."

The colonel's gaze never left Stanley's face. He knew better than to squirm under the eyes of an officer. He sat with his back straight, shoulders back, expression empty.

"Lord Hill has been quite concerned over you. We realize he is something of a soft touch when it comes to his men."

"Sir—"

Colonel Falwell raised a hand to stop Stanley's words. "No need to defend him. Hill is a born soldier and one of the finest officers this nation has ever had. The truth of the matter is he loves his men beyond what is probably advisable. It leads him to worry a great deal. Much of that worry has been surrounding you of late and the state of your health."

Colonel Falwell leaned back in the chair, his gaze sweeping over Stanley. "You are walking far better than I was led to believe you could."

"My balance and gait have improved a great deal these past weeks."

Colonel Falwell leaned his prominent chin against one fisted hand, the arm bent, the elbow resting against the arm of his chair. "And your seat?"

"I road at a gallop yesterday." That had been surprising and reassuring. Life in the army would be far harder if he was unable to ride well.

"A full gallop?"

"No." The rhythm of his mount's hooves had barely shifted to that of a gallop, certainly not reaching top speed.

"And your right hand? Is it usable?"

One thing could certainly be said for the army: efficiency always won out over tact. "I cannot grip a quill, sir, but I have been writing a little with my left." He'd been working on another letter for Marjie, a longer one, and it was taking a great deal of time and effort.

Colonel Falwell nodded but did not comment. Stanley waited. The mantel clock ticked loudly in the silence. Stanley wished the interview were over. He already knew the outcome. Drawing out the inevitable only made the tension worse.

"Are you eager to rejoin your regiment?" Colonel Falwell asked after an uncomfortably long moment had passed.

"I am anxious to return to my duties." He had rehearsed that answer. He believed in honesty, but one simply didn't tell a commissioned officer that one would far rather visit the teeth drawer on a daily basis than return to life in the army.

"Ah, but that is not quite the same thing, is it?" Colonel Falwell shifted in his chair, his hands clasped in front of him still, but his gaze locked on Stanley. The man could probably make Wellington himself feel disconcertingly evaluated. "Why did you join the army, Captain Jonquil?"

That was another unexpected question. Stanley found he did not have an immediate answer.

"I know the usual reasons," Colonel Falwell said, "and I can see any number of them applying in your situation. You are a younger son and are, therefore, obligated to earn your living. The army is a common choice for young gentlemen in your situation. You are also a natural leader."

Stanley had never thought of himself that way.

"After meeting the earl just now and having known your father for many years before his passing, I believe leadership ability is a common trait amongst you Jonquils."

"I did not realize you knew my father."

Falwell nodded. "We had occasion to work together at a time when Parliament had decided the army had quite enough funding, though that was not at all the case. He supported our cause but was a cautious allocator of funds."

That sounded like Father—giving and compassionate but always very careful.

"There are those who join the army for the glory they anticipate." Colonel Falwell motioned with his hand, though no one in that category was present. "Those are the men who suffer the greatest disillusionment. I do not, however, believe you are among their ranks. I think you saw the King's service as a means of doing good in the world."

Stanley couldn't prevent shifting in mounting discomfort. That had been one of his chief motivations in purchasing a commission, and it had proven an idealistic dream. He had, perhaps, helped lessen some of the suffering around him, but the good he'd done was frustratingly limited.

"We at Horse Guards have decided your regiment must be the most literate of any in all of His Majesty's Army."

"I do not understand." How had that change of subject come about so suddenly?

"I have received no fewer than thirty letters from men who served with or under you." Colonel Falwell appeared entirely serious, but something very like amusement lurked in his eyes. "They are worrying themselves into a decline over there in Paris, wondering what has become of you. 'Is our captain returning?' 'Is our captain well?' They are full of questions and even a few demands. At least half of them informed me that if you were still unwell, I was not to allow you to return. I am not, under any circumstances, to risk your life, limb, or happiness. If I ignore their instructions, I am positive we would soon have an entire outfit of mounted cavalry rushing Horse Guards with sabres drawn."

"I have never encouraged insubordination."

"I am not speaking of insubordination, Captain. I am speaking of loyalty."

Fortitudo per Fidem. Stanley understood loyalty well. Why else would he willingly return to his own personal purgatory?

"You are a force in this army, much the way 'Daddy Hill' is. That is what the soldiers call him, is it not?"

Stanley nodded.

"Your men would, as Stone put it, walk into the enemy's own drawing room if you required it of them. That amount of trust and dedication is invaluable. I will not prolong this interview any longer than needed. May I speak plainly and to the point?"

More plainly than he had been speaking? That would be something, indeed.

"Lord Hill and I agree—and we have discussed this with Wellington as well—that you would be a tremendous asset in the field.

We realize that even restored to health, there are limitations to what you can do. Yours would be an organizational and leadership position without the requisite marching and, heaven forbid, combat role, should the need arise."

It would. Stanley had been a soldier long enough to know that war would come again—if not on the Continent, then elsewhere in the world.

"We are offering you a promotion, Captain Jonquil. You would be made a major, though you will remain with the Thirteenth."

Stanley's lungs froze midbreath. He felt his jaw hang open. To be made a major while in his twenties was not merely unexpected—it was almost unprecedented.

"You could have a very decorated career in the army." Colonel Falwell leaned forward in his chair, his gaze penetrating and focused.

A decorated career in the army. Before he'd joined, before half a decade of warfare, Stanley might have thought that the most tempting morsel that could have been dangled before him. All he could think of in that moment, however, was that a career in the army meant a lifetime of fighting.

"You are walking well. You can ride. You *appear* well enough to return."

Stanley almost wished his conscience had been battered enough by war to allow him the luxury of lying. "I believe I am, sir."

The colonel's gaze narrowed. For several drawn-out minutes, neither of them spoke.

"Report to Horse Guards in one week's time," Colonel Falwell said. "You will leave directly from London to your regiment in France."

"Yes, sir." Stanley stood, recognizing that the interview had reached its conclusion. He saluted and received one in return.

As he stepped from the library, a weight settled into the pit of his stomach. He'd known his course from the beginning. Yet, fully facing it left him hollow and empty once more.

He reached the stairs. Marjie stood at the top, watching him, pale-faced and still. He couldn't manage an expression that held any degree of reassurance, so he simply nodded.

Marjie didn't speak a word. She turned slowly where she stood and disappeared down the corridor.

CHAPTER TWENTY-SEVEN

Marjie refused to cry. She'd known for weeks that Stanley would eventually be leaving. She understood why he had to and would not make doing so harder for him.

She watched two footmen load trunks onto the waiting carriage. Pluck was outside as well, in full uniform, climbing in and out of the carriage. He had been uncharacteristically somber ever since Colonel Falwell's visit.

"You are worried about him," Marjie had said the evening before. There had been no need to say to whom she referred; Pluck knew.

"'Course I am. Going back to all that is gonna kill him. Maybe not in the six-feet-underground way, but it'll kill him. Daddy Hill sent him back here 'cause he was a breath away from bein' dead inside."

Marjie had pushed back the panic that had automatically come at those words. The tension in the house had been thick as mud for days, and she'd struggled to prevent herself from adding to it by giving vent to her fears. Stanley kept his distance from them all, very much the way he had when he'd first returned to England.

"I ain't gonna let our cap'n be alone while his soul's gettin' chewed up and spit out again."

"But?" Marjie had sensed there was more.

Pluck had pushed a breath through his teeth. "I don't wanna go back. I joined the army 'cause I wouldn't be just another London street maggot or a worthless rumbibber like my da. There was some great guns in the army." Pluck had smiled a little. "We liked sayin' that in the artillery, we were all great guns."

Marjie had allowed a smile as well.

"But I like it here." Pluck made a vague gesture, obviously indicating Lampton Park. "I like that it's quiet. And there's good people here. Here, I ain't just another piece of useless trash like I was growin' up, and I ain't stuck loadin' guns, waitin' to be another name on a list o' dead soldiers."

"Could you sell out?"

"I could, but I ain't gonna." He'd shot a defiant look at her. "I go where he goes."

Marjie watched Pluck helping with the preparations for their journey, and her heart hurt for him. Were they all doomed to be unhappy?

Unhappiness certainly seemed Stanley's fate. Returning to his regiment would, as Pluck had said, destroy him. Remaining in England would as well. He would torture himself over what would, to him, amount to dishonorable behavior.

Marjie heard Philip before he ever came into view. A man who sauntered about with a dozen fobs on his watch chain did not move quietly.

"Are they about ready?" he asked, obviously referring to those preparing the carriage.

Marjie nodded.

Philip too had been heavier of spirit. He was accompanying Stanley to Town. He had business that needed attending to that he would prefer to complete before Sorrel's condition reached the point where he didn't dare leave her. For once, she had not insisted that she could take care of herself. They all understood that complications were unavoidable and that a happy outcome was far from guaranteed.

"Stanley will be down in a moment." Philip had apparently noticed her gaze wandering to the staircase.

"I want only to say good-bye."

Philip nodded. "I know. Only, try to make this easier on him. Stanley is struggling right now, and he needs us to be supportive."

"I will." She was determined to.

Philip stepped outside. Marjie could hear him speak to the coachman but could not understand the words. Her gaze returned to the staircase.

Do not make this harder on him, she silently reminded herself. *A brief, friendly farewell. A smile. Encouraging. Supportive.* She repeated the list several times, reminding herself of the role she must play.

She nearly lost her resolve when she saw Stanley coming down the stairs. To the casual observer, he would have appeared a typical army officer about to rejoin his regiment. His expression, though, was all but blank. Though he did not lean heavily on his stick nor seem to be struggling with his balance, he moved slowly, with an obvious reluctance in his step.

"Do not make this harder on him." She clasped her hands in front of her to prevent herself from touching him as he approached.

"Are you the footman this morning?" His false lightness pierced her.

She could not manage to respond but tightened her clasp. They stood in heavy silence. Stanley's gaze moved about the room, lingering a moment on an ormolu plaque of the Jonquil family crest that hung just above the door. Finally, he turned and looked at Marjie but quickly shifted his focus to the carriage just beyond the tall window they stood beside.

"I understand Layton and Marion are taking you to Town for the Season."

"Yes. In March." She dreaded it. More balls at which she would be forced to dance with gentlemen she cared nothing for, more evenings spent wondering where Stanley was and if he was well, more loneliness.

Stanley nodded. "I am—" He stopped abruptly. Stanley stood stiff and perfectly upright. She knew the stance; he had become a soldier once more.

She pulled her hands behind her back. Every inch of her longed to simply hold him, to try to find her Stanley beneath the empty expression and rigid posture.

Stanley spoke again. "I want you to—No. I *need* you to be happy, Marjie. I need to know that you are going on with your life."

Going on with her life? Did Stanley not realize that he was too integral a part of her life for it to simply go on without him? *Do not make this harder for him.* She didn't speak, didn't move.

"Will you write to me still and tell me how you are?" He finally looked at her. The bleakness in his eyes drained Marjie of every lingering hope she had. Until that moment, until she saw the pain he couldn't completely hide, she had held on to the possibility that he would find some joy in his career and in the life that stretched out ahead of him.

"Of course I will." She would write him epistle-length letters filled with completely fabricated reassurances of her happiness if it would bring him some measure of comfort. Knowing as she did that her letters had given him strength to survive, she would never cease writing to him.

Pluck poked his head inside. "Time to go, Cap'n." He left as quickly as he'd come.

Stanley stood still, watching Marjie. She didn't move either.

Don't make this harder, she kept telling herself, even as every instinct in her strained to hold him there.

"I have to go." He still did not move.

Marjie nodded. "Please be careful, Stanley." She had no idea how she managed the words without crying.

"I will. And I'll write to you, though the letters won't be long." He raised his gloved right hand, grimacing as he did.

"I will be happy to receive anything you send me." She sounded far more impersonal than she'd intended, but she knew if she allowed herself even a hint of emotion, she would completely break down.

"I have no idea when I will see you again, but—" Stanley's gaze slid away again. "I just wanted to say that—that I—"

Please tell me you love me. She needed to hear it but didn't ask. She would ease his way even if doing so required a stilted and disconnected farewell.

A footman came up the front steps to the door and opened it wide.

"I have to go now." Stanley's voice was quiet, empty.

"Good-bye, Stanley."

His eyes met hers. Marjie waited, silently pleading for some words of affection, but he didn't speak again. He simply nodded and left.

Dinner was a solemn affair, and not for Marjie only. Sorrel felt too ill to join them. Mariposa and Jason were the only Jonquils who had not yet departed following The Gathering several days earlier. Marion was near enough to her confinement that Layton remained at Farland Meadows. Only Harold, who had joined them for dinner, spoke. He quoted and expounded upon the thirty-first Psalm until Marjie was ready to strangle him.

Mariposa saved her the trouble. "We had a rooster once that was very much like Señor Harold," she said to no one in particular. "He made a great deal of noise and spoke very much, though almost no one heeded him." She lifted a forkful of fish but paused before putting it in her mouth. "He was delicious."

Jason sputtered but managed to hold back a laugh. Marjie genuinely smiled for the first time in days.

Harold raised an obviously disapproving eyebrow and continued eating in blessed silence.

Marjie liked Harold, for the most part. He had a good heart, as all the brothers did, but he also had the unfortunate tendency to become prosy. At that moment, the family needed compassion more than sermonizing.

Mater, who had not spoken a word all day, quite suddenly broke her silence. "I cannot bear this." A thread of determination ran through her words. "I have been a horrid, unfeeling mother."

"Mater?" Jason's confusion echoed Marjie's and, based on the looks on the others' faces, everyone else's as well. "How can you say such a thing?"

"I tried to not be emotional or to appear upset. I tried to ease his way. Stanley was unhappy enough. I tried to be impersonal as Philip suggested so as not to add to Stanley's struggles. But I am his mother, by the stars. There should be nothing impersonal about that." She set her fork down with an audible clink.

Mariposa nodded with her characteristic conviction. "Philip is a man." She waved a hand, dismissing and condemning all in one gesture. "These men, they do not understand anything."

Again, Harold's eyebrow lifted. Jason grinned.

"'Act like your heart is made of stone,' Philip says to you. 'Señor Stanley will be happier if his family treats him like a rag they will not miss at all.' I told Philip that he was, of all the men in the world, the most stupid. I threw my arms around Stanley and wept because my heart was weeping. You English, you are too afraid of emotions. You fight against your feelings." Mariposa shook her head and shrugged. "Of all things, a person ought to *feel.* Without feelings, what are we? We are nothing more than moving paintings."

Like a rag they will not miss at all. Marjie had stood stoically as she'd made her farewells, saying nothing personal or tender, simply stating that she would read his letters. Stanley must wonder if she cared for him at all.

"I have to see him once more." Mater looked from Jason to Harold and back again. "Please, boys. One of you must accompany me to London. I would be but a day behind him and could arrive, God willing, before he departs for the Continent."

"Of course you must go," Mariposa said. "This is not a question."

"I cannot leave Sorrel, but she is not well enough to travel." Mater's brow furrowed at the complication. "And Marion is near her time. Layton will worry."

"Mariposa and I will stay here," Jason said. Marjie had thought, from the moment they were introduced, that Jason had the voice of a barrister—logical, calm, and very persuasive. "We will send to Havenworth for Clara. Being a mother already, she will know what is to be done should either of our sisters-in-law have need while you are away."

Mater turned to Harold, the expectation in her eyes unmistakable.

"I can be ready to depart in the morning, if that is what you wish," he said.

Mater nodded, the lines of her face easing with relief. Instantly, Marjie began formulating a plan. She simply had to find a way to be included in the journey.

The family removed to the sitting room after their meal. Though there likely was a more elegant way of making her request, Marjie had not the patience to formulate one. She sat beside Mater, took a breath for courage, and pressed forward. "I wish to ask a favor," she said.

Mater met her eyes with a gaze deeply kind and maternal. "You wish to join me on my journey to London, I'd wager."

She wanted to explain, to lay bare the reasons her own farewell to Stanley had been insufficient. She wanted to reassure Mater that she would not be a burden during the journey. Her words, however, caught in her throat. All she could do was nod and blink back the mingled relief and sadness and worry that sat so heavily upon her mind.

"I will ask Harold to arrive early," Mater said. "We will waste not a moment."

Marjie rose once more. "I will go begin my preparations, then we need not be delayed." She left quickly, pushed onward by the hope that she would see her beloved one more time and could tell all that was in her heart. He needed to know that he was loved, and she needed him to understand how precious he was to her.

Upon reaching her bedchamber, she made a discovery that distracted her from her purpose: a single white rose on her dressing table and a folded, sealed missive beside it.

Her name was printed in blocky handwriting across the front. He had written to her, just as he had promised. Even before he had promised. The letter had to have been composed before their very brief, all-too-formal leave-taking.

She opened it, desperate for this small connection to him.

My dearest Marjie,

She lowered herself onto her bed, hearing that tender greeting echo in her mind in his voice.

> *Writing with my left hand is a slow process. I have begun this letter a full week before Colonel Falwell is scheduled to arrive in the hope that it will be completed before I leave for France.*
>
> *I have just now retired for the night after spending the afternoon amongst my fellow soldiers. Did I thank you for that? I'd like to think I did, but am certain I did not do so enough. You have given me something to cling to as I contemplate returning to that life I disliked in so many ways. I had, until this day, forgotten how truly good were the men I served among.*

But still, Marjie noted, he did not say how good he himself was, nor that he had done some good for his men. She was grateful to have helped but felt something of a failure in spite of that small triumph.

> *Colonel Falwell has just come and gone, and I find myself preparing to depart. Are you upset with me? I wonder. Perhaps you are disappointed. I hope in time you will understand why I must return.*

She did understand, and she applauded his integrity. If only her circumstances had permitted her to lay claim to that loyalty herself. But life had placed them both in an untenable situation. They could not be together but could not bear to be apart.

My bedchamber is once again packed and emptied of much that identifies it as having belonged to me. A soldier is, by nature, a nomad, a wanderer without a home. I should have liked to have had one though. I would, if I were able, choose a home with a vast stretch of land in some quiet and peaceful place. I find myself picturing a great many sheep.

A moment's laugh bubbled in her heart. She knew him well enough to recognize the remark as a humorous one. She hoped that meant his spirits were not entirely low.

I shall picture you in a home just like that, joyous and content. In doing so, I will worry for you less and will be at peace, knowing you are happy.

Take care, my dearest Marjie. Do not allow your sister to torment you with her defensiveness. Give Mater a hug from her "sweet Stanley." And whatever else you may do, write to me.

With all my love,
I remain your affectionate and devoted
Stanley

Marjie pressed the letter to her heart and closed her eyes. How perfectly she could picture the pastoral scene he had described. She could see him there as peaceful as he'd imagined she would be in such a setting. He deserved that more than she did. In returning to a life he disliked so much, one that burdened him so strenuously, he was not likely to find the peace he sought. She would content herself with knowing he had that dream of an imaginary sanctuary among the hills to which he might escape.

She would see him soon. She refused to believe they would be too late. All she asked was one more embrace, a kiss of farewell, and the chance to tell him she loved him. If she could have that, she could, somehow, someday, find a way of making her own peace with the too-often cruel hand of fate.

J

CHAPTER TWENTY-EIGHT

"What do you say *I* skip on across the Channel in the dashing uniform and *you* stay here and deal with Fallowgill?" Philip slapped a stack of papers onto the desk in front of him and leaned back in his chair with a puff of irritated breath.

"Trouble in Yorkshire?" Stanley appreciated the diversion. He would report in only two hours and was doing his utmost not to think on it too closely.

"Actually, in London. One would think that finding an estate manager who was both competent and honest would be a simple undertaking. Either all the desirable candidates have gone into hiding out of fear of being stunned speechless by my sartorial splendor, or London's hiring houses are capable of presenting to me only men who lack both credentials and common sense."

"I hate to tell you this, Philip, but you would encounter a great many incompetent buffoons in the army as well." Stanley thought of Major Horace-Fulton and smiled despite the encroaching despondency he'd fought all day.

He was dressed as a major, having been officially awarded that rank the day before. Never had he felt less himself in his uniform. It was as much a mask as the bright, flamboyant clothes Philip wore. He was playing a part and would continue to do so for the rest of his life.

"So I am doomed to deal with idiots all my life." Philip's amused expression took Stanley back to their childhood. Philip had worn a perpetual grin, by far the happiest of all the brothers. Stanley had often depended on that exact look on his oldest brother's face when he felt worried or unhappy.

"You could always abandon your estates and your responsibilities and go live a life of ease and indulgence in the Former Colonies," he suggested. "I hear that is the order of the day across the water."

"And yet, Holy Harry is smitten with an American. That is very nearly blasphemous. I wonder if the archbishop knows."

Stanley laughed, and after a moment, Philip's dry expression broke into a grin.

"A life of indulgence, you say?" Philip made quite a show of contemplating the suggestion. "I thumb my nose at all my convictions, my responsibilities, and turn my back on everything to which I ought to have been loyal. The idea has merit."

They both laughed again, knowing Philip would never choose such an absurd path.

"Father would have had your hide if you'd even contemplated such a thing."

"He walked out on Parliament once," Philip said. "I'd wager you didn't know that."

Stanley had never heard anything so preposterous.

"It must have been twenty years ago. The Reign of Terror had ended, but France was far from stable. War was raging on the Continent. There were riots throughout Britain. An air of panic and unease permeated the nation, as well as Parliament."

"Father would not have walked out if circumstances were so unsettled." Stanley knew that with perfect clarity.

"You wouldn't think so," Philip said. "I was young, but I remember everyone seemed a little on edge at that time. Mater was increasing. I was old enough to realize that, but I don't think any of the rest of you understood."

"Increasing?" That was too long ago for Charlie but would have been after Harold was born.

Philip nodded. "The child was stillborn. A girl. That, I think, made the loss even harder for Mater. She wrote to Father, but I don't think she expected him to come, he having committed himself to saving the country."

No. Father would not have turned his back on that responsibility.

"He arrived at the Park a couple of days later. Mater was shocked. I remember Father's exact words after she said she hadn't expected him to return. 'By the stars, Julia. I am the only husband you have! Where else would I be?'

"I had been with Mater. She had been sitting in the nursery, silently holding Harold. I had no idea what to do. He handed Harold to Nurse and led Mater away. I didn't see much of either of them for days. Father didn't return to London for months."

But Father had made a commitment to Parliament. He'd abandoned his responsibilities. Stanley stopped the thought the moment it formed. Father had had a responsibility to his family as well.

"I wish I knew what he said to her during those long weeks." Philip leaned back in his chair, rubbing his forehead. "How does a husband comfort his wife after the loss a child, especially when enduring that loss himself?"

Stanley recognized the question beneath the one Philip had posed out loud. "You are thinking of Sorrel."

Philip nodded, pain passing over his features. "I spoke with several physicians here in London—I wanted to come partially for that reason. Dr. Habbersham is growing older and told me he does not mean to continue his practice much longer. I need to find another man of medicine for the neighborhood. For Sorrel. I also wanted additional opinions on her current prognosis. I need to know if—" For a moment, Stanley thought Philip might actually cry. His expression held deep worry and barely held-back emotion. "They hold out very little hope. Each one believes she will lose the child."

Why was hope in such short supply? Of all things, a person ought to have hope.

"What am I going to do, Stanley?" Philip's words were choked to the point of near incomprehensibility. He rubbed his face with his palms, heavy breaths pushing through the cracks between his fingers. "This will tear her apart. I have no idea how to help her. If I could just take all the pain of this away, I would in a heartbeat. But I can't. I can't do a blasted thing."

"You will be with her, Philip. That will help."

"I've made arrangements so that I need not leave the Park for the next few months. My Parliamentary secretary will keep me informed on bills so I can communicate with my colleagues. If I can get my Yorkshire problem sorted out, all the estates should run smoothly without my interference. I hope nothing unforeseen arises. I do not want to have to leave her."

"Then don't."

Philip looked up at him.

"Suppose Fallowgill falls into complete disrepair or Parliament loses its collective mind," Stanley said. "Even if you could help, you're needed at home. Father would remind you that you are the only husband she has. That's where your loyalties lie, Philip. That will give you the strength you need."

Philip sighed and nodded. "*Strength through loyalty.* Sometimes I'm not sure to which loyalty that refers."

"Forgive me, my lord." Jeffers stepped inside the book room. Philip didn't bother with his dandy persona. "The Dowager Lady Lampton has just arrived."

"Mater is here?" Philip sounded as surprised as Stanley felt.

Before Stanley could summon a single thought to ponder why their mother had traveled all the way to London in the harshness of winter, Mater rushed into the room. His first reaction was panic—Mater looked frantic. He stood as she entered, his heart hammering out a concerned rhythm.

"Mater, what in heaven's name—?"

Mater had her arms around Stanley before Philip even finished the question. "Oh, my sweet Stanley," she said. "You haven't left yet."

"I have a few minutes remaining." He had planned to retrieve his belongings and leave within the hour.

"Philip." Mater skewered Philip with a look of warning that echoed a thousand different moments from their childhood. "I am about to be a gushing, weeping mother, and you had best not have anything to say about it."

Philip stood in stunned silence.

"As a matter of fact," Mater said, "I would very much appreciate your leaving us in privacy for a moment."

"Of course." Philip crossed to her. He kissed their mother on her cheek and left as she had requested.

Mater watched her eldest son, then turned to face Stanley once more. She looked concerned, perhaps even a little confused. "Has he been crying?"

Stanley nodded. "A little. He is worried about Sorrel."

"Yes. Hers is a situation not likely to end happily." Mater's voice filled with empathy, something Stanley would not have fully appreciated before Philip's revealing conversation. "She has a good husband though, and that will help. Our Philip has grown into a very fine gentleman. All of you boys have."

Stanley didn't know about that. Very fine gentlemen did not, he imagined, kill people nor send men to their deaths. He had not done so in cold blood nor with any degree of murderous intent. That was some consolation.

"Are you well, Mater?" He did not like the signs of fatigue and worry in her face.

"I had to tell you because I did not when you left." She touched his face with her hand. "I love you, my boy. You have ever been a comfort to me, and my heart aches to know you will be so very far away. I worry over you, over your well-being and your safety, and, most importantly, your happiness." Tears flowed freely down her face.

Stanley watched her, astonished. Mater did not cry often and not ever copiously.

"I am proud to have a son who is honorable, and I would never, ever ask you to compromise your integrity. Still, I wish with all my heart you did not have to go. Returning to that life will be so hard on you. It will be horrible for me as well. You bring me such joy and comfort, and without you here, I know I will struggle to feel that happiness. I did when you left the first time, and I did when you returned to the Continent in March."

Pain stabbed at Stanley's heart. He was hurting his mother, of whom he'd designated himself protector from the time he was a young child. He had to return to the army. He was needed and expected and committed. Yet doing so would hurt her.

"I did not say anything when you left the Park because I feared burdening you, but you need to know. Above all else, you must know I love you."

Stanley kissed her tenderly on the forehead. He'd done so ever since he was tall enough to reach. They stood, her weeping into his handkerchief, hers having already become too soggy to be useful, and he holding her in a tight embrace.

"I have to go back, Mater." How often had he said that over the last week, both to himself and to others? Father had often said that doing the right thing was not always easy. Stanley had not been prepared for just how difficult it was proving. "I pledged my loyalty to the kingdom in this way. I cannot break that pledge."

"I know." Mater spoke steadier than before. "*Fortitudo per Fidem.*"

"It is a powerful creed."

She stepped back and met his eye. "Harold told me once that he thinks the family might be mistranslating those words. He takes great pride in his grasp of Latin, you know."

"He takes great pride in a lot of things," Stanley said rather out of the side of his mouth.

Mater bit her lips, clearly holding back a laugh. "Watching him grow into his role will be . . . interesting."

Yet another thing Stanley would be missing. "What objection does Harold have to our interpretation?"

"*Fidem*, he insists, can and should be interpreted as 'loyalty,' but there is another translation he feels is just as important, just as crucial."

Stanley set his mind back to his long-ago instruction in Latin but could not remember another meaning.

"Faith," Mater said. "Strength through faith."

Stanley had not once thought of the family creed in those terms, and his mind would not, for a moment, wrap itself around this new version.

"'Strength through loyalty,' loyalty to one another, to causes we believe in, to those things and people and ideals to which we pledge our devotion. It is and always will be an important and necessary character trait of any good and upright person," Mater said. "But 'strength through faith,' faith in the promise of a brighter tomorrow, faith in the impact of a life well lived, and, my dear, sweet Stanley, faith in yourself, in your goodness, dear heavens, your deep and abiding goodness . . . That is just as important, just as crucial. Live your life with integrity, my boy, but do not live it without hope."

He breathed back the emotion that emerged, keeping himself steady for her sake. "You are asking me to be optimistic."

"I am asking you to believe."

"Each of us boys learned long ago that when our Mater tells us to do something, we do not argue."

"See that you don't." She smiled tremulously. "I love you, Stanley. I love you so very much. I did not want to make your farewell any harder than it had to be, but I needed to tell you that. I could not let you leave without doing so."

He could not even find the words to respond. No matter where life took him, no matter his struggles to believe in himself and the path life had put him on, a man needed to know his mother loved him.

"I will require another hug and a kiss before you leave," she said as if warning him, "but there is one more farewell that needs to be remade." She turned back to face the door. "Come in, child. I have never seen Stanley stunned into such complete silence. You'll have no difficulty saying whatever it is you wish to say."

Stanley followed his mother's gaze directly to Marjie. Neither of them moved as Mater left, but they watched each other silently.

By far, the most difficult and uncomfortable leave-taking had been with his angel. He'd wanted to say so many things but couldn't find the words to do so. He'd desperately longed to hold and kiss her, but he'd been afraid he would fall to pieces if he so much as touched her.

Marjie stepped inside. She turned back long enough to close the door.

What would she say? Stanley didn't think he could endure another heart-wrenching farewell. Not with Marjie.

She stepped up to him, the scent of roses filling the air around him. He would never smell roses again without thinking of her. She didn't touch him, did not reach her arms out to embrace him. Marjie lifted up on her toes and leaned toward him. Only their lips met in a kiss of tender farewell.

Stanley couldn't breathe. He had resigned himself to never feeling such fulfillment again. His arms encircled her, pulling her flush with him. He should not have allowed himself the moment's weakness, but he needed her comfort and the strength she gave him.

The world disappeared. Nothing existed beyond that stolen moment. The years that stretched out ahead of him faded into the furthermost regions of his mind. The hour of his departure disappeared, forgotten and unheeded. His Marjie was in his arms.

"Marjie," he whispered, attempting to make himself break away. He could not. A moment more passed before his soldier's instinct forced him to regain control of the situation. Prolonging yet another farewell would only be harder on them both.

He took a step back. He closed his eyes, forcing several breaths and lowering his arms determinedly to his sides. He had mere moments before he needed to leave. His thoughts must be brought down out of the clouds and back to his duties.

Marjie stepped forward, closing the distance between them once more. She reached up and took his face in her hands. "Please don't leave me, Stanley."

"Marjie—"

"I need you at least as much as they do. Please don't abandon me. Please."

Her words cut so deep Stanley felt as though his heart was bleeding. "I gave my—"

"I know. I am not asking you to abandon your duties. I am asking, begging, you to take me with you. Please."

Stanley held his hands firmly at his side, forcing himself to not reach for her again. Marrying her and taking her to France with him would be so much easier than leaving her behind. He could hold her when he needed comfort. She would fill the broken bits of his soul, the places that had cracked and shattered again and again since the day he'd witnessed his first battle. He would be able to turn to her when he struggled to endure the life he'd come to despise in so many ways.

"No, Marjie." Those were the two hardest words he'd spoken all day. "I will not force that life on you. I will not sacrifice your own happiness for mine."

"Do I look *happy*, Stanley? Does being left here appear to have secured my *happiness*?"

Stanley held his hands behind his back so he would not reach out and wipe the tears from her cheeks. He did not know if his self-control could endure touching her again. He feared he would give in and consign her to the misery that awaited across the Channel. "I know the life to which I would be taking you." He stepped back once more, and Marjie's hands fell to her sides. "Whether you believe me or not, you would be more unhappy there than you could ever be here, and I would hate myself for doing that to you. I cannot. Please do not ask it of me."

She stood silently for a moment. He saw her shoulders droop and her gaze drop away from his face. "I know," she said. "I know. I had not intended to beg you to keep me, Stanley. I had meant only to tell you I love you and I will miss you. I wanted to be supportive and comforting and—" She shook her head almost dismissively and shrugged.

"No, Marjie." He knew what emotion that shrug covered. He would not allow her to feel rejected. "You have been all of those things. Knowing that you love me will sustain me in ways you cannot possibly imagine." He did not deserve her love, but having it, he was determined to live worthy of it.

"I also wanted you to hold me just one more time."

With that simple sentence, he was back in Belgium, lost in the white fog of fever and approaching death. He'd heard her words fluctuating between the hoarse voice of Lieutenant Greenberry and her angelic one in his thoughts. Those words had taken firm grasp of him. *To hold her just one more time.* That had been worth living for, even if it had meant living a life haunted by memories and regrets.

"Oh, my Marjie." He sighed but stepped farther away. "Do you have any idea how you are torturing me?"

She took a shaky breath, tears still falling from her eyes.

"I cannot hold you again." Stanley forced back a groan of frustration. He needed her. "I am not strong enough to let you go if I do. But I have to do the right thing now. I have to."

"I know." Her voice broke.

"You do know I love you, don't you?"

She nodded but seemed unable to speak.

Stanley closed his eyes and pushed out a tense breath. Her words of a few moments earlier haunted him. "I need you at least as much as they do," she had said.

In a moment, he would leave to fulfill a commitment he'd made years earlier. In doing so, though, he would be hurting his angel. It was, in a word, impossible. How did a man find any degree of faith in such a hopeless situation?

CHAPTER TWENTY-NINE

STANLEY STOOD AT THE DOOR to Colonel Falwell's office, waiting. He had been instructed to report there and arrangements would be made for his transportation to the ship that would take him to France. Pluck stood beside him, quiet and rigid.

"What in the blazes are we doin' here, Cap'n?" Pluck hadn't yet adjusted to Stanley's change in rank.

"Fulfilling a commitment."

"Iffen ye nobs weren't so blasted hon'rable, we'd be back at Lampton Park 'stead of gettin' ready to ride some flea-bitten boat to France. Who the blasted blazes wants to go to France?" Stanley had never heard Pluck grumble as much as he had in the past few days. He knew better than to remind Pluck that he was not obligated to join him on his return to service. Pluck would lay into him with the viciousness of a rabid dog if he so much as hinted at such a thing.

The colonel's door opened, and a young man, a lieutenant by his uniform, stepped out. "Major Jonquil?"

Stanley answered with a quick half nod.

"Colonel Falwell will see you now." He held the door open. Pluck was instructed to wait on a bench near the door for Stanley's return. They would be traveling to France together, but this final interview was to be with Stanley alone.

He could see a narrow strip of the room within. He understood that he was to proceed forward, but he couldn't seem to move. His whole life would change the moment he stepped through that door. The documents he would be carrying to France for Lord Hill would be given to him in the next few minutes. The last few pieces of paperwork relating to his promotion and regimental assignment would be his as well. Stepping forward would put him firmly on that path. With Marjie's sobbing pleadings still fresh in his mind, combined with Mater's distress and Pluck's unmistakable reluctance, Stanley felt as though he were dragging his entire family into the direst of circumstances.

You promised to have hope. You promised to try.

Though his hesitation seemed to last for minutes on end, Stanley knew he'd paused but a second. He understood his duty. "Always a soldier." He set his shoulders and stepped through the door.

"Major," came the clipped greeting.

Stanley stopped directly in front of Colonel Falwell's desk. A tightness wrapped around his lungs, forcing him to work at every breath. The urge to run began creeping through his limbs.

Strength through loyalty, he told himself only to hear Philip's voice answer with the lament, "Sometimes I do not know to which loyalty that refers."

Father never had addressed the issue of conflicting commitments. Stanley was only thirteen years old when Father died. Perhaps that topic would have been covered if Father hadn't been taken from them so young.

"You are still not wearing your sabre." Colonel Falwell looked both curious and disapproving.

"No, sir." Stanley offered no answer beyond that.

The colonel's gaze grew more narrowed, though not angry. "Why is that, Major? It is a required part of your uniform, regardless of your inability to hold it in your sword hand."

"I choose not to wear it, sir."

"Rather, you *refuse* to wear it." Colonel Falwell wove his fingers together and rested his arms on his desk. "Why is that?"

Stanley maintained his tensely correct posture. He focused his eyes somewhere above the colonel's right shoulder. "It holds unpleasant associations for me." That was almost unemotional enough to prevent any of the tremors or noticeable paling he usually endured after speaking so closely to the heart of his worst battle scars.

"Are those associations in regard to your own wounds or to those you inflicted upon others?"

Colonel Falwell's insightful question surprised him. It nonetheless required a response—one Stanley did not wish to give. "Both, sir." He kept the sentence clipped to avoid a drawn-out conversation on such a painful subject.

"You are bothered to such an extreme as to willingly embrace insubordination? What if I were to tell you that you are, from this time forth, commanded to wear a sabre as your uniform requires? Would you still refuse?"

Stanley could feel his heartbeat in his throat. Sweat trickled down the back of his neck. To flout the orders of one's commanding officer was an offense worthy of punishment, court-marshal at times. Yet Stanley knew he could never wear that sword again, or any sword, for that matter. A sword in his hand made him nothing better than a murderer. If he was to have faith in himself, as Mater had pleaded with him, then he could not, would not, wear it again.

"I would refuse, sir."

"What, then, is your plan for enforcing adherence to uniform regulations amongst your men when they, seeing that their major is never in full uniform, refuse to comply themselves?"

Stanley had not thought of that. A major had greater influence than a mere captain. The men who knew him and understood his background would not question his defiance. There would be new arrivals, however—young cubs eager to test the limits.

Would he be forced, then, to wear his sabre? The mere thought of doing so made Stanley hate himself to depths he did not wish to plunge.

"Did you have a chance for a farewell with your loved ones, Major Jonquil?" Colonel Falwell abruptly changed the topic.

"I did, sir."

"It does not appear to have been a painless leave-taking."

Stanley instantly forced his expression back into neutrality. He must learn to hide his suffering once more. His men would depend upon him to do so. "I have, by my actions, disappointed most of those nearest me." He very nearly winced at the memory of Mater weeping and Marjie pleading with him to keep her.

"They do not support your return to active service?" Colonel Falwell's evaluative gaze never slipped.

Stanley kept himself still. He refused to shift uncomfortably like a raw recruit. "They are, in many ways, very dependent upon me. Also, they worry a great deal."

Colonel Falwell leaned forward. "How dependent upon you are they?"

"Sir?"

His forehead furrowed, the colonel motioned Stanley to the chair opposite his own across the wide desk. "Sit, Major. You have a few moments before you must begin your journey to the docks."

An indefinable change swept over the room in that moment, and Stanley didn't entirely trust it. Something had just shifted, though he could not say precisely what.

Colonel Falwell leaned forward, watching him from across the desk. "Tell me about your loved ones."

Marjie accomplished absolutely nothing for the first two hours after Stanley's departure. First, she had wept on her bed for a full thirty minutes. Following which, she had wept at the window, at her dressing table, in a corner of her room, and, finally, on the bed once more. Staring out the window had proven even less soothing. Only one thing would ease her mind and heart.

She slipped through the unnaturally quiet house and into the book room. Philip had left the house, though Marjie did not know where he had gone. Stanley had insisted on hiring a hack to take him to Horse Guards, and Philip had not argued.

Marjie pulled open the drawer where Philip kept the unused parchment. She would limit herself to two sheets. Marjie examined the quills laid out on Philip's desk. If she could find two well-sharpened ones, she would not have to stop partway through her letter to reshape the point.

She carefully shifted the papers on Philip's desktop to make room. He had an entire stack of papers regarding some place called Fallowgill and another lone sheet of parchment with several names listed under the heading *Reliable Correspondents in Lords Who Are Not Complete Imbeciles.* Marjie resisted the urge to search his list for a few of the more visible members of the Upper House if only to ascertain Philip's opinion of them.

With a space cleared, she set herself to work. She uncorked the ink bottle, positioned the blotting pad where it would be most useful, and picked up the first of her chosen quills.

My Stanley,

She briefly contemplated opening the letter with *My Major*, if only for the sake of poetic alliteration, but quickly dismissed the idea. Stanley had no love for his new rank and claiming his regard by using it would not express what she wished to convey.

Letters to Stanley were usually easy for her to write. They practically wrote themselves. Nothing, however, flowed onto the page this time. Her heart was full enough. She had pages worth of things she wished to say to Stanley. But she could not even begin.

She sat with her quill hovering over the nearly blank sheet as though her mind itself were as empty as the parchment before her. What was wrong with her? She needed to write to him. She simply had to have that connection, and yet she couldn't do it.

Her hands began to tremble. What if she found herself unable to write to him from that point on? What if she could never manage it? She laid down the quill, attempting to force an air of calm over her mind and body. The frightening idea had taken root and was swelling to formidable proportions.

"You are simply overset," she told herself. "This will be easier after he has been gone a day or—" The words stuck in her throat as a realization hit her. Stanley was not returning, and the passage of time would not make his absence any easier.

She rose and crossed to the window. A driving rain pelted the windows of the book room. The sun had set already, the sad influence of winter on the allotment of sunlight. She brushed the moisture from her cheek with the palm of her hand. How could she possibly have more tears to shed?

A clock in the room began to strike the hour. She pressed her hand to her throat, fighting back a sob. Stanley was to have reported to the captain of the *Triumphant* no later than four o'clock so that the ship of the line could disembark with the tide at five. A fourth time the clock struck, followed by a fifth, and then the room fell silent.

Marjie closed her eyes. He was gone.

The dinner dressing bell sounded, bouncing off the walls of the empty house. Though they were in London, country hours were being observed. Dinner would be at six. Marjie had no desire to eat. She opened her eyes and sank onto the window seat.

A light had been lit in the mews at the back of the house, enough to illuminate the gate leading to them. Gusts of wind opened and closed it with fierce determination. Though she could see little beyond shadows and sillhouettes, she knew the trees jerked and bent under the same influence.

Would the wind help or hinder the departure of the *Triumphant*? She didn't know which she preferred. Should the ship remain docked, Stanley would be nearby longer, though he would still be beyond her reach.

How sorely she missed him already. How would she endure a separation, not knowing when, if ever, she would see him again?

"Oh, Stanley." She wrapped her arms around her middle. "Do you have any idea how desperately I miss you in this moment?"

She listened as nature punished the grounds below. A drop of only a few degrees would likely turn the rain to sleet, rendering the night as miserable as Marjie could imagine it. She pulled her legs up onto the window seat and wrapped her arms around her bent knees, resting her head on them, her skirts draping about her.

How far away was he? How long must she wait to receive a letter? Would she always struggle to write to him, having known the completeness of being in his embrace only to lose it again?

The deluge continued. The gate slammed in the wind. The inherent loneliness of the scene, so poorly lit by one tiny spot of light amidst the unrelenting dark, tore at her tender emotions.

One of the stable hands stepped into view, a caped coat held over his head. He fumbled with the gate a moment, obviously attempting to latch it despite the gusts. If only all difficulties could be solved so easily.

She sighed. Sorrel would have condemned the melodrama of such a thing, but Marjie found she simply had to release some of the tension building inside.

The stable hand yet struggled with his task. A change in the wind nearly pulled the large coat from his grasp. Marjie sat up straighter, her face nearly pressed to the windowpane. Beneath his coat, the stable hand wore what appeared to be a dragoon's uniform.

"No." She would not allow herself to hope, but she did not look away. If only the night had not grown so dark already and the window weren't covered in flowing water, distorting her view. She could not be entirely certain of what she was seeing.

Apparently conceding defeat, the unidentified man below shifted his heavy coat to his shoulders. He moved a walking stick, previously hidden beneath the long coat, from one hand to the other as he slid his arms inside each sleeve. *A walking stick.*

Her heart pounding in her throat, she jumped from her seat and ran.

J

CHAPTER THIRTY

Marjie threw open the French window that led onto the terrace at the back of the house and paused only a moment, drinking in the sight that met her eyes.

Stanley. He stood at the gate, still, dimly lit by the light from the mews, his face turned up into the falling rain.

"Stanley." A rush of wind whisked the strangled whisper away. She pulled a breath into her lungs. "Stanley." Her voice carried.

He looked in her direction. Could he see her despite the dark of night? Some light spilled out of the house behind her but not much.

She dashed out from beneath the covered terrace's protective roof and into the falling rain. Mud and water seeped through her house slippers. She called out his name again.

He rushed toward her. Marjie braced herself against a sudden gust of wind, shuddering as it cut through her damp dress.

Stanley reached her in a moment. He wrapped his arms around her and, though he was even wetter than she, his embrace warmed her through. He whispered her name again and again as his lips brushed over her rain-drenched face. She clung to him, only the bite of the wind convincing her that she was not dreaming.

"You've missed your ship." She closed her eyes for a moment, concentrating on the feeling of his arms around her once more.

"Yes, entirely," he said very near her ear. He pressed a kiss to her hair.

Marjie lifted her hand to touch his rain-drenched face. She could see so little of him. Her fingers ached and shook with cold but told her what her eyes could not with certainty: he was real, and he was there with her.

"The *Triumphant* has left." She fought for clarity despite her heart's insistence that she not lose a single moment of his company. "Why are you not on board?"

"I needed to hold you." His whisper echoed her own pleadings, and a suspicion as horrifying as it was hopeful formed in her mind.

"You've sold your commission?" Hope warred with fear at the thought. "What of your commitment, your loyalty?" He would grow to regret allowing her pleadings to convince him to act against his own conscience. He would resent what he saw as his own dishonorable conduct, and he would come to blame her for it.

"Tell me you needed me here, Marjie." He kissed her right eyebrow. "Tell me you needed me to return." He kissed the other.

"I needed you before I even knew you." Why the sudden need for reassurance? Did he not know how desperately she'd longed for someone like him, someone kind, affectionate, and gentle? Or had he realized as much and turned his back on his own convictions as a result? "What have you done, Stanley?"

Pluck sauntered past, unbothered by the downpour. "Ain't polite keeping a lady out in the rain," he said.

"What has happened, Pluck? He won't tell me."

But the young man continued up the path without explanation, whistling a jaunty tune.

Marjie turned back to Stanley once more.

"Come stand under the terrace," he said. "You are beginning to shiver."

He stepped in that direction, but Marjie took firmer hold of his coat and forced him to remain. "What have you done? I am panicking at the possibilities. Are you returning still, only later than planned? I cannot imagine you selling out or, heaven forbid, deserting, but you were supposed to have been on board—"

He traced the line of her lips with his thumb. "I am soon to become the youngest retired major in the history of the British Army, or very nearly, at least."

"Retired?" Her brain had gone entirely numb.

"In light of all I have done these past years"—a moment of pain passed through Stanley's words. She ran her hand down his sleeve, urging him to continue while acknowledging the difficulty with which he spoke of his time in the army—"Colonel Falwell, with the backing of Lord Hill and Wellington, has declared my service complete, honorable, and . . . enough."

She held her breath, waiting, watching.

"I have been placed on half pay while the details are finalized. I will undertake some domestic responsibilities on behalf of the army but am otherwise released from my obligation to continue actively in His Majesty's service."

"Retired?" She repeated that word, uncertain what exactly it entailed.

"Yes, my love." He held her face tenderly in his hands.

"How is that different from selling your commission?" She knew that was something he would consider an act of disloyalty.

"I am not choosing it. I kept my word, and I went back, and *they* are releasing me." His words emerged nearly breathless. "I could never have simply walked away, not while they still wanted me there, not while the army still felt I needed to serve."

"They no longer feel that?" To know his departure was not viewed as abandoning his duties would make all the difference for him. "They are ending your time there, not you?"

"Falwell said I have given all that was ever expected of me and more," he said. "They are releasing me. I can retire without choosing to leave."

Her mind continued to spin, struggling to make sense of his return, of his future. "I did not realize that was a possibility."

He pushed a strand of her water-soaked hair off her forehead. "It was not a path I could have chosen for myself, so I never considered it. One either sells out or continues to fight. There was never a third option for me."

"But you . . . ?" She hardly dared speak the ending she hoped belonged to that sentence.

"I am done, Marjie. I am done."

Her heart pounded hard against her ribs. "Done? You do not have to go back?"

"I don't have to go back."

"Not ever?"

His voice caught on his response. "Not ever."

A sob escaped her throat. She buried her face in the front of his unbuttoned coat. She slid her arms inside so that she might truly hold him. He wrapped his arms around her tightly, and they stood in the rain, the sound of her tears mingling with the rhythm of raindrops.

"Marjie." He spoke softly but without the heaviness that had laced through nearly every word he'd uttered in the past weeks. "Even in a siege, we were occasionally allowed to seek shelter in a downpour." She felt the smallest chuckle in his chest. "Might we at least step beneath the terrace covering now?"

He did not wait for her reply. He held her close to his side as he guided her back toward the house and up the stairs. He stepped back from her and shrugged out of his greatcoat. She felt the nip of cold in the air more acutely when not within the all-encompassing comfort of Stanley's embrace. She wrapped her arms around herself as she began to tremble.

He settled his coat about her shoulders and motioned for her to sit. He took his seat beside her on the backless bench. A light shone in the window behind them. "You should go inside and get warm, of course, but I must explain to you while we have a moment to ourselves."

Marjie leaned against him. The rain had not entirely washed away the smell of him.

"Not being on active duty, I am currently at half pay and will continue at such after I have been granted retirement."

What cared she for remuneration details? Stanley was at her side, alive and whole, and he never had to leave again to live a life he despised. In the peace of home and with the support of his family, he could begin to truly heal.

"I have a small bit of income from my father's estate, but it is not sufficient to support a wife."

Marjie found she quite suddenly cared very much for the particulars of his financial situation.

"I will require some time to find a position that would allow me to support anyone beyond myself," he said. "I was always meant for the army and never learned to do anything else. I may find that I have no skills that make me employable."

She snuggled closer to him. "Only an hour ago, I would not have believed you could be here with me now, nor that you could have been released from your duties in a way that was both honorable and permanent. I refuse to lose hope now."

"Hope." He smiled a little. "Mater says hope is the strength that comes from faith. I told her I would try to believe that something good was coming, but I could not see how that could be true."

"All that is changed." Marjie laid her hands on either side of his face and looked into his eyes, praying he understood that she was in earnest. "If I am at all capable of doing so, I will see to it that from this moment forward, hope fills your life to bursting."

"My angel," he whispered before kissing her lingeringly.

Her heart swelled inside her. Could it all truly be real?

"Say you will marry me, dearest." Stanley kissed her again before she could respond. He trailed light, airy kisses along her cheek before resting his jaw against her temple, his hand gently smoothing her damp hair. "A retired major with half a leg and a mangled hand is not precisely a catch, but I will love you all my life, and that life will be worth living again if you are beside me."

"I told you I would marry you even if you were a highwayman." She settled herself into the crook of his arm, her neck bent so her head could rest on his shoulder.

His arm squeezed her shoulders. "Yes, though I had inquired after your acceptance of a mere farmer."

"Either one would be fine with me." She wished to remain there always but found she was beginning to tremble rather violently in her drenched clothing.

"Personally, I find farming the far more dapper choice." Marjie's head jerked up at the sound of Philip's voice. He stood just outside the french window Marjie herself had stepped through. "One can cut such a dash dressed as a country squire. Black masks and capes are so melodramatic, don't you think?" He swung his quizzing glass on its ribbon, eying them both.

"Stanley is returned." Marjie blushed at the inanity of the remark.

"Yes, so a certain cheeky young valet informed me a moment ago." Philip expertly lobbed his glass into the tiny pocket at the front of his waistcoat and sauntered a bit closer. "From what little I overheard of your conversation, Stanley is about to descend upon Bath."

"Bath?" A smile lit Stanley's tone. Marjie leaned against him once more. His heart had lightened.

"Is that not where all the retired gentlemen of His Majesty's Army spend their declining years?" Philip raised an eyebrow. Marjie had seen every one of the Jonquil brothers make that exact face, though Corbin's rendition was far more subtle and Harold's bordered on a prediction of divine retribution. "If you have not yet been fitted for a bath chair nor claimed your place at the pump room, I believe I may have a proposition for you."

"I do have some duties Horse Guards requires of me." Stanley sounded quite curious. Marjie had not heard such unfettered anticipation in his voice since their earliest conversations. He was coming to life again!

"I am not suggesting anything so drastic as to interfere with the workings of the powerful and influential at Horse Guards." Philip opened his eyes so dramatically wide, Marjie couldn't help a smile of amusement. "This proposition leans toward the long term, unless you have iron-clad plans for your future."

Stanley took hold of Marjie's hand. "Only one thing is iron-clad."

"Perfect." Philip nodded. "Allow the poor girl to dry off and warm up. I will give you a very brief and undetailed account of my ingenious plan while we seek out Mater. In return, you can explain to me just what brought Colonel Falwell to make such a complete change of position."

Stanley helped Marjie to her feet and kissed her hand before escorting her inside once more.

She kissed him on the cheek when they were obliged to separate.

"I love you," he whispered.

Marjie smiled. "I love you." As she turned the corner to climb the stairs to her room, she heard Philip ask Stanley, "Tell me, brother, how do you feel about sheep?"

Stanley stood amongst his brothers in the Lampton Park entryway. Mater stood beside Layton, Marion not being in attendance, having been delivered of a very small but blessedly healthy boy only one week earlier. Sorrel leaned upon Philip's arm, her own health noticeably waning. Corbin's wife had remained at Havenworth to nurse their daughter through a cold, though Corbin had made the hour-long journey. Jason and Mariposa were scheduled to depart for Thornton Manor the next morning. Harold had, thankfully, divested himself of his clerical robes, though his facial expression hadn't changed. Charlie, the youngest, had arrived from Cambridge a mere two days earlier with Fennel, Marjie's brother, whom he'd retrieved from Eton. Marjie's mother had not come, though none of the Kendrick siblings appeared to have expected her to attend, nor did they seem upset at her absence.

The day was clear, the weather fine but cold, as expected for December. The roads were not overly muddy, neither were they icy. Stanley wore his uniform, his retirement not yet official and feeling a keen obligation to be true to what remained of his commitment to the army.

Not one of these happy circumstances compared to the joy he felt simply looking at his Marjie. Her smile lit her eyes as she descended the stairs to where he stood. She loved him in spite of all he'd confessed about his life in the army and his misgivings regarding his conduct there. He had admitted to her that he had not shared all of his experiences, that there were aspects of his service unfit for her to hear. She loved him anyway.

"Mrs. Jonquil," he greeted her, unable to resist the urge to call her that yet again.

She blushed, as she had the first dozen times. She slipped her arm through his.

"Are you ready to depart?"

She nodded. "I am sorry I have delayed us a little."

"No matter." Stanley laid his hand atop hers, where it rested on his arm. "We do not have far to travel today. We will make up time during the remaining legs of our journey."

Their progress would undoubtedly be slow. Stanley traveled relatively well, but the roads to Yorkshire could not be counted on in the winter. They were journeying by way of two Lampton holdings and a small estate owned by Marion's cousin, the Marquess of Grenton. Should they find continuing impossible for a time, they would not be holed up at a chance-met inn.

Stanley hoped the trip was uneventful. Philip had offered him the running of Fallowgill. Though the property was entailed, rendering Philip unable to sell it outright, he had proposed that Stanley use his "skills of leadership and organization" to see if he couldn't turn a profit there. The undertaking would require time, years, most likely.

Should Stanley manage to turn Fallowgill around, Philip had pledged, by means of a formal contract, to grant Stanley 50 percent of Fallowgill's profits. Stanley and Marjie were also to be given use of the manor house. Given enough time, Stanley could save his income and they could find a home of their own.

Good-byes were offered as they made their way to the door. The wedding ceremony that morning had been small, as both Marjie and Stanley had wished. Only the family remained for farewells.

Marjie lingered over the hug she shared with her sister. Their relationship had changed in the previous weeks. Sorrel had learned to depend upon her loved ones more. Marjie had accepted that Philip and Mater could be trusted with her sister's well-being. What had once been a strained connection had soothed into one of acknowledged need and necessary distancing.

Stanley exchanged a glance with Philip. "She is unwell," he whispered, indicating Sorrel.

Philip nodded. "But she wished to see the two of you off." Philip looked at his wife. The expression on his brother's face told him beyond a doubt that he was mentally preparing himself for the worst.

"You fought for years for the peace and safety of your family, Major Jonquil," Colonel Falwell had said during that fateful interview only a few weeks earlier. "You have earned the right to see them happy. If their happiness requires your presence, then that is what they shall have."

As Stanley passed Harold, he found he could not hold back one last request. "Let me know if any visitors arrive in the neighborhood from America."

Harold raised his pontific eyebrow. The other brothers grinned, even Charlie, whom they had wasted no time informing of their discovery.

Stanley and Marjie stepped outside toward the waiting carriage.

Pluck held the carriage door open for them and bowed deeply. "Cap'n. Mrs. Cap'n."

No matter that Stanley was no longer a captain, Pluck still called him that. The name he had fashioned for Marjie he spoke with utter deference.

"I am so pleased you are coming to Fallowgill," she said.

Pluck had accepted Stanley's offer with unfettered enthusiasm. The boy had hardly stopped speaking of it since.

"I never lived in the country," Pluck said. "Glad to try my hand at it."

The country, Stanley firmly believed, would be a healing balm to them all.

A warm brick had been placed in the carriage. Stanley climbed in after Marjie and laid his walking stick along the bench opposite them. She snuggled close. He settled a carriage blanket about them both and wrapped his arm around her.

He allowed a sigh of contentment.

"Do you realize we first met one year ago today?" she said.

Stanley brushed the back of his knuckle along her cheek. "I did realize that."

"You are happy?"

"Words cannot express how happy I am, my dearest."

Marjie's arm wound about him. Stanley pulled the blanket more firmly around her.

"Tell me again about Fallowgill," she said.

He had done so many times since Philip had made his offer.

Stanley leaned his head back against the squabs and closed his eyes, a picture forming there. In his mind, he saw a combination of the few memories he had of the small holding and Philip's description of it as it stood presently. "Fallowgill lies in a lush green valley. Several streams run through the property. The house sits on a small rise and is surrounded by fields of white sheep. Philip said the nearby village is small and remarkably friendly. York can be reached in a day's journey. There are no large roadways nor cart paths running nearby. Fallowgill is quiet and fairly remote."

"Peaceful," Marjie whispered.

"Yes."

"I know we will be happy there."

"Yes, my love." Stanley kissed the top of her head. He had known enough sorrow for one lifetime. "I am determined that we shall be very, very happy."

J

ABOUT THE AUTHOR

SARAH M. EDEN is a *USA Today* best-selling author of more than seventy witty and charming historical romances, which have sold over one million copies worldwide. Some of these include 2020's Foreword Reviews INDIE Awards gold winner for romance, *Forget Me Not*, 2019's Foreword Reviews INDIE Awards gold winner for romance, *The Lady and the Highwayman*, and 2020 Holt Medallion finalist, *Healing Hearts*. She is a three-time Best of State gold-medal winner for fiction and a three-time Whitney Award winner.

Combining her obsession with history and her affinity for tender love stories, Sarah loves crafting deep characters and heartfelt romances set against rich historical backdrops. She holds a bachelor's degree in research and happily spends hours perusing the reference shelves of her local library.

www.SarahMEden.com
Facebook: facebook.com/SarahMEden
Instagram: @sarah_m_eden

PROPER ROMANCE

Ready to find your next romance?

Let us help.

@shadow_mountain

@properromanceseries

Proper Romance Series

The Proper Romance series is a collection of sweet romance novels from award-winning authors, with strong heroines and handsome heroes.

PURELY ROMANTIC.
PERFECTLY PROPER.

SHADOW MOUNTAIN

J